CUZCATLÁN

CUZCATLÁN

Where the Southern Sea Beats

MANLIO ARGUETA

Translated from the Spanish by Clark Hansen

AVENTURA
The Vintage Library of Contemporary
World Literature

VINTAGE BOOKS
A DIVISION OF RANDOM HOUSE
NEW YORK

An Aventura *Original*, June 1987
First American Edition

Translation copyright © 1987 by Clark Hansen

All rights reserved under International and Pan-American Copyright
Conventions. Published in the United States by Random House, Inc., New
York, and simultaneously in Canada by Random House of Canada Limited,
Toronto. Originally published in Spanish as *Cuzcatlan Donde Bate La Mar Del
Sur* by Editorial Guaymuras, S.A., in 1986. Copyright © 1986 by Manlio
Argueta.

Library of Congress Cataloging in Publication Data
Argueta, Manlio, 1936–
 Cuzcatlán.
 (Aventura)
 I. Title.
PQ7539.2.A68C813 1987 863 86-46197
ISBN 0-394-74253-2

Manufactured in the United States of America
10 9 8 7 6 5 4 3 2 1

. . . I set out for another town known as Acaxual, there where the Southern Sea beats. . . . I saw fields full of people at war . . . with their offensive and defensive weapons, in the midst of a plain. . . . And arriving at that city of Cuxcaclán, I found the entire town in rebellion; and as we took our lodgings, not a man among them remained in the town, for they had all gone into the mountains. . . .

—Report from Pedro de Alvarado to Hernán Cortés, July 27, 1524, referring to the conquest of Cuzcatlán, now El Salvador

You think this mountain is beautiful? I hate it. To me it means war. It's nothing but a theater for this shitty war. . . .

—Response of Comandante Jonás to a foreign journalist's request to take pictures of the mountains, eastern front, El Salvador, 1983

CUZCATLÁN

I / MICROBUS TO SAN SALVADOR

JANUARY 9, 1981

MY ALIAS IS BEATRIZ. Ticha is my nickname. Age: twenty-four. Peasant background. Currently living in San Miguel, though I travel frequently to San Salvador; sometimes, but not that often, I get off the bus near San Vicente to visit my two sons, who are living with my parents outside Apastepeque, near the lagoon.

Favorite pastime: reflection. Or daydreaming, some people call it.

Element of nature which is special to me: *metate*. It's a precious stone, made from the lava of volcanoes; my parents, grandparents, and great-grandparents all made a living from it. They made grinding stones. For grinding corn. We peasants grind corn using the strength of our arms. On a *metate* base shaped like a small washtub, using a pestle, also made of *metate*, we mash corn that has been cooked in water and ashes. The ashes help to soften it. After a few pounds of the pestle, which is also called the handstone, the corn becomes a spongy white dough, which has a pleasant feel and a very agreeable taste. That's what we peasants live on. We form the dough into a tortilla by kneading it with our fingers and palms, then we put it over the fire on a *comal*, or clay griddle. The tortilla is our bread. It is life.

No peasant home is without a grindstone. I used to help my

parents make grindstones. That's why *metate* is my favorite stone. The flower I prefer is: mignonette.

I wonder where we would be without corn. Nowhere. We eat tortillas with salt our whole life. We *campesinos,* peasants. I grew up on them. We live and love on them. Sometimes there are beans. We also eat leaves, a lot of leaves; flowers of all kinds; the top shoot of certain plants, especially pines; and herbs, quite a few herbs. Also, we run across small game every now and then: *garrobo* lizards, iguanas, rabbits, coati, pacas; or tacuacines, which are large rodents that are very good to eat, seeing as nobody eats their chickens anymore.

But we like tortillas with salt best of all. There wouldn't be a meal without them. Anyway, that's all we need to fill us up. Because, of course, that's all there is.

To us, life is a miracle of God.

Living is something else: keeping your body free of disease, not dying from rickets or diarrhea; or starvation. Over half the small children in a given family die from these causes.

Maybe that's why we always want big families. It's a kind of defense to keep the race alive. Besides, the more hands a family has, the better its chances to earn its daily bread.

We must also survive. That's something else again.

They're after us. The authorities haven't been able to even look at a peasant since 1932 without being filled with rage. Now, half a century later, things have gotten out of control. There are no jails. If you fall into the hands of the law, you're dead. They say our country is too small for the amount of people who live here. People who say that have studied abroad or they're foreigners who support the authorities. The government says it too. They claim there are too many of us, that's what the problem is. They teach that in the military academy. The advisers teach it. I don't know how they rationalize it, but from time to time they shout: You're a plague, you poor people are a curse from God. People were happy before Cuzcatlán got populated. You've been multiplying, like the fish and loaves. It's time to wipe out poverty. They say it in a way that makes it sound pretty.

However, we live by the strength of our hands and produce the wealth that those who are well-off possess. The rich used to be happy. Not anymore. It's our fault. That's how a lot of professional soldiers—those who have studied in military schools both here and abroad—put it. Because the advisers are the same way.

The advisers don't know anything about us. That's the problem. They come to our country in big airplanes. They tour the countryside in their helicopters. They wear dark glasses so they can't see our light. They drive bulletproof Cherokees. They don't speak Spanish. How are they going to understand us like that?

They are happy. We survive.

They're after us. They murder us. The most common cause of death for someone like me is decapitation. Dismemberment. Just as the conquistadors did five hundred years ago. They used to threaten you with jail. Every estate, every hacienda, had its own jail. Whenever a person didn't want to work for the *patrón*, the owner of the estate, he was jailed as a vagrant and a troublemaker. There's still a law against vagrants and troublemakers, but it no longer applies. Now they apply a swift death instead. If the advisers knew our history, would they still treat us the same? I don't know. Besides, our history is sad and boring. Maybe they're not interested in hearing about it. We're interested, though, because it gives us strength. It teaches us to survive.

We've learned how to survive. That's why I use an alias.

———

I have two sons. I will never have a big family. I don't live with them right now. They live with my parents in a hamlet near Apastepeque. And my grandmother lived just a few miles from there, north of the lagoon. For a long time, before I was born, my grandparents lived on the south shore, but it was flooded and they were forced to move. They planted annatto trees and beans on a little parcel there, together with their children and Grandma's father, Emiliano. For a while they made a living making grindstones and selling things like cottage cheese and *conserva de leche,* or milk pudding. Recently they decided to abandon the grindstone trade. People weren't buying them anymore. Since the stones lasted for many, many years, longer than a lifetime, people stopped buying them. Everybody already had one. My family sold them. They've had them in their huts since my great-great-grandfather's time, and they treat them like jewels. That was a problem, so we had to give up the trade: the stones lasted forever.

I always got along well with my grandmother. She died a few months ago. She was sixty. It's her name I use as my alias. She's a symbol for me. You wouldn't think that with the age difference and the distance between us I would take her name. But it's symbolic. Her name was Beatriz.

Besides our ages, there were other differences between us. She never left her hamlet, never cared for cities. I did, because one day I decided to leave the zone of Apastepeque; in essence, I was following in the footsteps of my older sister Antonia. It was actually my father's aunt who got us to leave home; she took us to work with her in a cooperative in Chalate. This aunt was my godmother. "You must come with me," she said, "so you can have a better life." And so you can survive.

———

I was forced to take the children to live with my parents when my *compañero,* their father, died. I realized it would be impossible to take care of them. They went back to the place of my birth. I don't know what will become of them.

When my *compa* was alive, we took turns looking after the kids. I worked in the Social Improvement Textile Factory, which was run by the government in San Miguel before they turned it into a garrison. Now you can't even use that street to get to the train station if you want to go to Colonia Belén. At night I had plenty of time to study the principles of nursing—we called it first aid—which was a course given by the trade union. And my *compa* was involved in his own affairs, though I was never quite sure what they were. I did know that he hadn't worked in the factory for over two years because they fired him for being a union member. We got along all right, living and surviving. He went under an assumed name like me.

When the factory became a garrison, we were all laid off. No severance pay, nothing. The union helped out a lot, though, because we decided to keep it going even though the factory no longer existed, so we went to San Salvador to the Ministry of Labor to see if they wouldn't give us at least enough to live on for a month.

That was our excuse to stay organized. Because once they fire you, forget it. You could drop dead asking for handouts. So we didn't press too hard, but we did have an excuse to get together and go to San Salvador to meet with other trade unions. And that's how I got so deeply involved in the struggle. I had some previous experience from the cooperatives in Chalate, which was good because it helped me learn what it means to defend your rights.

Once they killed my *compañero,* things changed. I couldn't keep on living in San Miguel with my children. My reputation as a union member and the wife of a slain worker was a direct threat. I explained the situation to my parents and they understood. So did my grandmother. The little ones could live in both places. It was barely an hour's walk between them.

Together we'll fight the war.

If I hadn't been organized, I would have wound up dead like thousands of other people. The vast majority of the forty thousand people killed in the last three years are innocent. It's part of the extermination plan.

I don't include myself among the innocent. I try and fight back, so that's why I use an assumed name and do other things. We're at war. If I hadn't left the hamlet, I wouldn't really have known what was going on. I would have been a victim. Thanks to my father's aunt, we're advancing and seeing life in a different way. Both my sister Antonia and I. We both went to Chalate. We worked in a cooperative there; but to get organized we went to San Miguel. Fleeing practically.

That woman was very advanced. I never would have guessed. My father's aunt.

You never know when you'll get caught by the authorities. They're strong. Maybe stronger than we are because they don't have to hide or use assumed names. We have to, in order to survive.

We do have one big advantage: we've organized ourselves. That's where we excel. And in conscience, too.

Sometimes I think this whole life is a dream.

After being away for a few years, I have to go back to Chalate for a couple of days; they have asked me to identify someone whose name doesn't even deserve to be mentioned. We'd like to be forgiving. We're an emotional people, maybe because of the life we lead. They show us only their cruel side to arouse our feelings. They think if they take their rage out on us our contempt will turn to hate and then they'll have an excuse to exterminate us. That's been the authorities' policy for the last three years. If we speak out, they kill us. If we're suspected of speaking out, they disappear us. And if we keep our mouths shut they think we're hiding something. So they kill us for that, too. We used to have a right to remain silent, at least. Now they make us talk so we don't keep our hatred to ourselves. Then they have another excuse to kill us. "Everything that moves in the zone is suspicious," the military chief has told the pilots who drop bombs from their airplanes. We even have to be careful about the way we look at people. We have to choke back the tears for our dead. If we mourn them, that makes us their accomplices. So we get killed. The key is to learn how to hide your emotions. That's very characteristic of this war. We're not even allowed to cry.

So I don't know what will happen when I meet Corporal Martínez, prisoner of the guerrillas in Chalate. I have to give testimony on him. That's where I'm going, to Chalate. It's a difficult situation. Though they say people are at their best when things get tough.

I've always enjoyed reflection. I think of it as a way to live two lives. Especially now that the authorities show no mercy and use us as targets for their new weapons, which we've never seen before.

I'd rather forget Corporal Martínez. And think about my *compañero* instead, about the last time we traveled together on this same microbus. He really gives me strength and confidence. He was like a brother. I liked it that way. We lived through a lot of hard times and a lot of separations. One time he was gone for six months. Without a word. But I knew nothing would happen to him. Because he was working for our survival.

The last time I saw him we were together on the bus.

To tell the truth, it's very sad being alone with nothing but a shadow or the thought of him suddenly appearing with the same old smile and greeting, carrying a couple of oranges in a plastic bag.

I was just thinking—not about the last time I saw him but about the time he disappeared for six months. We didn't have any children yet. It's harder to be alone when you don't have children.

Always waiting for him to appear. I got far in my first-aid studies. Without a husband or kids around I had time to spare. Each night when I came back to our room at the hostel, I hoped he would be there to surprise me—sitting quietly on one of our two stools, like all the times before, waiting to pick me up and hug me, and then we'd squeeze each other tight, never wanting to let go, and we'd walk together still clinging to one another. Then I'd stand on his feet and he'd spin me around the room. Both of us laughing wildly. We could stay that way for a long time.

But he wouldn't be there. And I'd be filled with sadness. Those were six desperate months. Now, to think we'll never be together again. Not me or his two children. Separated for the rest of our lives.

It took a lot out of me to give my kids to my parents; but they understood. My *compañero* was dead and there was no way I could keep them in my room and take care of them—I was working both at the factory and for the union.

The day he was killed we were traveling on the bus together. He was only going as far as San Vicente and I was going all the way to San Salvador, because we were on two separate assignments.

It was just a mile or two to the San Vicente stop, where he would get off and continue on foot into the city—there was a mile and a half to go on the highway when the microbus was pulled over by a patrol. There were over a hundred *guardias* hidden on a side road with "mazinger" trucks.

It's an awful experience running into them. You never know what they'll do next. They told the driver to pull over. We thought they would search us. I made a mental note of the contents of my purse: I had my identification card, a picture I took in Barrios Park, San Miguel, with my two kids, a couple of *centavos,* and all the other odds and ends you carry around for goodness knows what reason. I felt better.

My *compa* and I were sitting together without saying a word. Like total strangers. When the patrol surprised us like that, coming around the bend, we thought they'd open fire and people got nervous. My *compa* took my hand and surreptitiously slipped it around his waist. This surprised me. But then I realized what he was doing, because I felt a metallic object beneath his shirt. I squeezed his hand for several seconds to let him know I didn't want him to shoot it and get killed. What could he do, anyway? He let go of my hand when he knew I'd found the weapon. Clutching his hand for those few seconds made me feel like they would never end. Life walks right up and slaps you, just like that. Standing on his feet, whirling around the room, holding on to each other. For dear life, so nothing would break us apart.

We have a humble home. A single room with a hallway leading out to a patio surrounded by other run-down rooms— communal toilets right there in the middle of the patio, which is how you can tell it's a *mesón,* a hostel. Our room is big enough to fit a bed, a pinewood table, and two stools. On the table there's an instant-coffee container filled with some crepe-paper flowers: a vase. There's also a closet which we bought with our savings after our first year in San Miguel. The closet is divided in half: on one side there are a few shelves and on the other there's a pole for hanging dresses and shirts; below, there are two drawers to which my *compañero* added false bottoms for storing sensitive documents. Hanging from a nail on the wall is a print of a little boy with curly hair holding a globe in his left hand; his right is near his heart giving the sign of benediction; there's a halo over his head and a slight smile on his face; a white tunic hangs from one of his shoulders; the other is bare. He is El Salvador del Mundo, the Savior of the World. Between the curly haired boy and the cardboard backing that holds him in the wooden frame there is another, hidden print of Monsignor Romero.

We keep it hidden in order not to cause problems with the authorities; it could cost us a disappearance into one of their subterranean jails.

The hallway leading to the patio is divided by a newspaper-covered partition, and that's where we keep a kerosene stove.

We lived in that room for almost six years. Both our kids were born there. Mesón Las Flores, San Miguel.

We were happy at the *mesón*. Despite the fact my *compañero* occasionally had to leave for long periods of time on union business. But I knew he'd come back sooner or later, even if he'd been gone for months. He'd always come back at night, knocking three times with a long pause between each knock. I opened the door and he stood there, not coming in; he just looked at me, hunting me down with his eyes and his smile. I, the nervous doe. Whenever we got together again, we played this happy game for the first few seconds. Then he came in, took my head in one hand, and closed the door with the other. We never took our eyes off one another. We never stopped smiling. And the minute the door was shut, we'd leap into each other's arms.

We were lucky to have a room on the street. It was better for catching the breezes that blew through the open door. It's hot in San Miguel. So nobody closes doors facing the street. That way everybody knows everybody else, because no one can hide behind four walls.

We were happy there. And scared sometimes, because we weren't natives and it took a while to adjust to the way people did things: you had to let your neighbors know everything you were doing that day—where are you going, where have you been, what did you do there, can I help you, let me come along, I'll join you, what's your name, would you like a piece of sweetbread, may I borrow a pinch of salt. In other words, all the things that make you feel a part of the community—making contact, talking in doorways, on the street, at the corner. People think you're strange if you keep to yourself. People like us who were involved in union activities after work had to tell our neighbors at the *mesón* that we'd be late, but we'd be back by such and such a time. And then I had to explain my *compañero*'s long absences. Naturally we were always making things up.

But from another point of view, it's an advantage, it's not so hard to be alone. In fact, you're never alone. You just have to get used to it. You get to know people and you realize they don't mean to pry, they just want to help. In spite of the difficulties, we liked San Miguel. We were happy as long as we could be together. The long separations didn't matter. They made us feel that much closer. It was a terrible blow. If it wasn't for our two sons, I would never have gotten over his death. And that wouldn't have been good, because it would have affected my work and my prospects.

II / BEATRIZ, EUSEBIO

1936

WHEN A MALE child is born, you cook a rooster. You cook it with *chicha*, a fermented corn drink. And when it's a female, you just thank God. Eusebio and Ticha ate three roosters in their time. The first two sons were only a year apart; the third came along much later; then they were blessed with two girls. Their worst experience was with their first boy; they didn't think he'd live long because he came before the nine months were up. He looked like an abandoned kitten, all skin and eyes. The neighbors insisted they eat the rooster three weeks after the little boy was born. Both girls died in their infancy.

The minute Ticha announced she was pregnant, they started fattening up the rooster.

"We'll eat this red rooster, he's the most colorful," Ticha tells Emiliano, her father, and Eusebio, her *compañero*, flashing them both a flower smile. Two flowers, one for each dimple.

"I kind of like that yellow one with blue spots," says Eusebio, just to say something, since he knows the color of the rooster's feathers has nothing to do with how good it will taste or the outcome of the party they're planning. The announcement has made him happy. You can tell by the look on his face, how the whiteness of his teeth reflects the light in his eyes. It's the light of a father-to-be who loves his *compañera*.

"Any rooster will do. What gives it flavor is the *chicha*," says

14

Emiliano. As usual, he speaks as though giving lessons on life.
The two men are sitting on a log which serves as the main
seating area; they use it for visitors. It sits next to a stick wall
in a small open-air shed attached to the hut.

Ticha keeps feeding the chickens. She tosses a handful of
millet to the rooster she's picked, the showy red one. Then she
tosses another handful to the rest of the birds so they'll stay
away from the rooster.

"Ticha's eyes are happy," says Emiliano.

"Of course they are; they're looking at me, aren't they?" says
Eusebio. Then both pairs of eyes meet, as though seeing each
other for the first time; they have the radiant look of people who
could be the men of the future.

They made quite a fuss in town. Especially the men he worked
with. Eusebio, the stranger, the newcomer, had conquered
Ticha. Maybe Ticha got bored seeing the same old faces and got
interested in the first man who came from somewhere else.
That's what everybody thought. "That's probably what happened," they all agreed with indifference, since they had nothing
against their new neighbor Eusebio. Also, no one had ever
caught Ticha's eye before, so Eusebio had no rivals who could
cause problems for the couple. "She was just a kid; no one would
notice a skinny thing like Ticha." This is what Emiliano thinks,
already feeling like a grandfather.

"We should tell Lastenia," says Ticha, the mother-to-be.

"Who's Lastenia?" asks Eusebio.

"The village midwife," Ticha answers, still looking after the
chickens, paying no attention to what the men are saying.

"There's plenty of time for that," says Eusebio.

"Lastenia also makes tortillas, gives massages, and lends a

shoulder for people around her to cry on," says Emiliano, happy about his future grandchild. "Besides, if everybody else knows you're pregnant, Lastenia must know, too," he says with a touch of malice. He doesn't want to admit that he's already told her. So they don't think he's a loudmouth.

"I bet you already went and blabbed the news," says the daughter, interpreting her father's barbed comment.

"You're right," acknowledges Emiliano.

"So what did she say?" asks Eusebio.

"She said don't worry and watch for a full moon, because we should count nine moons from the last day of Ticha's period," Emiliano says.

"How are we going to keep track?" Ticha asks.

"By making slashes on the mango tree with a machete," answers Emiliano, once more adopting the attitude of popular sage.

You measure weeks by counting mornings and evenings. To calculate months you count moons. And you count years from the start of the rainy season. Six months of rain, six months of sun. Invariably May is the first month of rain. The peasant year begins in May. It's a month of happiness, green-corn parties, fruit festivals, green iguanas, and the warbling of the *zensontle* bird. Five hundred years ago they possessed a perfect calendar, and could gauge the movement of the stars and calculate eclipses with precision. It is different now, as if time has been destroyed and everything has regressed. It has all gone to shit.

"There's nothing to it," Lastenia told him. "But you shouldn't have had a girl." Emiliano's eyes cloud up. In exchange for a daughter he had lost a wife. He didn't like to be reminded of it. Lastenia had slipped and spoken about nooses in the hanged man's house. She realized her mistake when she saw the shadows in Emiliano's eyes, as when a cloud blocks the sun and it stops shining. "Just have some clean rags and a pot of water ready," Lastenia said, trying to make up for her gaffe, looking at him fondly as if to say: Forgive me, *compadre*, forgive me, brother, I did it without thinking.

Memories are sometimes thorns in your feet. Lastenia won't stop talking:

"The girl is strong, looks like she's having a boy—you better get the rooster ready." She says this with glee, as though she's ringing bells and each word is a bouquet.

"May God hear you, Lastenia, and let us eat a rooster," and the shadow of his beloved Catalina, dead for sixteen years, crosses the wrinkles in his forehead.

Ticha knew Eusebio from a young age. She left home with him when she was fifteen. She had seen him before it even occurred to her to pay any attention to men. Before she'd grown wings to fly alone. Nothing but care for the animals around the house and go to the cutting fields. The life of a normal little girl.

"Papa, there's a man here to see you." Father was spreading a layer of wet clay over a hemp sack to make a pitcher. He made all his own containers.

"What does he want?"

"He says can you come outside for a minute."

"Tell him to wait until I'm done with this clay. Ask him what I can do for him."

"He wants to know if we can sell him some tortillas."

"I'll be right there."

"That is, only if we have any to spare."

"There's a few left from this morning; they're probably hard by now."

That was her first memory of Eusebio. She would not forget him. Her father sent her to get the leftover tortillas off the shelf. And when she returned with two tortillas in her hand, he

17

stretched his long arm out to her. That's how she saw it: a long arm like a *chinchintora* snake. He offered to pay. Father said no. So he said thank you. And to forgive him, but could he fill his gourd with water. So she went in again to get cold water from a pitcher.

"Where are you from?" Father asks, since this is the first time he's seen him in the zone.

"From Chalate."

"That's a long way."

"I'm looking for work, on my way to the coffee plantations in Chinchontepec."

"We've got a mill nearby; they've got plenty of work for people your age."

"I'd rather find a coffee plantation; they pay well."

Father looks him in the eyes to see if he can trust him.

"What's your name?"

"Eusebio Martínez, at your service."

"Much obliged." Then father said good-bye so he could go back in and dry the clay; he was making a pitcher. She rushed to the door where she had given him the tortillas and brought him water. She watched him leave. And that was all. It was her first impression of the man who would someday be her *compañero*.

Then he started coming around more often, sometimes on his way from Chalate, other times from San Vicente. Always on the back of his mule. He and Papa Emiliano became friends; he took his siesta under the *nance* tree, fastening his hammock to its branches. He usually came by in the afternoon and left before dawn the next day. By the time the family woke up—before sunrise—Eusebio had disappeared. Sometimes he just lounged in his hammock the whole time, not even bothering to go to the hut and talk; other times he helped draw water from the well. As he began to feel more comfortable, instead of taking siestas he would do things like work in the yard or give the chickens water. And one day he even sat down to polish a grindstone. Another time he and Emiliano had a few drinks together. Eusebio and Papa grew to be very close.

Ticha speaks:

Then one day we had a tempest that turned into a tropical storm; Eusebio had to take down his hammock and we told him he could hang it from the posts supporting the shed next to the hut. Well, there was no way he could leave that morning—how could he cross the ravines and torrents pouring out of the hills? —it was dangerous, he could get swept away; the best thing would be to stay and have a tortilla with us. His siesta lasted three days. We all remember that storm because it kept us from going to work. I took a good look at him for the first time. I still wasn't interested in men—I was barely twelve. While my father finished a stone, Eusebio went out in the rain looking for clay —he said he wanted to make us a new *comal.* I said: Let me help you. How are you going to carry all that clay by yourself? Papa said don't even ask, go out and get some clay. So we went out in the storm and immediately got drenched, even though we covered our heads with a *petate,* a straw mat, to keep from getting pneumonia. It was the first time we'd ever been that close —we weren't even friends. See, he always talked to Papa, not me, when he spoke—except every once in a while I caught him looking at me; but like I say, I wasn't at the troublemaking stage yet, so I just repeated a song we girls used to sing when a man we didn't like was looking at us:

> *Don't look at me with lust*
> *Keep your frog eyes in the dust.*

I didn't say it out loud. It just came to mind. But you only sing a song like that when something's gotten to you, when you're not indifferent anymore, and that's why I think it came to mind, because he was getting my attention. That's as far as it went, though, because once the storm was over, he was gone the next morning. I will say that when we were under the *petate* getting the clay, I found out how nice and warm he was; that was a new sensation for me. And that's when you start getting ideas, even though he may not have had any designs on me at all. Looks don't mean a thing. By the time I turned fourteen, Eusebio was a good friend of the family, and for me something of a hero: all those miles alone on his mule loaded down with everything from beans, brown sugarloaf, and salt to clay dolls from Ilobasco. This, despite the fact he was a farm worker and not a merchant. He said he always carried things with him to trade for other things he might need on his long journeys. The most extreme case was the time he gave us a calf as a present—he said he found it wandering on the highway and waited all afternoon for someone to come and claim it, thinking it belonged to somebody nearby. But nothing. So he said to himself, Finders keepers, losers weepers, I guess, and tied the calf to the mule's tail. We had quite a laugh when we saw a calf attached to his mount. Such antics made us stop and think. Maybe he's nuts, Papa said. In the first place, you don't go walking the Lord's roads with nothing but a mule for protection. There were barely footpaths in those days, and bandidos could appear at any time and kill you for anything of value. He wasn't out of his mind, of course, but as I got to know him better, that's exactly how I saw him— crazy as a goat. And that's what I liked about him.

This time the moon was wrong. Or Lastenia the tortilla maker. Or maybe it was Ticha's weakened condition. Or the strain of cutting too many indigo plants. Or bad luck. Ticha started to feel pains in her belly a month before she was due. She thought maybe the baby was suffocating and was trying to get out. Emiliano didn't let on, but his heart was trembling, the way water on the lagoon trembles at dawn.

Ticha didn't feel like going to cut indigo plants that day.

"You go on," she tells Eusebio and her father, getting their tortillas ready to take to the hacienda.

"If you don't feel well, call Lastenia," says Emiliano.

"It hurts me to have to leave you here all alone," Eusebio tells his *compañera*.

"Ticha knows how to take care of herself," Papa thinks. And if you don't work, you don't eat. And if you don't eat, you die. And they wanted to live. By sharing the work they were able to share their food.

"It's nothing, just a little pang," says Ticha, trying to convince her *compañero*, who has by now firmly planted himself inside the hut. Emiliano tells him it's getting late. They watch the rays of the new day stretching like a lazy cow behind the cordillera.

"Don't worry," Emiliano says. "It's not her time yet, I just checked the notches on the mango tree and there's still one moon left." He says this calmly even though the solitary lagoon which is his heart ripples. He thinks of his Catalina, dead just days after their only daughter Beatriz, called Ticha, was born.

As the dirt was shoveled onto Catalina's pinewood coffin, Emiliano's eyes filled with black earth. He lowered his head so no one could see him cry. He tried to make himself feel better by thinking about the newborn creature who needed a name, and for whom he had to live and provide. At that moment a neighbor woman was looking after her; she was barely two weeks old and he was thinking of baptizing her Beatriz—Ticha. Men don't cry. That's what his parents taught him, and like him they had known what it was to work like slaves, under the whip, bitten by watchdogs that never left the hacienda gang boss's side. Emiliano didn't want to be different from other men, and he wasn't glad they could see him cry. He didn't want to stand out. But his heart was betraying him. The same heart that the torturers and gang bosses at the hacienda wanted to turn to wood, the better to withstand the rigors of work in the mill. "I hope my friends don't see me crying," he thinks. He hangs his head. Why did he have to be like everyone else, if each heart is a universe? he reflected. And then he cried, like a river, or the breeze off the sea. He wiped his nose with a red handkerchief, a memento from his Catalina. He didn't want to show his eyes because they might reflect his sorrow. He might infect others with his pain, his suffering. His hunger. We don't like to share our troubles. That's the way we poor people are in Cuzcatlán. "If we weren't as strong as wood or stone, we never would have lasted at the hacienda." The race would have died out. Working conditions were deadly conditions.

And as the dirt was shoveled onto the pinewood coffin, he thought once again of the hope raised by the priests who visited the hacienda every three years to celebrate the mission feasts: they proclaimed life everlasting in heaven after you died. He quickly put this thought out of his mind; he'd rather have Catalina nearby, in the song of the *zensontle,* the chattering of the *guacalchía;* in the humming of the *colibrí* that sipped honey from the bellflowers; or in the refreshing breeze which, at that very moment, buffeted his face. "I hope Cata doesn't go to heaven. I hope she stays under the cool shade of the mango tree." She'd be with him in the indigo fields, or when he was quarrying *metate* for a grindstone. From the moment the dirt was shoveled, he tucked her away in his heart, a birdcage for Catalina's voice. God, I hope she doesn't go to heaven, because that's where the landowners, their gang bosses, and the managers of their estates go, since they were closest to God's emissaries on earth. He didn't like the idea of Cata spending all of eternity side by side with those who had been their wardens and executioners in life. These crazy reflections fascinated him. He lifted his head to show his eyes were dry. He had just wiped them with his red handkerchief. No trace of tears. What difference did it make, anyway, if they saw him reveal his innermost feelings? They were his neighbors, his blood relations, after all. They'd keep his crying a secret.

"Why do you have to go all the way to Chinchontepec to find work?" questions Macario, Emiliano's father.

"Because they've got a coffee plantation in Chinchontepec," Eusebio answers.

"Do they pay well?"

"Very well. You'd be surprised how many people from around here crowd onto that plantation."

"It's worth traveling all that way to pick coffee?"

"It's a living." Eusebio is only twenty-four, but you'd think he was nearing a century from the way he talks. He has the pallor of someone who was sick and never cured; however, neither his energy nor his bearing shows any trace of weakness; instead he possesses the muscular arms, sad eyes, and happy heart of a strong peasant. Tall and lean, like all the peasants from Chalatenango. Only in his eyes can you detect sadness. That's the way peasants are in Cuzcatlán. Their pallor is covered by sunburn when they work beneath the sun's scorching rays all summer long. From sunup to sundown.

"We could never have gone that far even if we'd wanted to—there was no place to stay," says Macario.

"We're not allowed to build huts on the coffee plantations, so we just sleep under the trees they plant to shade the coffee plants. The cold's the only problem; it gets worse the further up Chinchontepec you go."

"That's fucked," says Macario.

"Why do you say that?" Eusebio asks.

"Because of the volcano." Macario's eyes take on a rare quality of light that comes through his pores and permeates his entire being. His ingenuousness transforms him into a gentle man, with the beautiful, natural expressions of one who has lived long enough, but whose end cannot be foretold. He is the eternal old man. You can tell by the look in his eyes.

"What about the volcano?"

"They say the entrance to hell is through that volcano."

"Not at all, Macario, sir. Hell is right here in these dry valleys, where it never rains anymore because the indigo ate all the earth and trees; and when there's no fresh earth or groves of trees, the clouds flee and it doesn't rain, except for the occasional odd thunderstorm, and all that's good for is scaring you half to death when the lightning strikes."

"Don't forget the tropical storms," Emiliano interjects.

"A tropical storm once a year is nothing; at worst, it ruins the crops."

"But at least there's still a little bit of indigo around, that's what we live on," says Macario, getting back into the conversation.

"I worked in the indigo mills when I was a kid, until I realized either I was going to starve to death from the measly salaries, or my lungs would kill me, the same way they killed everyone else in my family."

"It can't be any worse than wandering to hell and back like a dog without a master. I bet you get sick a lot on those cold volcanoes

you were talking about. Right here they've got a mill, last one left in the zone, they say."

"What, and starve to death on what they pay? No thank you. Anyway, indigo water makes me itch, it really affects me. That's why I had to get out."

"Then work as a zacatero, *clearing the fields; we wouldn't suffer. There's only three of us in the family and we don't need that much—after Catalina died, Emiliano settled down, got rid of all his bad habits, and Ticha's an angel. We don't spend what we don't have, and we don't ask for much, either; maybe that's why we make enough clearing fields. All three of us have kept ourselves going as* zacateros. *And there's the grindstone business. Of course, around here people are saying indigo is a thing of the past, it's only a matter of time. That's probably true, because every day more land is abandoned and the owners let the grass grow, then they put cattle on it and make more money that way. There are also those who just let it sit and don't do anything with it. They just want to hang on to the property.*

Eusebio laughs:

"Maybe someone like me, who doesn't even have a petate *to drop dead on wouldn't do so bad as a* zacatero."

"Don't you have anybody?" Emiliano interrupts. He's been paying close attention while carving a stone.

"Well, I've got an aunt in Chalate, but she's much younger than me; everybody else went to the coast, looking for new horizons, as they say."

"And there's no woman, no compañera?" *Emiliano asks.*

"The only compañera *I've got is my mule. I hope you don't take that the wrong way," laughs Eusebio.*

"God spare us," says Emiliano, not amused.

"I really don't mind wandering from place to place, though," Eusebio continues.

"*You young people sure like being out and about, don't you?*"
says *Macario.*

"*It's better like that, then life just rolls right along and you don't
even notice,*" says *Eusebio.*

"*You people are fortunate to be able to find your next meal
wherever you go.*"

"*Sometimes when you're looking for your next meal, though, you
find death instead.*"

"*May God keep you, son,*" says *Macario. His face glows with
the radiance and strength of the undying old.*

Lastenia asked to be left alone in the hut with Ticha. She
wanted someone to boil water with mint in which to bathe the
little one. Babies born in the eighth month need to be rubbed
down with warm water to open their pores. Steamed mint and
chest massages help purify their blood. She explained this all to
the two men when she saw the pained looks on their faces. Both
anxiously awaited the future Pedro.

"Don't worry, I haven't lost one yet," she says, putting her
hands on Eusebio's shoulders, encouraging them both to leave.
Eusebio lingered by the door.

Emiliano went out into the yard. He knew women need to be
alone to perform the magical act of giving life a new start. He
lit a cigar and wrapped himself in tobacco smoke and shadowy
memories. At this point sixteen years before, Catalina's presence, Catalina's shadow, had been kicked out. The fact that his
grandchild was being born when the moon wasn't right reminded him of how his *compañera* died giving birth to their only
daughter, who was at this moment there inside with Lastenia.
He preferred to drink his bitter cup in solitude; that's why he

had quickly left and got away from Eusebio at Lastenia's bidding.

It's hard for Emiliano to deal with his feelings. His son-in-law understands and tries to cheer him up by sharing his own thoughts.

"Don't worry, Emiliano, maybe we got the moons wrong," says Eusebio.

"I'm afraid not, son. I made exactly eight slashes with my machete on the mango tree; but I won't be worried if you're not. I'm sure everything will turn out all right," Emiliano says.

"Do you think there's any danger?" Eusebio asks, seeing strange shadows on the other man's face.

"No, there's no danger," and he banishes the doubts from his face, and from his eyes. He's been infected by his son-in-law's confidence.

"I don't think either Ticha or the baby are in any danger," says Eusebio. "I felt his tiny body in her belly; he kicked and I could hear his heartbeat." Eusebio laughs like a man who knows no fear, spreading confidence and serenity.

Eusebio was nervous about his firstborn, Emiliano was remembering Catalina; so they shared the silence and waited for Lastenia to come out with the news.

For half an hour each of them gnawed on his hopes and fears, watching the birds fluttering about; digging holes in the ground with their machetes, lulled by the movement of the clouds above the hills; listening to the sound the wind made in the sky and on the ground; hearing faraway rivers and streams of water pouring off the volcanoes.

Lastenia appears in the doorway to the hut.

"You can come in now," she shouts in a way that bodes well. "We're going to eat the rooster," she adds, displaying her toothless grin and a long life well spent.

"Is everything all right?" Eusebio asks.

"I've got a grandson," Emiliano says with the joy of one who finally sees his life passed on for generations to come.

"You must register a name," Lastenia says.

"We have one," Emiliano replies.

"His name will be Pedro," says Eusebio. "That's the name my father-in-law picked."

"I called him Pedro before he was born, but I kept it a secret. I didn't want it to bring bad luck," Emiliano adds. He pushes past Lastenia so he can get into the hut where a newborn baby cries and a mother says soothing words. Like the sound of birds in a thicket of flowers and leaves. Words that are only spoken once in a lifetime, unrepeatable like happiness itself. Pedro was the name of the son he never had, so he made Beatriz, his daughter, give the name to his grandson.

"Are you pleased?" asks Lastenia.

"Yes I am," the grandfather replies. Because from now on that's what he would be: the grandfather of the house; the man who would live on through the children of his daughter, whose blood was the blood of his Catalina.

"You're acting like he's your son," teases Lastenia, smiling and reveling in the success of her skills as the village midwife.

"You don't know the whole story," says Emiliano, who felt like dallying with Lastenia before going in to meet his grandson. For the moment it was enough to hear voices inside the hut, like nesting birds. Their warbling was music, the only music his ears had ever heard in a lifetime of tracking in the indigo fields, or searching for iguana and *garrobo* in the ravines.

He can smell the lagoon. The clouds wave from the treetops to which they are tied. This day is different from any other in the life of Emiliano, who is over thirty years old. Deer dream in the distance.

Catalina was a victim of indigo. She suffocated to death. After she gave birth. Her lungs couldn't stand the stress; they had been weakened by indigo effluvia. The dye had slowly poisoned her.

At one time their fabrics had been so colorful! Now their clothes were white. The indigo had gone to other worlds. Their land was gone, too. They survived on what the mill gave them, they earned their daily wage; but the mill was severe and the ships' holds greedy for more. Hundreds of children were employed to pack the tanks, submerging the plant to the level necessary for extracting the highest-quality dye. The landowners exempted neither childhood nor old age in their efforts to secure the manual labor required to meet their exportation needs. That's why their shirts, pants, skirts, blouses, and underwear were white, made of cheap white cotton. The natives had lost their color. As well as their land.

The entire population participated in the process of manufacturing the dye, from the harvesting of plants to the transportation of the finished product to the ports of the Southern Sea, in their own Cuzcatlán.

The oldest died first. Then the younger ones took their places at the hour of death. After that came the babies. Regardless of their good or bad luck, mortality knew no age limit.

"Hunger has the face of a dog," says Emiliano.

"The face of death, you mean," Catalina interjects with irony.

Poverty is worse without land. Then all you've got to rely on are your hands and the willingness of employers to hire you in the haciendas and mills. This gives you the opportunity to earn a few *centavos* to spend on small things like salt, corn, cheap cotton for your clothes, a hand mirror, a comb, a machete, and some sandals.

He kept his red handkerchief, the one he used to dry his tears, in his back pocket. He swore he'd never go back to work at the mill. And his baby daughter would never work in the mills either.

So he concentrated on making grindstones. Walking over rough and parched terrain, he found *metate* in the brush and reeds. It took a few days to clear the ground before he got to the blue-gray basalt required for the grindstones.

"If you're willing to help, we can keep on living without having to work in the mill," he tells Ticha, who has just turned eight.

"I'll do whatever you say," the little girl answers, drenched in sweat and fatigue. At the age of eight she was scarcely aware of the importance attached to her father's words; she was, however, aware of the risks of working in the dye factory.

"The fumes from the dye ate away at your mama's lungs," her father had told her. "Even healthy young people can't resist it —if it doesn't get your lungs, it eats away your skin," he says as though he has to convince her. At eight, all she knows is to obey her father. "Your mama died ten days after you were born; her lungs couldn't take in enough air to support two lives."

"My poor mother!" she says. Her voice is muffled behind a stream of sweat.

"We can clear fields because that can't do any harm," her father says.

"Even though *zacateros* don't even make enough to buy salt," Ticha responds.

"At least they make something," Emiliano says cheerfully. "But no one of my blood will ever work in the mill," he says, barely able to finish the sentence, choking with fatigue. "Do you hear me?"

"Yes, Papa."

"We will not be the slaves of death," he says, not to his daughter, but as one would let loose a flock of butterflies. Once men like Emiliano had been poets and sages. Then they became slaves and serfs. In the last century they had become wage earners, but their living conditions were those of slaves.

"We retain an ounce of wisdom," thinks Emiliano. "It gets passed through the blood," he continues. Grandparents pass it to their grandchildren, and they to their children, in a luminous chain like St. James's Road to Heaven. "We will not be the slaves of men, do you hear me?" Despite the fact that all this has been running through his mind, it's as though he's been speaking out loud to his daughter. Together they strike the stone, causing chips to fly.

"I hear you, Papa," says Ticha, or perhaps she thinks it.

Unemployment could be added to slavish working conditions as another sign of their penurious and miserable state. Thousands of peasants were denied the opportunity to find work. Indigo had ceased to be the Old World's vision of the ultimate in color. Hence an immense floating population was rounded up for vagrancy by the *guardia rural* and forced to work on the new coffee estates located at the base of the volcanoes along Cuzcatlán's central cordillera. Peasants in the north, like Emiliano, clung to their meager trades and tiny parcels in an effort to prevent the Keepers of the Peace from forcibly removing them to the volcanoes, where you weren't allowed so much as a roof or a garden. Or a *petate* on which to drop dead. They had to prove they had a trade or were awaiting harvest, just so they wouldn't have to undergo the transfer to the plantations, where people slept under trees or open canopies made of avocado leaves or squash vines. Sometimes all the workers on the estate had to sleep under collective canopies, lying on the ground with nothing but leaves to cover them. Working conditions on the estates were just as harsh as those in the textile mills; except that in the latter case you could rent a plot of land or work as a tenant farmer. It wasn't easy for the *guardia rural* to uproot the peasant masses from the north and move them to the region of the volcanoes.

"They'll have to kill me before they take me from this place," Emiliano tells Ticha.

"They'll never get me to leave, either," says Ticha, who in the last few months has begun to develop. And her mind has begun to clear and mature as she gains more skill as a maker of grindstones. Sunbeams brown her skin and illuminate her thoughts.

III / EMILIANO

1950

EMILIANO WAS THINKING about grindstones. And about subsistence. He also contemplated the sea. He watches sea gulls, pelicans, and uprooted tree trunks from God knows where. Stones made smooth by the water. Footprints made by other men on the wet sand. He also observes ships in the distance carrying off the last historical shipment of indigo, processed into compact, turquoise slabs. The color of the sea.

His father Macario was the first to bring him to this place. Many years ago. Going to the sea is the baptism by fire that initiates you into life. An old Salvadoran custom.

See the sea and die.

He had journeyed from Apastepeque, near the lagoon, to Acajutla, where the Southern Sea beats. "A lagoon is too small for the eyes," he said. The trip took longer than a week. He loaded his cart with sacks of salt to sell in the village. But the important thing was to go and dream before the blue expanse. Use the trip to go beyond the real.

Emiliano's eyes are lost when they reach the point where the waterline meets the tail of the sky. Behind him rise the cordilleras covered with roads for man and beast. The animals made paths with their hooves, men with their bare feet. White paths sprinkled with the dust of centuries. Men who had knelt before the whips and guns of the landowners. These were the new land barons who defended their right to property with armored cars and fearsome, terrifying horses that destroyed hamlets and trampled children and plants in the fields.

"One day we shall know the world." The first time Emiliano felt like knowing the world he was twelve. Watching the sea and ships in port. He sensed a world and a civilization beyond the wall of water that quenched the fire in his eyes. Perhaps that is why his parents and the parents of his parents' parents brought their children to be baptized in the sea, as a way intuitively to draw closer to other nations.

It was a pleasure looking at the sea; it brought you back the dream contradicted by the land at your back, of which Emiliano owned nothing but the vista of its cordilleras, clean mountains, and cloud-covered volcanoes.

The ships left with indigo and returned with cannons and gunpowder. To be used against his grandparents, his own flesh and blood, and future generations. This had been going on now for five hundred years. "We are the victims of those who came with the ships." Persecuted in their own country, exterminated, exploited. Emiliano, his daughter Ticha, and his grandchildren were caught up in the conflict. They sensed it, they smelled it with their innocence.

There are so many things that can happen to you, Emiliano reflects. When will we know happiness? His inner voice resounds like an echo:

I remember 1932; I was around thirty. They rounded up large numbers of people and forced them to dig the trenches that would be their graves. They made the people line up in front of the trenches. Then they shot them where they stood; then the soldiers came to cover the bodies with dirt. Any part of the body

—arms, legs—not in the trench was kicked in by the soldiers. Any two people together in a house or on the street were considered a Communist gathering and became candidates for death. The authorities spared no one. They were coming to the defense of the nation, imposing order and Christianity, as they put it. Civilization.

The Protestants hadn't shown up yet, nor had any of those churches that send gringos down here like traveling salesmen, going door-to-door with their ties and black attaché cases, white shirts, and babyfaces—looking like they've never so much as broken a plate. They tell you they're merely investigating anything relating to the insurrections of the poor. Because anything remotely connected to demand for higher wages or any sort of rights is considered Communist, and then they bring the machine guns in. There's no way out and no law offers any protection—it is the law itself which indicates we should be treated with an iron fist: it's the only thing we poor understand and the only way to get rid of poverty. Our laws are rather special in that regard. I don't know what they're like in other countries. They are based on a desire to shit on the poor. For that reason we have no faith in the gringos who go from hut to hut with a Bible in their hand and a pistol in their attaché case. We've had a lot of experience with that type.

So my papa tells me to go to Oriente, to San Miguel, because that's one of the few places they're not killing peasants. So off I go. I'll miss my sisters and my mama, but what else can I do? Stay here and die for no reason, hurting the ones I love and leave behind? I went to the maguey plantations in San Miguel, where they extract fibers to make sacks for coffee exportation. I worked there a year, harvesting maguey plants and then on machines that ground the leaves, removed the fibers, and made them into the kind of string called mezcal. It's hard to imagine the big green sea of maguey stretching over the hills. You close your eyes and you just can't believe it.

I had to leave my family behind—I didn't want Ticha, who had already lost her mother, to lose me, too. So I had to go to San Miguel out of necessity. But I thought about it and decided it was better to be with my daughter and my parents, Macario and Emérita. If I was going to get killed, I might as well be among my own people.

My mama and papa were so glad when I suddenly appeared out of the blue—actually, they were scared because even the chickens cackled and they only do that when they've seen a ghost, a soul in torment. I don't know, maybe it was because deep down I sensed I had been saved and brought back to life. Anyway, I wouldn't be telling this story if I hadn't left. I was in San Miguel for over a year.

"What are we going to call it?" Catalina asks.

"Either Beatriz or Pedro," says Emiliano. "Depending on whether it's a girl or a boy."

"I can't wait until it's born," Catalina says with all the love of a mother-to-be.

"Does it feel heavy?" her compañero *asks, without giving much thought to his question.*

"Like a feather," she replies. Her voice has acquired the grace of someone walking out of a cornfield ripened in the sun.

Beatriz was born and Cata died. He wanted to be able to remember without making distinctions. Without being affected by it. Like hearing rain on the roof in bed with the lights out. A light rain, barely audible, like the silent steps of a wildcat on the thatched roof.

"I like both those names," says Catalina, her eyelashes lit by

*the embers of the dying fire. "I think it's going to be a girl," she
adds. "It's so quiet, it hasn't moved in five days."*

"Maybe it's a sleepy boy," says Emiliano.

*"It doesn't even wake when I'm grinding corn or cutting indigo."
She strokes her belly, searching for signs of life.*

"It's happy in there," he says.

"Just think, in a few more weeks it will be born."

Emiliano wanted to be happy. He wanted to be able to sing
or say wonderful things. He keeps the memory of the way
Catalina moved and the way she looked when she was happy
buried like a treasure chest, so he can take it out whenever he
gets lonely or needs inspiration. He drinks deep drafts of Catalina and transforms himself into a happy man every day before
he goes off to the mills. Once again he reflects: When will we
know happiness? And he is answered by the sound of the river
in the distance. Or by the dreaming of the lagoon nearby.

Every day he constructs realities with his hands, but he has
no sound answers to his reflections.

*"Having two more hands around the house will be a blessing,"
he tells Catalina. This is how he consoles himself for having a
daughter instead of a son.*

*"But it will be a long time before she can do her share of the
chores," says Catalina, leaving off dreaming to plant her feet
squarely on the ground. That's the way she was in life.*

*"Seven years from now she'll be able to cut indigo," Emiliano
says. This is the way he answers his question about happiness; the
way he keeps his spirits up. His body is getting more and more worn
out working at the mill every day. Children are the hope of the
future. He never expected to have to give up his* compañera *for a
child, though.*

"Seven years is an entire lifetime," says Catalina.

Children are like fruit trees: you must plant them without

worrying about whether they'll bear fruit, because if you worry you won't plant—the sight of such a tiny seed so far from the abundant tree it will become is disheartening. So you plant the seed anyway and when you least expect it, there you are gathering bushels of fruit. This is what Emiliano told himself in those days in order to give himself encouragement and go on dreaming.

Suddenly Ticha realized Eusebio was a member of the family, even though he only passed through every now and then, quite unexpectedly, once every four or five months.

She was finally learning to look him in the eye without getting embarrassed. Maybe it was because she was older. She had begun to develop. Now when Eusebio is visiting and she's washing corn, she looks him in the eye. Calmly, without wanting to take flight. She lets her eyes wander from the tip of his sombrero to the pigskin sandals on his feet.

Eusebio takes his sombrero off and hangs it on a nail. He's just come from Chinchontepec on his way to Chalatenango. At least he's got an animal to ride, Ticha thinks, looking at the mule their guest has tied to the tamarind tree.

Her gaze rests on Eusebio again, on his smooth hair falling into his face. He's wearing a white shirt and gray drill pants. Their eyes meet. Ticha looks away, toward her grandfather, Macario, who is finishing a stone; then at Emiliano, who is absorbed in shaping a stone. Eusebio offers to help Emiliano. No one says a word.

"Ducks are passing," Macario says, referring to the long stretches of silence hanging over the hut.

"If you want, I can give you a hand," Eusebio says to Emiliano.

"That's all right, I'm almost done," says Emiliano.

"I didn't mean to disturb you, compa," says Eusebio.

"You're not disturbing me." Emiliano holds the stone up to the light coming through the doorway.

More silence, broken only by the purl of grindstones being scraped. Ticha grinds corn. Grandfather Macario breaks the silence:

"How did your family die, Eusebio?"

"From many things, but mostly lung disease and cancer. The same things most people in Chalate die from, on account of the indigo. I'm glad they got rid of that shit. . . . Pardon my language, Ticha." Eusebio pulls up a bench and sits next to old Macario. He follows the movement of the hog machete in the old man's hand as he scrapes the metate, finishing the stone. *"Unfortunately that was the only way to make a living in Chalate—here you have basalt for making grindstones. In Chalate we couldn't even raise pigs— no water, they die of thirst in the summertime. Millet's the only thing that grows. People are very poor, but it's better now that the indigo's gone."*

Eusebio pauses.

"I don't know what's worse: starving to death or dying from some disease."

Still chiseling, Macario replies:

"Hell, Eusebio, what you're saying is it doesn't matter whether you shit on yourself or not—either way you're dead."

"The difference is at least if you don't have anything to eat you can go out and pick flowers, scrounge up some leaves, hunt animals, even catch fish if you can sneak down to the lagoon without the landowners' permission; with diseases you just waste away," says Eusebio.

"Life can get pretty sad, can't it?" says old Macario.

"Let's not even talk about it—here, give me that hog machete and I'll help you out."

"I think I'm all done; the stone is as good as it's going to get.

What do you think?" He holds the stone up for Eusebio to inspect. His hands shake. "He's old," thinks Eusebio. "His hands are shaking, he must be over seventy."

There are another few moments of silence as Macario adds the stone to a pile in a corner of the hut. Eusebio gets up and joins Emiliano. He's decided to come right out with it:

"Emiliano, look . . ."

"What is it, Eusebio?"

The younger man fidgets with grandfather's hog machete.

"That girl is growing up fast . . ."

"What girl, compa?"

"Your daughter, Ticha."

"Aha. And?"

"I might like you for a father-in-law."

Silence once again. The sun streaming through the doorway illuminates the most humble objects in the hut: an old hammock, the fire, the grain bin, papaturro-wood cots, hanging baskets for leftover tortillas, brown sugarloaf, and other things to eat. But it was their faces in particular that became more radiant, as though some kind of interior renovation were taking place. Then he is aware that he has a daughter who is turning into a woman, though she's only fourteen.

"That might be what you'd like, compa, but don't be deceived by appearances—remember, he who sleeps with little girls wakes up in shit." He means it, though he knows Eusebio, the stranger, will be Ticha's compañero.

Sometimes Emiliano's interior voice is exuberant like an erupting volcano:

After 1932, at the time of our great tragedy, for that is what the government's slaughter of the peasants was, I had to go with my father Macario to sell some pigs in San Vicente; in those days I usually accompanied Papa. People had finally gotten over their fear of eating pork; up to then these animals had fed on corpses, the victims of 1932. Their bodies were only half buried, right near the surface. Nobody wanted pork. People saw the animals going around with a piece of leg or part of someone's arm hanging out of their mouths. These celebrated hogs gorged themselves on the dead people they dug up, and since it was a time of famine—there wasn't even any corn—they were content to nose around in ditches looking for their macabre meals. So people stayed away from pork, as it was unthinkable to feed on an animal whose diet was made up of Christians. It was the Guardia's fault for improperly burying the peasants they shot— a shovelful of dirt and a shove of the foot and that was it. There were too many to bury. Thousands upon thousands in four short weeks.

So anyway, it was around 1934 and people were eating pork again as long as they were raised on corn and human excrement; people accept this because in our country porkeaters know that the animal's principle diet is shit, since there aren't many out- houses and the pigs are waiting to clean up after you. That's no problem. So I went with Papa Macario and a herd of twelve pigs. When I think of all the bad luck we've had with these animals I have a hard time talking about them, I'm afraid people will think we're just plain stupid. I remember it was May, because we had just planted corn and my papa said: Look, son, now that the corn is in we can take a little trip to San Vicente—the pigs are getting fat and they say people are eating pork again.

So I said, Okay, let's go. I was glad to be able to get out of the village and look around—I always liked to get away. It wasn't easy to travel in those days. Maybe it was in my blood. Who knows.

By afternoon we were pretty close to San Vicente and Papa said we shouldn't go into the city because it was getting late and it might be hard to find a place to sleep in the plaza, especially since a lot of people visit the so-called City of Lorenzana at that time of year. He says to me: Let's stay here, get out your hammock and we'll find someplace to hang it.

All right, I say. So I went and looked for a *nance* tree. I asked him if he wanted me to hang a hammock for him, too; he says no, he feels like sleeping on the ground, which is why he brought a *pepeishte*, because he didn't like hanging in midair—the swinging back and forth didn't agree with him.

It wasn't even dark yet—you could still see fire in the afternoon sky—when my father asked me if I'd felt an earthquake. Well, I thought he was joking, so I say maybe it was all those beans you ate. He protests, saying when have you ever known me to be a farter? So I asked him what he's talking about then. And he says, maybe since he's lying on the ground he was in a better position to feel it, like sounds coming from underground. Maybe I better have a little swig, he says, just in case. Then it dawns on me that all this talk about earthquakes is an excuse to get into the *guaro*—he never wanted to set a bad example drinking and he needed some justification; he never drank excessively in front of his children. Maybe that's why we don't have any big drinkers in the family. "I just like to have two or three drinks so they say bad things about me and don't call me a saint or claim I'm not interested in things men like. Because around here, drinking *guaro* has always been a symbol of manhood and strength."

"Look, Papa Macario," I say. "Go ahead and have a drink, but be careful, you don't want to sleep too late because we have to be at the market in San Vicente early."

"What are you talking about, Emiliano? If I need advice, I'll ask a priest." He's teasing me because my insolence amuses him. In those days you respected your elders, particularly your father. I drank, too, but not in front of my father.

"I didn't mean to give advice; it's just that we've got business to do and we can't afford not to make a sale in San Vicente," I say, reminded that the best deals are made early in the day.

But with all the small talk and give and take, he managed to get quite drunk.

Sometimes Emiliano's voice is a tree of birds and flowers:

So there we were when all of a sudden the ground began to rock. Because of all our bantering back and forth we hadn't tied the pigs up properly. I swear, one minute I was facing up, towards the angels, and the next—once the quaking had stopped, because that's what it was, an earthquake, sent by our Lord and Father—I was facedown. That's how strong the first tremor was.

Our hearts were still racing from the first wave of fear when a second quake hit. Papa Macario was saying *Santo Dios, Santo Fuerte,* which are the magic words for preventing earthquakes, and I joined in clutching my hammock as it swayed back and forth; by now Macario was sitting up. The fear must have sobered him right up. I saw him hunting around for the bottle.

"Sonofabitch! That quake made the bottle roll off somewhere," says Papa Macario.

"Listen to you! Obviously God's wrath means nothing to you," I say in a quavering voice.

"Shut up and help me find that bottle," he says.

Then came the third quake. Things were getting serious.

"We're in deep shit now, papa, because any minute the ground's going to split wide open." He was still groping for the bottle; so I said, more nervous than mad: "Pop, forget about the *guaro.*"

"Who said anything about *guaro,* boy? I can't get up."

"Let's untie the pigs and get out of here," I say.

"And where do you plan on going with all this shaking going on?" It was true, the strongest tremors had passed, but there were still aftershocks.

"God is punishing us," he says. I can see now he's as nervous as I am. And when the fourth quake hits I say that's it, I'm out of here; but Papa stops me and says stay put, the ground could give way at any time. You don't have to tell me. I've never been so scared in my life. Then a big cloud of dust or sulfur came up, or maybe it was volcanic ash, I don't know. It was like the dust storms that hit the roads in December. Then we heard Chinchontepec erupting. All this happened in the space of half an hour, although I'm not entirely sure about that because it was hard to judge, and that's when we saw people coming. We were just outside the city gates, and people were trying to escape. They came out crying, saying San Vicente had been destroyed and the city might be buried, houses had collapsed and many people had died. I can't believe the tragedy in our towns—the persecution of 1932 was barely over and now this had to happen. We had been so frightened that we didn't notice the pigs had gotten loose and were grunting—we hadn't heard them because of the pounding in our hearts. People were pouring out now, trying to get to the Acahuapa River and spend the night on its banks, where it was safe. I tell Papa I've felt over twenty tremors, and I'm not moving for the rest of the night, and maybe the earth won't split open because if it were going to, it would have split when all the people were going by.

———

That must have been the saddest night of my youth. Chinchontepec wouldn't stop erupting and people kept fleeing to the Acahuapa River. We spent the night alternating between prayers and plagues and before we knew it we saw the sky lighten, and since our souls had yet to return to our bodies—there's nothing worse than having to go through something like that in the middle of the night—the light of day was very welcome indeed. Your fear diminishes when you can see things, so I was glad everything seemed to be going away—the eruptions had ceased and the tremors were leveling off. That was when we saw a group of people headed our way, with a bunch of kids and a few women crying. My old man asks them what happened, like if their house had caved in or maybe someone died. They said, yes, the father was badly injured when a wooden post fell on his head. They were carrying him on a hammock hanging from a pole—two boys each carried an end on their shoulders with the injured man lying in his hammock between them. Then papa asks how it happened and they tell him the man had been drinking when the first quake hit and everybody but him had fled out of the house—he wanted to be the brave protector, or maybe it was just the drink talking—anyway, the roof caved in. So then they had to get him out—luckily the post didn't pin him. Now they were taking him down to the river because if the eruptions went on for much longer the whole city would be flattened.

"Well," says my old man, "if you say he was drinking, then I might happen to have just the medicine he needs." Macario, always the troublemaker—of course there was no such medicine, just the bottle he'd been drinking out of before the earthquake and which he'd lost in the panic.

"But he's passed out, how can he take any medicine?" asks the woman who appears to be the wounded man's *compañera* and the mother of all those kids.

45

"Just leave it to me, he'll take that medicine even if we have to funnel it in."

"Where are you going to get a funnel?" the woman asks. She shouts at the boys carrying the invalid to wait, come back. So they bring him back in the hammock.

"We'll make a funnel out of a corncob," says my old man; that's what he's good at, invention.

Soon Macario was siphoning *guaro* down the man's throat—first he sliced one end of the cob to look like a real funnel, then he opened the man's mouth, inserted the cob, and started pouring. While the woman was commending herself to God, Papa let him have two big swigs.

"That smells like *guaro,*" says the oldest son.

"Right you are," says my old man. "That's *guaro,* all right. I didn't mean to get your hopes up, but I do think it's good medicine, because what this man has is a bad case of fright."

"Well, don't give him too much or he'll get drunk again and die in his sleep," begs the woman.

"That won't happen, my good woman," he says, addressing her more confidently now. "This stuff is called Dead Man's Cackle, you just wait and see."

"Let me have a little, don't give it all to him," says the oldest son. And as he says this the man opens his eyes and speaks from his hammock: "You better let me have all of it because that's good shit."

You should have seen us laugh. After being so scared we were grateful to have something to laugh about.

It was unbelievable, after all that and the man says set me up with another, chief. Right there, hanging from his hammock. The words weren't even out of his mouth and his sons let go the pole and dropped him on his ass. The woman begged her sons not to leave in case the man had broken his ribs or something.

I tell you, the things that happen in this life. Just when things look darkest, there you are laughing your ass off. We forgot all about the earthquakes and lost pigs. Life isn't always sad, never forget that, my father used to say. That was then, though, and things weren't half as bad as they are now, when people are left without homes, children, or food. Times change, but the thing is, you don't even notice.

Emiliano's interior voice continues:

One day—it was one of only two times I ever went to San Salvador—a couple of friends and I decided to go to Soyopango and then on to the capital; they did have trains back then, but they weren't meant for poor people and we didn't dare take one. Our plan was to go to the plaza where they were celebrating the August Fair. This must have been around 1946. We got as far as the corner of La Garita when we heard gunshots. We had two choices: either go north in the direction of Aculhuaca, and wait for the shooting to stop, or keep on going into San Salvador and pay no attention to the gunfire.

So we got as far as La Tiendona, where there was lodging for the poor; besides, it was a fun place right in the heart of the August Fair. Suddenly we saw a demonstration, a handful of people coming down the main street. We asked what was going on and some people told us it was a demonstration organized by General Castaneda Castro, who had recently been installed as President of the Republic. The men and women in his group were wearing blue and white, the colors of his party as well as those of the national flag. Coming from the opposite direction we could see another group of demonstrators, all dressed in red and white. These were the supporters of Dr. Arturo Romero, who, according to them, was the presidential candidate of the poor.

Both groups were coming from opposite directions, and met at the corner. When they met there was a lot of shouting and rock throwing. Dr. Romero's people were at a disadvantage, since they were armed with only sticks and stones; Castaneda Castro's people were carrying pistols—after all, his was the party of the military.

We had barely enough time to duck into a doorway which, fortunately for us, was open, since most people locked their doors once the shouting began. We heard more shots. We were crouching there in the doorway when the owner of the place shows up and asks what we think we're doing, because he's about to lock up and we'd better get lost before he calls the police. We told him we didn't know San Salvador well and gunfights were new to us. Well, you'd better get used to them, he said, then gave us a shove. "Eat shit, shepherds, Easter's over," he added. We had seen the police around the corner calmly letting General Castaneda Castro's people by and waiting to ambush Dr. Romero's people. We were up against a wall at that point, hoping to find someplace to hide. We felt pretty stupid since we hadn't a clue in hell where we were. I remember I even lost my sandals in the commotion. Then we heard shots coming from a different direction.

About that time we saw a girl selling tortillas coming our way. We asked where the shooting was coming from. She said the Parque Centenario and that two students had been killed. We asked if she wasn't afraid to be going towards the police; she replied she was used to it and besides she was only going as far as Plaza Ayala, right around the corner. I can still see her with her tortilla basket around her waist. She said we'd better find a place to stay right away because martial law started at six. We asked what that was and she said martial law meant they could shoot whomever they pleased on the street and leave him there to rot. When we asked what time it was, she said about five-thirty. How can you tell? we asked, and she said she could tell what time it was by the color of the sun; it had just started turning red. We thought it was cutting it pretty close—a miscalculation could prove fatal, and you could be damn sure the police knew the precise moment when they could open fire on whatever unfortunate soul they found on the street.

This girl was so unconcerned that her courage amazed us— here she was walking home as though everything were fine and we stood there with our knees knocking together. We spotted another open doorway and asked the girl if she thought it would be all right to go in. She said, If you want, but I promise you're not going to get shot before it's time; she was so sure about the time, so positive the police would hold off for another few minutes. So she just went on her way as though there were nothing to fear.

Meanwhile we had found a cart and were squatting under it when this crusty old fellow walks up and says hey, who told you you could stay under there, and we said no one, but we were kind of lost and we were willing to pay; it was past six by then and there was shooting everywhere, as though it were a national holiday. The old geezer told us he wasn't running a hotel and if we wanted a place to stay we'd better go to Plaza Ayala. All right, we said. But we knew we could get shot. "Stay close to the wall and the police won't see you." It should come as no surprise that we heard someone crying in a nearby house whose doors were open. As we had nothing better to do, we went in— if they wanted to kick us out, they'd have to find us a room somewhere. We heard more people crying. On the far side of the room (we came through the front door when we heard the crying) was a girl covered in blood, lying on a bed of straw. To avoid getting thrown out, we asked what happened, trying to act like we belonged there. Everyone who lived there—it was a rooming house—was crowding around the girl. They told us the girl had been killed as she was coming in the door, hit by a bullet in the shoulder.

It came as quite a shock when we realized she was the girl we had just seen with the basket of tortillas; she had been off by a few seconds. Everyone was crying, and we'd just seen her alive, so we were pretty upset ourselves. And we cried right along with them, big tears, too, because we'd only known her a short while and now she was gone.

So that's where we stayed, no one threw us out. We tried to make ourselves look like stray dogs, which wasn't that hard because we were honestly affected by the tortilla girl's demise.

After that I promised myself never to return to San Salvador.

The next day we left for Soyopango on our way to San Vicente.

Everywhere people were crying. We figured that's what usually happened after martial law took effect—people would forget and get caught in the street at the hour of slaughter. The law states that any Christian observed on the street as of 6:00 P.M. will be subject to armed intervention, which is the same as saying they'll shoot you like a mad dog. I just want to know one thing: Who wears a watch to be able to tell the exact time? The officials who give the *guardias* the go-ahead, that's who.

The authorities took great pleasure in shooting Christians caught in the street at the appointed hour. That way they got a taste of real blood, so when our enemies invaded, they would already be trained to see people dead.

That was the last time I ever went to San Salvador.

Ticha lights the oil lamp. The light spreads across her nahuilla *dress, bathing her in poor-quality gold, like one of the sculptures the conquistadors melted down to obtain pure metal. She places the lamp near the two men conversing. One is her father; the other a brother who came late. As she goes off to bed her resplendent, eternal body leaves a luminous wake.*

Coyotes come near. It is the hour of the prayer which says: With God I sleep, with God I wake, through the grace and mercy of the Holy Spirit. The rain has stopped. The coyotes continue to howl.

It is the hour of damp grass and wet leaves; and trees stirred by the wind walk in the night. Fireflies alight on dark branches and shine their phosphorescent tails. Occasionally the silence draws its silver dagger and pierces the night with a bolt of lightning. Flashes cross the sky, nervously winking like phantom planets, stars that never were. The corner where the men of tomorrow rest is illuminated.

Emiliano and Eusebio speak of strange things. The younger man and the older one come from the same family; they recognize one another after a long time of not seeing each other, of not finding each other. They are of the same blood that comes from distant generations. They are the same flesh and blood because they are made of the same stuff: corn and clay. They are related by the same whisper. Their soft speech is the sound of a cornfield blowing in the breeze. Blood brothers recognize one another because they share a common affirmation of poverty and abiding affection. They resemble one another in their eyes and attitude toward life. They long for something to please them, something they will never know. They make love to their women on wooden cots covered with petates *or cotton quilts. Their blood is red like that of other men but inspired by something else, something that makes them sensitive to the river, the volcanoes, animals without masters, a future life that exists only in their dreams. Their eyes see into the night; they penetrate the darkness and discover the mystery which holds them in poverty. But they are afraid. There have been five hundred years of terror. They are afraid because they are sensitive. Their eyes see more than the eyes of cats, or jaguars, or pumas. In dreams they see golden hillsides of corn and flowers: pumpkin flowers creeping among the shoots in the fields; bean flowers crawling to the tops of the cornstalks.*

It is the hour to remember Catalina as the purest being on earth, and to love her in her solitude and poverty. They were born inseparable, it is true, but the night further consolidates them; though she's not present. They have the energy they need not to be destroyed; nor will love or memory be annihilated. It is a different love, a love without borders, without the limitations of bodily presence.

He remembers when he loved her they were like harmless, newborn animals; they had the indeterminacy of an unreality. She made him sensitive. Perhaps it was she who brought Eusebio to the hut so she would be mentioned again. Emiliano had not said her name since the day of her death. His mouth never formed the word Catalina, *not even when he spoke to Ticha about her. Eusebio came to resurrect her in words.*

He had not confided in anyone for fourteen years since his compañera's *death; no more than hellos and good-byes, good morning and good day; greetings from afar, raising an arm and waving.*

The coyote continues to howl in the distance. The lamp lights the hut with an orange glow that is a butterfly keeping sleep at bay.

IV / MICROBUS TO
SAN SALVADOR

January 9, 1981

WE HAD A WAY of looking into each other's eyes. And of finding each other. Now we're together even though we can't communicate.

what difference does not being together make if, though they can't talk to each other, at least they are traveling together

on this day his eyes glowed, clothed in a soft light which masked the long and deadly fatigue

after sixteen hours of work

being together is a joy but it also gives you the sensation that everything has been put on hold

now their feet are touching. Their hands meet, bound by the heat of the sun and their bodies. United. Welded together

by the energy of a million suns

or a million nerve cells. The same light they see shining wherever they look in the sky above the hills and water

their bodies calm and beautiful because they love each other so much

relaxing and getting ready to go to sleep

sounds of the sea and animals making noises in the trees planted on the mountainside facing the sea. He met her by chance in a place that looked like a station where dreams arrive

but where was she really? what could she have been doing

that night that morning that he would have been somewhere else working to survive, emerging from the sea spray, rising out of the rubble of sunlight and luminous hues? He is her *compañero* and somebody else

if she is not there then who were those two people coming together and touching bound by humanity eternity hope

she who is a grassy white sand dune when she curls up

in which location of time and space does she purr like a contented mountain lion with gleaming eyes that reveal the calm waters within

when his fingers trace red roads on her skin made by a five-legged spider that stirs everything it touches

a place in time every day every hour when they are truly awake holding their hearts in their hands beneath the protective shadow of the tall mountains or in the salty blue phosphorescent sonorous waters covered with a special mixture of gray, yellow, and sky-blue light

and out of these waters come ships to destroy them to wage a dirty war on them a war of hunger a war of misery a war of desperation and daily terror a war that lays waste destroys burns kills maims a war of the powerful who possess ships and guns versus the barefoot and hungry and naked who have learned much from the dreams handed down from generation to generation by their grandfathers. And the grandsons who became fathers and grandfathers

they feel themselves growing like the beautiful and perfect trees looking down on the Southern Sea which has belonged to them for hundreds of centuries and which threatens them now with angry dogs that come over the horizon

exactly there where unknown and fraternal worlds are. There where the horizon barks like a spreading problem whose solution is recorded in the poems inscribed by the grandfathers on rocks and memory

they know they are not alone on the path of flames traced by
the ships on the horizon but they touch
so they know they remain they exist and everything they
touch turns to honey, dripping honey
his *compañera* in life and death something as real as dreams
in Cuzcatlán
where the Southern Sea beats and defeats

They met by coincidence. No one introduced them or arranged for them to meet. She rode the same bus every day to
San Salvador. She enjoyed watching the road. The way it disappeared every so often into groves of *maquilishuat,* cashew, and
olive. Other times she felt as though she were floating on the
heat melting the asphalt and making it shimmer like a river of
steam. Especially during the first twenty miles from San Miguel
to the Zona Paracentral.

She wasn't surprised to find herself traveling with the young
man for a fourth time, sitting so close their legs could touch.
There is an odd sound which she can't place. Heartbeats, maybe.
Or the sound of the watch he always wore, even when he slept.
A gift from his grandfather.

By dress he is a worker. His eyes are glued to a book. They
have been stuck there ever since the third time they traveled
together. The pages of the book are always open. "How can he
possibly read with so much jiggling?"

Like two friends who have never met. However, they did
develop a certain rapport from being in such close quarters.
Their legs touched. She thinks these kinds of encounters are
always suspicious. She had to be suspicious of everything. Especially now that she knew first aid and worked as a nurse—her
collaboration to aid those who struggled, her *compas* in life,
friends in death.

What an imagination!

She must always try to act natural. That's why she wore a blue Mexican dress, a present from her *compañero,* in order to keep up appearances in a country where one has to be either clever or a monk. "When you dress, you must keep in mind the possibility of being stopped by a patrol." You are considered more or less suspicious depending on the clothes you wear.

At the moment she is pretending she's on her way to a fiesta. Complete with high-heeled shoes she's never worn before. She's even wearing lipstick, but not too much because she's afraid of smudging it, staining her lips with an artificiality that doesn't become her.

She's already licked her lips twice. As she's about to lick them a third time she worries it's all come off and that wouldn't do if she wanted to look the part of being on her way to a fiesta.

I must be natural, she almost thought out loud.

They had ridden together in the same vehicle a number of times before: the 6:30 A.M. micro. Quite a coincidence actually, since she was always aware of the people around her. "Of course, he probably has to be in San Salvador by ten in the morning every Monday just like me." The last time they traveled together she noticed that he rushed off in the direction of the Mercado Quartel bus stop as she was crossing Doce Avenida on her way to Esquina de la Muerte and got lost in the crowd on the street leading to the Parque Centenario. "Maybe I should at least say hello." What would she gain by saying hello? Maybe it would be the most natural thing to do. She was used to hiding her feelings. Being suspicious of everyone, without letting it get in the way of her particular sweetness and sensitivity. In a way, her behavior was not uncommon. "We've lost our faith in people," she thinks. Then she asks what time it is, just to say hello with a glance. I love you.

Her traveling companion answers:

"Twenty to eight." He feigns indifference, but his silence speaks for him. I love you, too.

Your fear of enemies must be greater than the fear of God, her grandmother Beatriz had said. Great-grandfather Emiliano said the same thing: "Because our enemies are strong and better equipped than us; but we must never show them that fear, that is how we have survived." She can hear her great-grandfather saying it.

Circumstances obliged them to travel together, though they couldn't talk to one another; however, it may be possible to talk and still maintain your distance. That's what she's thinking. Why wouldn't she talk to him if he's sitting right next to her? She's aware that in dangerous situations any gesture is suspect.

"Here's the San Vicente turnoff," she says to no one in particular, but, of course, since he's right there obviously anything she says is directed at him.

"Right, right," he says, repeating the same word either to indicate he doesn't want to talk or to grant her an extra word.

She isn't afraid anymore; his voice has instilled her with confidence. She feels her heart swell. An imprisoned sea beats in her breast wanting to break the levees and overflow like a river. That's the way her heart was: when she was sad, her sadness would flow into her breast. And when she was happy, her joy would spill over into laughter and wide smiles that drew dimples on her cheeks.

She felt like a seasoned traveler. Ninety miles by microbus was always an experience, especially when they got to Puente Cuzcatlán, where there were always military posts, either those of the government or the guerrillas; the latter charged a war tax, the former searched the very soul of each and every passenger. "What would happen if we got caught in crossfire?" she wonders. "Between the government and the subversives." She'd gotten used to calling them subversives instead of *muchachos,* in order to avoid unforeseen difficulties. "I should at least call them *muchachos* in my head." A flock of wild birds escapes from her heart.

Saying *muchachos* was a way of not offending her conscience. Or getting used to saying either of the two words without making distinctions: "*muchachos,*" "subversives"; she used the second word if she had to say it aloud in front of someone she didn't trust; and she used *"muchachos"* when she was with her brothers-in-blood. She was even careful about what she said in front of her sister. "You should stay put in San Miguel and quit taking your life in your hands every weekend," Antonia had told her.

She had replied, I travel to carry out tasks of which you're well aware, sister.

Besides, it gives me a chance to visit Apastepeque every so often. "Our parents wouldn't appreciate your visits if they knew the risks you were running," Antonia responded. Her brief interchange with the young man unintentionally and even unconsciously pressing up against her leg afforded her a strange self-assurance. In reality, the man at her side is her *compañero.* But she has to pretend she doesn't know him, and to make it more believable, she insists on dreaming. Like always.

"He *was* a stranger seven years ago." Now she knows him inside out. But under the circumstances she had to act as though there were nothing whatsoever between them. "It's best not to trust strangers." To conceal her agitation she takes out a piece of paper that has *Lucía* written at the top. It's a letter from her father, Jacinto, in Apastepeque, written by a neighbor on lined paper with big letters and bad spelling. She reads the letter over and over again. Having a letter to read makes her feel better and puts some distance between her and her seatmate. She adjusts the skirt of her Mexican dress, colored blue with mahogany dots that make it look like her skin is showing through. Her skin had been bronzed by the sun for all the twenty-odd years of her life. She worked outside as a little girl, with her family, picking cotton, shucking corn, piling earth around coffee trees, covering the roads from plantation to plantation, hacienda to hacienda, on foot. She remembers the big sombrero she wore on her head to keep the sun off when she went down to the coast to comb cotton, but her little shoulders got so sunburned that she almost had to scream. She was thin and fragile like a flower then. She felt better in the city. She arrived in Chalatenango when she was fifteen, in search of her aunt and her sister Antonia. Soon thereafter she decided to get involved in a mass organization. She felt like a woman enlightened by living an intense life full of high hopes. She had lost the anemic pallor of a country girl as well as the signs of having been malnourished. She had the complexion of a woman now. Her cheeks were no longer hollow; rather, they had filled out like those of the city girls. There was a marked change. Her body had shot up like a colored mountain peak. She was radiant in her poverty. As beautiful and lovely as her own spirit.

In the reflection of the windshield she can see the breeze blowing her hair. Up ahead is the road through the hills dotted with cashew and olive trees.

She takes endless pleasure in this road she knows so well— the way it climbs past the Lempa River and winds through hills scorched by airplane fire. Gutted by bombs. She breathes the special, refreshing air of the river. A fresh wind blows through the valley of the Lempa. "Poor thing!" She looks at her *compañero.*

The young man beside her naps or reads. She wanted to touch him. Snuggle up next to him. But she knows she must control herself. Those are the rules. "He's also one of my brothers-in-blood," she remembers. She doesn't know why she said "poor thing" to herself. It's as if she knows something strange and remarkable will happen today. Or maybe she just feels sorry for him because he has to climb up and down mountains.

Beatriz's hair whips in the north wind. Her head is a dark sun. Her body is stirred. It is cold.

"We were just talking about droughts and then this storm comes up," says Eusebio.

"I pray to God it's a storm," says Emiliano with a smile that shows how happy he is when the rain comes. "If it rains, the corn and beans will grow taller."

"I don't believe it," Eusebio says with a note of complaint in his voice. "A few minutes ago it was so bright you had to shade your eyes to keep from going blind, and now a storm threatens."

"It's not a threat, man, it's a blessing, because now there will be work."

"There's no way I can leave now. Why do I have to wander all over the place?"

"If that's all it is, you can stay here, compa, *and wait for the storm to pass—we can set up a corner for you to rest in," says Emiliano, trying to console him.*

"You have to cross two ravines," Eusebio says.

"And this storm will bring out frogs and snakes—it hasn't rained in weeks," Emiliano reminds him.

Not five minutes before, the hills were bathed in the warm glow of the afternoon sun; now wind and water are cascading down, uprooting trees and wildflowers and swallows unable to return to their nests.

"*Now that the clay has gotten soft, I'm going to make a new* comal. *I notice Ticha's other one is falling apart. . . .*"

"*But isn't that too much work, Eusebio?*"

"*What are you talking about? Anyway, I don't want to sit around and do nothing while I'm here.*"

"*Maybe you should untie your hammock before everything gets swamped—hang it in the shed, where we keep the cart,*" *Emiliano suggests.*

"*First I want to run out and find some clay.*"

"*Wait another half hour, so it gets nice and soft.*"

Ticha breaks in:

"*You can't carry all that clay by yourself, let me help.*"

Eusebio notices the girl grinding corn at the moment.

"*You could hurt yourself.*"

"*You should both go and save an extra trip. The way the rain is coming down there's no telling when it will let up.*"

"*If you've got something we can cover ourselves with, we can go,*" *says Eusebio, addressing the girl.*

Ticha leaves the grindstone and looks for a petate. *She's barefoot and dressed in* nahuilla. *Tattered but clean, like her coffee-colored eyes. Her* nahuilla *is the color of her eyes, a nice coincidence. Her feet are thin and strong, with the taut muscles of one who has worked in the fields for seven years from sunrise to sunset, from rainfall to rainfall. Her gaze is black, blacker than the darkness of the storm. Her eyes are lively. Even beautiful, not so much their size as the black light they cast.*

The last thing to die in poor people is their eyes. It's also the first thing you notice. A perfect, penetrating, expansive light. At the age of twelve her eyes seemed moistened by the afternoon showers. It's hard to tell whether from sorrow or hope. And when she's thirteen they'll come even more alive. She will be a woman then and she will meet the love of her life. Men will seek her because she works hard and she's full of potential offspring. Children improve a family's prospects. They bring blessings and food upon the house. Men admire Ticha because she spends five hours in front of the stove making tortillas three times a day, and she helps her father rain or shine. Planting or carving grindstones.

There are more than enough to love her. That is what her father thinks as he watches her, happy and proud like the animals of the field when rain comes from the volcano. She's reached the age when you can love somebody and be covered with children. Children are as shade to sun. They protect.

He's thought it over carefully. And now that his mind is clear, things begin to shine. Especially when he sees his daughter go out the door and into the yard with Eusebio, their heads covered with an old petate *mat.*

She was barely fourteen when Eusebio asked for her. After consulting with his father Macario, Emiliano expressed himself with a mixture of confidence and resignation: "Well, life goes on, and if that's the way it's got to be, then so be it."

V / BEATRIZ, EUSEBIO

1948

TICHA HAD MADE life with Eusebio beautiful and happy.
Years become minutes when a person disappears. Not knowing
where his body rests to be able to put a flower there. Not to be
able to cry for him, since you don't know whether your tears are
in vain and you're mourning his soul when he's not dead. Being
disappeared is another, awful kind of death: it's a death both for
the one who is not there and for those who love him and hope
to see him again. That's why they decided not to mention
Eusebio, so as not to grieve his presumed death, far worse than
real death. But she does remember him; she remembers the way
he walked, limping from the indigo venom laying siege to one
of his legs; she remembers the texture of his hair, still imprinted
upon her hands; she remembers the warmth and color of his
skin; she remembers his taut arms, his hardwood muscles,
sculpted by the energy expended in wielding a machete since
childhood. She knows the heat and sweat of his body from
memory, impregnating the hut every day at five in the afternoon
with its smells, a sweat that bathed and coated his body twelve
hours a day throughout his life under the cruel sun of March or
the benign and beautiful sun of December.

Beatriz felt that life with her *compañero* had been short; she
also had the sensation that it had been just yesterday that
Eusebio went to El Divisadero and he'd be back in a few hours.

She couldn't get it out of her mind, though several years had passed since his absence. He left her with three male children. In them she saw the gestures, look, and voice of her *compañero* for life.

A baby girl was born and they named her Paula. She was born right after Emiliano had made the eighth machete slash on the mango tree, figuring the number of moons. Or months. This time they saved the rooster dinner, but they were happy just the same. It was a short-lived happiness because Paula died three months later.

"Two years passed before our third son came along," says Ticha. "God did not want to favor us. Eusebio was worried because children are a blessing—they say children eat more and bring us greater poverty—but that's not how we see it. To us children grow up to give us more help around the house, and whatever they eat they earn themselves, past the age of seven. Not only that, but whatever they bring in keeps the family from starving." Ticha speaks with her eyes, with her hands and a few facial expressions, as though she's talking to the things that surround her in her home: the *guacal*—a corn-filled calabash— the grindstone, the wooden cot, and the log where people sit and smoke tobacco. "Then we had María Rosa, but she wasn't meant to live either. Lastenia barely had time to sprinkle the baptismal waters on her. God didn't want to leave me with any girls; he knows.

"Then I had two sons. We ate the roosters, too. Manuel and Jacinto, that's what we called them." Ticha uses the time by herself to talk things over with herself; outside a flock of white doves dusts the treetops with the sound of their wings. "Eusebio left for the mines in Morazán, poor thing; maybe he didn't want us to see him suffer, because one winter morning he left at dawn, at the time of year when dawn is as dark as a bat cave. He made no sound when he closed the door, so we wouldn't hear him leave. The children didn't suspect a thing, but I did. I gnawed on my sadness. Bit back my pain.

"His traveling taught me how to live alone. And my oldest boys, Pedro and Manuel, didn't even have a chance to grow up before the patrols came and took them away to do military service." She never saw them again. Sometimes she wanted to bring them back, imprison them with her memory—such was the vehemence of her thoughts. "They were barely fifteen and sixteen when they came looking for them; the country was in danger and they had to go back to the city with the military patrols, to the garrison; they were tied up like *garrobo* lizards; they cried, maybe they could tell we'd never see each other again." The wind catches the words as they come out of her mouth and carries them off into the mountains, where they bounce off of rocks, as though they had weight, as though her words were lead. She's lucky Jacinto was still too young, otherwise they would have taken him, too. Ticha draws a timid smile.

"Listen, girl, God calls the shots, he gives children and he takes them away; same with *compañeros.* It's not up to us. Even though they come out of our bellies, even though we love them very much. We must get used to worse than that. God tests us every day.

"Maybe if Paula and María Rosa had lived, our lives would be different. Women are a blessing to the family. I don't know where they got the idea to eat roosters only when sons are born. As if we weren't equal."

Ticha shouts something to Eusebio, something he can't hear because the words are lost in the sound of ducks in flight.

"What was that?" he says without looking up from the water,

intent on his pathetic fishing attempt; every day there are fewer fish on this side of the lagoon. He searches the bottom, inspecting every submerged rock.

"I said Lastenia came over to the house yesterday," Ticha repeats. This is what she said seconds before. She doesn't wait for a response from her *compañero* as she pounds clothes against the rocks, her usual method of doing the laundry, using soap made of pig tallow.

Eusebio came over holding a net, still not taking his eyes off the water's surface. He was close enough to hear what Beatriz was saying now—before, the ducks were flapping and clothes were slapping against the rocks, and the sound carried around the lagoon and up into the lush hills.

"Hm," he grunts; he's gone back to concentrating on a school of *olominas* he's discovered on his way over to Ticha. Now he can hear what his *compañera* is saying.

"And she asked about the children," she says softly, not wanting to disturb Eusebio as he casts his net.

"Who's Lastenia?"

"Don't give me that. She's the tortilla woman."

The sound of the net splashing the water gets tangled in the willow branches, slithers up the lianas, and, reaching the tops of the willows, becomes a bird soaring over the branches of other trees all the way up the hill serving as the lagoon's backdrop.

"What? I forgot who she was, that's all."

"She spoke to me."

"And what did she say?"

The net has sunk to the bottom of the lagoon.

"She asked if we wanted to send our children over to her to learn to read and write."

"And what did you say?" He hurries the question because the answer he wants is *olominas,* the few he's spotted in the depths of the lagoon. His eyes settle like two planets lost in the cool, sparkling waters.

"I said yes."

"And then what?" he asks as he scans the net, his eyes gleefully spinning like the *olominas* in his net.

"I think the kids are old enough to learn how to read."

Once Eusebio has given it some thought, he gives a more complete response:

"I don't think a one of them should go; the older boys are needed for work, and Jacinto is very young—he could get confused. Besides, is it even possible to learn at the age of six?"

He speaks with the full conviction of one who has never even seen a written letter or number, much less been able to tell them apart; to him, letters are the mystery and privilege of the *patrones*. "Also, everybody who learns to read goes off to the city." It's as if he already knows that one day, when he's no longer around, his children will take off for the city.

"What good does knowing how to read and write do for poor people?" he thinks. "What are they going to read if there's nothing written down around here? It makes sense for the *patrones* because they have to count large amounts of money and they deal with the city. I'm sure even the gang boss doesn't know how to read." He keeps these things to himself because he doesn't want to disappoint Ticha, who's excited about the mystery of the written word. "The only reason I think it's a good idea is maybe the tortilla woman would knock some sense into them."

"They've already got plenty of sense, Eusebio."

"Don't count on it—sooner or later they'll take a wrong turn somewhere."

"So you agree, then. Besides, the tortilla woman will teach them the Christian faith."

"No, I don't agree. I was taught the Christian faith by being whipped with a bull pizzle, and look at me now: I'm being eaten alive by indigo vapors and I barely make enough for salt and tortillas." He's convinced, as if all the wretchedness were played before his eyes.

Ticha wanted to have a favorable answer from her *compañero,* but she didn't want to argue with him—she herself wasn't sure about the need to read. She knew nothing about writing either. And she agreed that you only needed to know how to read if you went to the city. This wasn't as much of a problem for her as it was for Eusebio, because she knew that once her children were on their own they would inevitably wind up in the city and it was better if they had a way to protect themselves. "I figure if children are going to get lost, they might as well have a machete so they can do something about it." That's what she thinks. Besides, the tortilla woman would also teach them how to mend their clothes and patch them up, which was important; she'd teach them the Christian faith, and the importance of being clean and well dressed, so they wouldn't go around in rags. They could go around in patches, but not rags. She knew God had given them water for baths and washing clothes, but he didn't teach them how to take care of their clothes or keep things in order, because even she couldn't do that. "We mamas like to spoil our babies and so we need a tortilla woman every now and then to knock some sense into them," she thinks. She knew Eusebio's main objection was about the time they'd waste, the loss of manpower, of their contribution to the household, their ability to stave off hunger in the dead season, when the harvest was over. So she made a final proposal:

"What if they only went Sunday? Maybe one day a week would be enough."

Eusebio put his net in a sack and got ready to leave the

lagoon. He watches Ticha, naked from the waist up, washing her hair. She was done with the wash. "I love you like my right arm, like my eyes," he thinks. He waits with his answer since another flock of ducks has just flown in. "Watching ducks is like sleeping," he thinks. But Ticha's eyes cast their fishnet over him. And he comes back to reality and replies:

"Sunday is the Lord's day, it is a day of rest."

Far away you can hear the *güis,* the bird that fights with hawks and announces Christ's birth. "Christ-is-born," its song says. Long ago somebody discovered in this bird song the promising message about the birth of Christ and passed it along to succeeding generations. So the *güis* is considered a bird of good omen. It's a sin to kill one. Their meat is no good because the minute they hit the ground and stop breathing their bodies become infested with worms. It's the same if they're caught. That's how the *güis* protects itself. It brings good news. It also announces visitors. If it sings in a tree near your hut, that means you'll have visitors; also, the first person to hear it will have a visitor.

"That's the Lord's way," says Ticha whenever she can't understand something. She's very clear about the mystery of the Nativity, though. And if the *güis* announced the birth of Christ, then it must be a sacred bird. The missionaries had taught them about the Virgin Mary, the stable in Bethlehem, the cow, and the donkey. Also about how God and his Son were poor. That's where their resignation came from, as well as their knowledge of Christian doctrine.

"How many times have you been to confession?"

"Four, Father."

"Is that all? But you're an old woman."

"Not so old, Father; poverty makes me look as I do; besides, the four times I confessed were the times you people came here."

"I see your point, but you must have at least ten confessions to gain the Kingdom of Heaven."

"It will all depend on how long I live, because you people don't come around that often."

"We're going to come at least every three years."

"Then I won't live long enough to have ten confessions, Father."

"You must embrace the faith and everything will be granted unto you."

"May God hear you, Father."

She rarely spoke to the missionaries; when they came to the village, people did nothing but attend services: to confess and receive the sacraments. They always had doubts. No one was capable of voicing their doubts. The priests weren't always in the best frame of mind. They accepted their lot in life, but they mingled with the peasants as little as possible, only when it was absolutely necessary: for confessions, baptisms, counseling on dying children. Sometimes they asked questions:

"Are you with God in respect to your husband?"

"What does that mean, Father?"

"I refer to the sacrament of marriage."

"Eusebio is my *compañero* for life."

"In other words, you are living in sin."

"The only thing I know is that we have no problems, we get along well."

"And that's how you expect to earn the Grace of God? Misfortune can arise at any time, so don't say you have no problems, because one day they will rain down upon you."

"What should we do, Father?"

"We're not performing any marriages this time because we

didn't come prepared to do so; at any rate, we must warn people in advance so we can perform collective marriages; they're cheaper."

"Say the word, Father, we'll be here, we're not going anywhere."

"The important thing is to recognize the sacrament, to know that in order to walk with God and earn his Grace, you must refrain from living in sin."

"I had no idea, Father."

"Fine, now you know, and that's the first step. Three years from now when we return we'll have a good group together for a collective wedding ceremony. We make great sacrifices, coming out here in the middle of nowhere to save your souls. Imagine—you've already got two children and you're expecting a third. And that doesn't count the baby girls that died. My, my! God's wrath is mighty!"

"Thank you for saving us, Father."

Nobody told Ticha, but she could tell that in the beginning everything was calm, silent, waiting, immobile, hushed; the expanse of sky was empty. There was no Adam, no Eve, no birds, no fish, no crabs, no rivers, no ocean, no ravines for catching coati, no stars, no suns, no trees, only the sky like a vast, dark mountain range, infinitely black. Immobility and night. And Gucumatz, the Creator. When he made the mountain and river guardians—birds, pumas, snakes, pacas, coati, and ants—he also opened a door letting in the light. And there was day. When the door closed it was night. God was the light. The Maker of Forms. It is light that gives everything form.

Everything was motionless in the immensity of sky. Only lightning flashed. Then the first man appeared, made of earth and water. A clay man that couldn't move his face, stiff, empty-headed, and he couldn't turn his head—he was a clay doll. He talked and had no understanding; he listened but didn't respond to questions and couldn't follow the conversation. He spoke in monologues, hearing only himself. He laughed but wasn't happy; he breathed through his mouth, which was always open, gaping in awe and wonder at the immobility of things. Finally he dissolved on the spot where he sat, because he was absorbing water through his clay feet. It was a god that ripped time apart, like a dirt clod worn down and turned to dust between the fingers.

Then Gucumatz ordered the men of wood, or *chintos de palo* —stick men—made, with movable arms and heads that turned on their necks. Their faces were stiff, they didn't laugh, their muscles were rigid, their bodies hard and sickly; they had no veins, no heart, and they didn't breathe. These were the first true men on earth, though they were different from men today. With fire and souls inside. They lived for thousands of years. They didn't think, which was too bad. Men that don't think are a disaster. Gucumatz ordered them destroyed with a rain of stars and a hurricane of thunderbolts. They did not fight back.

And then came the war of things.

Comals and kettles hurled themselves upon the *chintos de palo,* who launched the fire they carried inside themselves, intending to burn the things, but they didn't burn because they were fireproof. And the things threw water in the faces of the wooden men, the *chintos de palo* and *chintalalas,* or stick women. Finally the men of wood and the *chintalalas* were extinguished from within. They were left without souls. The wooden humans did not survive; they were dolls who had mistreated things, and the things destroyed them, causing them to cry out in pain. The *chintos de palo* and *chintalalas* had been bad because they didn't think, they were imbeciles and tyrants. Some were saved, but they walked on all fours. Today they are monkeys, apes, gorillas, and those inclined to be dictators.

One day Gucumatz discovered a white seed, fragrant when cooked in ashes over a slow fire. It was ground into a white pulp. The cooked grain was ground with a grindstone. The seed was corn. Man was made from that white pulp. The man with understanding, that loves, that cries, that is happy on earth. On the back of the deer. The man that flies. They multiplied and had children and survived wars and fires, earthquakes and floods, meteor showers and massacres.

Above all massacres.

They went naked and barefoot. Like savage angels. They endured hunger and thirst. They survived for thousands of years, because they had hearts and understanding. They could not disappear from the face of the earth. We are here.

We are corn and water. The species will not perish. That is how it is told from generation to generation.

VI / PEDRO AND MANUEL

1945

TICHA SPEAKS:

In the months after Eusebio was gone, Grandfather Macario died. He didn't even say good-bye to anybody. He said he was hot and was going to rest under the tamarind tree. He'd never done that before. Even though he was an old man, he never said he wanted to rest. Especially not in the middle of the day.

It's his age, let him be, said my father, who had asked Grandfather not long before if he was getting tired of carving stones.

I've been doing it for sixty years, why would I get tired now? Grandfather protested.

Those were the last words he spoke. I remember him walking toward the tamarind. It was the first time I noticed he was old. His body was bent, his head sunken between his shoulders, his feet dragged. We didn't know how old he was. Grandfather himself figured he was past eighty. No one knew.

Goddam, said my father, how can anybody live so long?

Some people make it and others don't, I said, remembering my mother, Catalina, who died at the age of eighteen after I was born.

That afternoon, when we called Grandfather to come eat his bit of tortilla, he didn't respond. He was dead.

———

Pedro and Manuel got bigger every day. They both accompanied Emiliano to the *metate* quarry. All three quarried stone. One is ten. The other nine. They handle the hog machete with great skill; they shape the stone, heft it, run their fingers along the edges, trace the oval at the base with their fingertips. Meanwhile Emiliano looks for the right chunk of *metate* to begin a new sculpture, which is what the grindstone is. Emiliano gives it its initial shape and then leaves it for his grandsons to smooth the edges and make the groove where the corn is deposited to be ground and made into dough. When they're finished, Grandfather cuts the base to take to the hut. As the final step, he gives it a last polish at the hut, until it feels soft to the touch, like stroking skin. Everyone in the family gets involved in this step. They put aside their usual tasks to work together and contribute to the exigencies of life.

"Work dignifies a man," says Emiliano.

"It makes me sweat buckets," says Pedro, wiping away the perspiration that drips into his eyes and mouth and soaks his shirt.

"It's those buckets of sweat that dignify you," Emiliano insists.

Grandfather is satisfied with his work, with his independence. He had decided not to return to the indigo plantation, where all he could do was meekly submit and hope for the good fortune not to be poisoned to death.

"Life is hard," he says. "And my grandchildren must be prepared to face life as it is."

His life is like the rivers, whose waters are never the same: each second they change without ceasing to be the river. But grandfather is also a fruit tree. A grain of corn. The fertile earth. Rain. Wind.

———

Ticha's oldest sons, Pedro and Manuel, have gone to catch *garrobo* lizards. Stick chickens is what they call these small lizards that live among the leaves of trees or under rocks. They bring a dog for reinforcement on the hunt. Jacinto, the youngest brother, wanted to come along, but the older boys said he'd just get in the way—he was only five and they had to walk a long way to get to the ravine.

Pedro is nine and Manuel eight. They both go out and catch reptiles or white-winged doves on the days they don't go to the hacienda—usually Saturday.

The boys watch the tree branches. Suddenly they discover the first *garrobo*, which looks like too big a prize to let get away. The animal leaps from a higher branch to a lower one. The boys watch it from the top of the ravine.

"Where did it go?" says Manuel when they lose sight of the *garrobo*. The dog barks, pointing his head to the other side of the high rock wall that forms the ravine.

"We lost him," says Pedro with his hands on his waist, looking in the direction the dog is barking. "Or else he's playing dead in some hollow along the wall." He assumes the lizard jumped out of the tree, because they can't locate it in any of the branches. "Get the dog and go down into the ravine," he says. Sweat and sun on his face.

"All right, but we should go down, too," says Manuel, rolling his pants up to his knees. Then he starts down to the bottom of the ravine, sliding carefully on the ground, clawing the dirt with both hands. Pedro watches him. Behind him the dog barks.

"Hey!" Pedro shouts at the dog, which continues barking at the wall, which is covered in moss and oregano flowers. "This damn dog must have lost its mind," he says, scrutinizing the vegetation along the ground. "There's nothing there, because if there was you could see it from here," he shouts again from the lip of the gorge.

"Get down here, brother," says Manuel, jumping onto the dry riverbed, followed by the dog.

"He must smell something," Pedro answers. He too rolls up his pants in anticipation of the slide down.

"There's no place down here for it to hide."

"Wait, I think I hear scratching," says Pedro.

"I can't hear a thing with this dog barking."

"Sounds like dry leaves," Pedro says, stopping to catch his breath. "I think it's over there, Manuel." Pedro points to a ledge on the wall.

"Ssshh! I think you're right," Manuel answers softly. "I'm going to climb that branch to get a better look." He presses his legs together and shimmies up the trunk. "If he's there, we've got him."

"Shut up, you damn dog," Pedro shouts.

"The *garrobo*'s too big to hide on such a small ledge," says Manuel.

"The dog must be barking at something—don't forget how good *garrobos* are at hiding."

"I don't care if it's as small as a needle," says Manuel, sitting on the branch. "We could still see it."

The *garrobo* knows how to hide in small places; it hugs the ground, it is slow and silent—incapable of fleeing once it has been trapped, it prefers to await death without moving, camouflaging itself among the branches and dry leaves. Only its eyes are visible among the leaves. It is already a dead animal, besieged by the boys and the dog. For centuries it has been called the poor man's chicken, the tree chicken, the stick chicken. It grows up hidden among the green leaves when its skin is green;

it also mimics dry branches, turning gray or light brown as it sees fit. Meat of the poor. Catch of the day. *Garrobos* spread like the plague, they grow in the woods like fruit on trees. It is a domestic lizard that makes no sound, won't attack or bite, and will not fight back. Its defense is to be able to transform itself to adapt to the medium in which it hides. It can grow to be five and a half feet long, from head to tail. Sometimes it is green, like in May when the rains begin and it is young; when it is old it acquires an orange hue. The *garrobo* is gray and the iguana is light or dark green. Both turn orange as they age. Male and female, *garrobo* and iguana.

"Something's moving in the tree," says Pedro.

"Give it a jab so it'll jump—the dog's ready for him." He hands his brother a stick. "Don't lose sight of it or else it'll get away," says Manuel. "Look it straight in the eye so it stays still and doesn't jump too soon."

Pedro probes the place where he thinks he's seen the *garrobo*'s eyes.

"There he goes, get him!" he shouts to the dog. But the *garrobo* clings to the oregano flowers. Now it's gotten under the plants and is trying to dig into the earth and hide, causing dry leaves under the vegetation to crackle. It was the sound they'd heard moments before.

"Give it a good shove so it'll drop," shouts Manuel. Meanwhile the dog keeps jumping up and down trying to reach the top of the ledge.

The *garrobo* finally leaps to the only available spot. Manuel hangs from a branch and drops to the ground. Then he takes off after Pedro, who's got a stick in his hand. The dog howls deliriously, desperately, running, surprised by the *garrobo*, which has fallen at an inopportune moment. Manuel rubs his backside as he runs, for when he jumped out of the tree he landed in a sitting position. The creature does not succeed in getting away; he crouches under a rock, where the dog can easily get him. Manuel takes it out of the dog's mouth before the dog has a chance to kill it. He must take it alive and try to sell it in town. If he doesn't sell it, the family will eat it.

"Get a rope and let's tie him up," says Pedro, directing Manuel.

Pedro has the *garrobo* on the ground, its head pinned under his foot. The dog has stopped barking and paws at the sand around Pedro, pleased with the catch. The other boy ties the lizard's feet behind its back, bending them backward.

"You're a big one," says Manuel.

"We can get ten *centavos* for him."

"You must be dreaming," Manuel replies. "I think he's male, and if they don't have eggs people won't buy them."

"We'll see," Pedro sighs.

"It weighs as much as a small pig," says the younger brother.

"Probably we'll eat it ourselves."

"Mama doesn't like them, she says they're disgusting."

The sun shines on the leaves of the *guarumos* that grow along the edge of the ravine. Bees buzz around a hive hanging from a *conacaste* tree. A *torogós* cries in the distance. The *torogós* is a bird that looks like a king dressed in royal blue. It has long feathers and at the tips of its tailfeathers there are two diadems, like two eyes.

Then an unexpected thunderclap. A storm.

"Hurry, it's about to rain," says Manuel.

"Not yet," says Pedro. "Can't you see the sun's still out?"

"Yeah, but look how fast the storm clouds are gathering."

It will rain within a few minutes. Sacred rain, rain that makes the corn grow, that dislodges clusters of pine nuts and ripens the red-and-yellow hog plums. Rain that makes the purslane in the field green again; that makes the *chipilin* grow and bloom; that ignites the bellflowers in the treetops and opens the blossom of orange and lemon trees.

"The dog is still back there," says Pedro.

"Leave him there, he knows the way home."

"So what's the rush? If it rains, so what, we'll get wet, and with this heat, that's not such a bad idea," says the older brother.

"It's a long way home," says Manuel.

"It's getting dark and the Cipitio could get us."

"The Cipitio only goes after girls."

"You never know what the Cipitio might do," says Pedro, "He could make a mistake."

"Eat shit, he's not going to make any mistakes with me because if he does I'll ram a machete down his throat."

"Let's get out of here—you take one side of the *garrobo*, I'll take the other and let's run," Pedro replies, trying to change the subject.

"Now look who's scared," says Manuel.

"Scared of what?"

"Of the Cipitio."

The boys grip their prey and take off running. This is a kind of happiness they rarely enjoy: getting lost in the mountains and making new discoveries. They imagine all sorts of things and tell stories along the way. There is another thunderclap. Much louder now. It will rain all afternoon.

Emiliano tells Eusebio to go ahead and stay because night has fallen and the great storm has flooded the roads
    it was going to be very difficult to lead the mule through the ravines
    he should wait

besides Eusebio has already hung his hammock in the cart and granary shed, over the granary actually

maybe there's a chance I'll be able to get away in the morning Eusebio thinks and anyway he's in no hurry to get to Chinchontepec

and then again it's preferable to walking the roads alone now that it's afternoon or rather evening since the storm has obscured the day it must be four-thirty or five

walking the roads like a soul in torment

one of God's souls out on the road what the hell I'll stay and I'm grateful

no need to be grateful I'd offer a corner to anybody to say nothing of you and the friendship between us

what better excuse to throw some more wood on the fire it's gotten so cold

the family fire is also a very warm stove

might as well toast some of the tortillas left over from lunch or if you prefer there are a few hot off the comal

he tells Ticha to put some lard on the tortillas if there is any then he asks Eusebio if he likes toasted tortillas with salt and pork lard

of course I like tortillas with pork lard says Eusebio but I don't want you to go to so much trouble

no trouble at all don't worry Emiliano replies and then orders Ticha

put the tortillas directly on the coals

soon they're eating tortillas with salt and lard while they talk and Ticha goes looking for a clean perraje *to offer him since the afternoon shadows have fallen and it is cold*

there's nothing to do but sleep at the same hour as the chickens and save your strength because tomorrow is another day and you never know it all depends especially now that the thunder has stopped and that means it's a tropical storm I hope not since work will be called off no one will be able to get out people will stay at home and do only what is absolutely necessary during the storm

Ticha is a little machine going back and forth putting things away old clothes the top to the sugarloaf on the shelf light an ocote *branch to illuminate the hut*

look for the lamp instead it's a more dependable light her father says we've got visitors and he offers Eusebio a cigar so they can smoke while they talk

Ticha can't unscrew the cap to the lamp to add kerosene it's rusted shut they only use it for special occasions

give it to me mamita *I'll open it for you Eusebio says at the corner where he sees her trying to force off the top*

but she holds off lighting it because during a break in the rain a ray of light suddenly parts the clouds and the countryside shines as though all that water had washed the afternoon clean but it's a vain hope because a moment later it gets dark again and they must resign themselves to waiting out the storm

the smell of wet earth penetrates even the most inaccessible corners of the hut

it is the hour of prayer

the birds have fled the rain and sleep in their nests

the guazalos *go out hunting and the pumas take shelter in caves the coati also emerge with their beady red eyes like the tips of lit cigars*

off in the hills a lone man shouts maybe because he's lost or to chase away his fear so he doesn't feel so isolated his shout multiplies in the hills and people say Ave Maria Purisima *and a chorus responds "conceived without sin" and like a thousand-ringed serpent a shiver crawls up the spine under the peasants' weatherbeaten skin*

you can hear murmuring on the other side of the stick wall rivers have entered the huts

or voices hushed for fear of the night

sacred breaths sighs weary sobs laments simple loving words tree sounds are the life of the peasants

the lightness of airborne seeds released by the pochote *the* ceiba
the pacún *the* maquilishuat *trees*
    air moistened by rain and in the deep night crickets bore into the
silence the fear the night the dread
    a question what will happen tomorrow when another new sun
appears which is the same old sun that opposes the nocturnal gloom
    full of timid stars

Pedro turned out to be a lot like his grandfather Macario: he
sold pigs and grindstones. Barefoot and thin, malnourished and
hungry. Hungry stomach, hungry brain, hungry eyes. However,
he was untiring in his efforts to leave the zone to earn his tortilla
and salt. Manuel usually went along, and so did Grandfather
Emiliano, every now and then. The presence of supernatural
beings such as *cadejos, siguanabas,* and *cipitios,* as well as
haunted wagons, hangmen, headless priests, men that turned
into coyotes, and women that turned into pigs, made those
perilous times to live in. Same with the highwaymen.

The fear of mortal danger was offset by the need to live. He
launched a survival offensive from the little village where,
thanks to the indigo inheritance, men's skins were yellow. They
had been yellowed by the indigo effluvia.

Of Eusebio and Ticha's three sons, Pedro was the only one
who suffered from the dye—the last mills were shut down as he
reached adolescence. The product was known to be lethal at the
turn of the century, but it could not be vanquished, particularly
in the northern zones of Cuzcatlán. It was gasping its last breath.
Pedro had worked in the dye factory—the mill. He was charged
with the task of inserting and removing logs from the water
tanks to soak the plants and keep them submerged to the correct
depth. He had also been a presser—he would get into the indigo

vats along with other men, women, and children and press the liquid out with his feet.

Not long after he turned eleven he left his job at the mill, not so much because he wanted to escape the hellish working conditions but because of the crisis in natural colorings, precipitated by the rise of synthetic dyes in Europe; hence workers were being laid off.

For over four centuries the process of fermenting and precipitating the indigo in those rural factories had been turning the area's inhabitants yellow. Tubercular. Cancerous.

Meanwhile it had enriched the landowners who lived in the city.

The cultivation of this plant, discovered by the Spanish in the late 1500s, had afflicted many people. Thousands of peasants continued to die until finally the population was decimated. Pedro was one of the surviving 10 percent of the population descended from half-dead, half-alive Salvadorans imprisoned in the dye factories—mills—for the last four hundred years. The failure of the indigo industry saved Pedro from death in childhood.

The plant was so toxic that merely by touching it with your hands or feet you could contract skin cancer. A great number of women and children were employed at putting rocks and logs in, and later removing them, to keep the plants underwater, effecting the physiochemical process that determined the high or low quality of the dye. The men were employed in cutting the plants on the plantations and in manufacturing the dye as well as the tablets—the form in which the dye was exported.

"It eats the flesh off your legs and when you stir the water it releases fumes that go straight to your brain and make you go crazy," Eusebio, the father, says.

"But Grandfather Macario and Papa Emiliano didn't turn

yellow from the indigo," says Beatriz. "Neither did our son Pedro."

"We got out in time," says Macario. "Thank goodness our family had other ways to make a living: we had a cart, and we weren't totally committed to the mills," agrees Ticha.

"Though we men did work as *zacateros,* meaning we cut plants on the plantation, we were reluctant to get totally involved because smoke from the fermentation poisoned your blood and your lungs. When I was little I did work in the mill, but I was always in favor of getting kids out early, by the age of twelve, because it's better to starve to death than have to live with poisoned blood, because that's a living death. There's no harm in cutting. There is in milling or manufacturing," Macario tells Pedro.

Indigo enriched the landholders and the owners of textile factories all over the world. "We were dumped on by the fucking indigo, that's how I feel," Eusebio says indignantly.

"We had always been rich—the word *Cuzcatlán* means 'land of riches, fruit, jewels, and rivers'; but the mills killed us," says Macario. "Rich in corn and fruit."

Pedro left the mills when he was eleven, when indigo was no longer worth anything. When it was in its death throes. You made almost nothing. What the landowners paid couldn't even buy tortillas. The landowners were going bankrupt. So the boy devoted himself to traveling in his cart trading grindstones for salt. Stones made by his grandfather Emiliano and great-grandfather Macario.

"I don't even know how long we've been making grindstones at home—maybe since my grandfather's time or even further back than that—no one knows for sure," says Macario. "The stones saved us from having to rely on indigo and from death; we were the only people making grindstones in the region," Macario stresses to his great-grandson Pedro.

"Your father has suffered so much from the dye that he's thinking of going to work in a gold mine in Morazán," Ticha tells Pedro.

Pedro didn't go out to sell hogs alone. His brother Manuel went with him.

"The minute they meet a woman they'll forget all about pigs and carts," Emiliano says, criticizing the excursions made by Beatriz's older sons. "They're never around anymore. If it wasn't for Jacinto here, we'd be alone in the hut."

"Leave them alone, Papa," their mother protests. "At least we know they're working and not settling for being mere farm workers, giving all their sweat to the owners of the haciendas."

"It's just that the cart makes them so footloose," Grandfather insists. "It's all right for Pedro to go, he's a grown man." Being a grown man means he's over eleven. "But this one here," he says indicating Manuel, "He just lost his baby teeth." He exaggerates the youth of his second grandson. "He doesn't want to come back to the hut anymore; nowadays everybody wants to be a businessman."

"And that's not the last of it," says Beatriz, "Wait till Jacinto grows up."

People say, "The Martínez family's going to end up being rich, they work from sunup to sundown."

The people saying this also worked from sunup to sundown, but the Martínez family also worked from one rainfall to the next. From one setback to the next. Through thunder and catastrophe. Dragging their cart back and forth and back again.

"God will watch over them," their mother says as she watches them load the cart: the grindstones, two sacks of millet, one of beans.

Mother's voice expresses such vehemence that it's as though she sees God looking down on them.

They'd been making grindstones for as long as they could remember; they had inherited the thing from Great-grandfather Macario. It had been in the family for generations. Their other line of work also came from that side of the family: raising and selling hogs. Macario tied them to the back of the cart. He didn't always sell them outright; sometimes he traded them for tobacco, sugarloaves, eggs, or candles. When he was younger.

The neighbors watch the Martínez brothers go down the highway.

"Where are you two going?" Pedro and Manuel's neighbors shout.

"We're just rolling down the road."

"You stole what down the road?" the neighbors would tease. This would have offended the Martínezes if they hadn't taken it as a compliment. Besides, these were neighbors. Neighbors are sacred. They share the same blood, the blood of the village.

Sometimes they were gone for two months, depending on how far they went. Once they were out the door, they would make tracks, goading the oxen from the back of the cart, first jabbing right to left, then left to right. Quickly moving the goad from side to side, poking the oxen's flanks. The cart was loaded to capacity and made a sound like rocks rubbing together; the whisper of the wind when they headed into the wind. The sound of wood falling into potholes. Road marimbas.

"Now that they've got their own cart, they're never around anymore," Grandfather Emiliano complains insistently.

Beatriz understands the boys better:

"Let them be. At least we know they'll bring back some salt; besides not everyone has a cart—we're lucky we didn't burn the undercarriage and those old wheels, and they decided they wanted to fix it up—what a big help it is to have a rig like that."

"I was thinking about the risks they take," Grandfather says.

"Don't you remember that Grandpa"—Beatriz refers to Macario—"left the cart for junk and now we have the luxury of traveling and being able to sell things."

"We're not the ones doing it," Emiliano corrects her. "The cart belongs to the boys."

"It doesn't matter who it belongs to. Whatever the boys earn from using it goes to everybody," says Ticha.

"That's right," Grandfather concedes, "Everybody."

Eusebio was cut off for three days by the tempest that turned into a tropical storm. Once again he found himself there with Beatriz's coffee eyes as they flitted about the hut. Suddenly they rested on Eusebio's face. He repeats the exact same words, from memory, that he said to Emiliano:

"That girl is growing up, Macario, sir."

Ticha pretends she's not listening. The stranger doesn't take his eyes off her.

"I hope she finds somebody worthwhile," replies Macario.

"Of course she'll find somebody," interrupts Emiliano, "and don't think I'm exaggerating just because she's my daughter. Her mother was just like her." His eyes cloud up and it starts raining inside; to remember is to go and meet shadows you once loved. "Ticha knows her mother died ten days after she was born."

"Her mother died?" Eusebio asks Emiliano.

"Yes. Twelve years ago." And he sees the face of his Catalina.

Emiliano has gone to a corner of the hut to find a grindstone. He has the hog machete in his hands, getting ready to put the finishing touches on a grindstone. This permits him to dissemble. He thinks Eusebio can see the images of his dead compañera through the clouds in his eyes. He prefers not to talk about her although he enjoys remembering. It's his way of bringing her back home. But he doesn't like to see her lying on the floor that way. Nobody knows what to do; Emiliano runs out to find the tortilla woman—maybe she knows what to do. Macario puts a rag soaked in hot water on her head; he tries to lift her onto the wooden cot. For months now she's been spitting up blood and coughing a lot. This time she had a chronic attack. Emiliano heard it from out in the yard, where he was unloading the cart. He'd just returned from the quarry with a load of grindstones. He ran into the hut when he heard screams coming from within.

"So you were all alone?" asks Eusebio.

"That's right, all we had was Ticha. Catalina died right after she was born. Catalina didn't want to stay in bed, poor woman, and she went downhill rapidly. She didn't even last two weeks after the birth."

"It's the indigo, Emiliano. My family died the same way, both my mother and father; that's why I hate working in the mills."

Emiliano sits on a bench and puts the stone between his legs. Eusebio spreads a ball of clay out on a petate *lying on the ground. He plans to make a pitcher.*

"You're good with clay, Eusebio. . . ."

"I'm all right, but the comal *I made yesterday turned out kind of lopsided."*

"Not that much, it turned out beautifully."

"Well, we'll see what happens when it goes into the fire. This house needs somebody else in it," Eusebio dares to propose with compassion in his voice.

"We were all alone."

Nobody told Eusebio that the death of Catalina, mother of Beatriz, was not mentioned around the hut—you weren't even allowed to say her name. She was buried far away in order to avoid any reminder of her in the hut. It's best to forget her in front of others. Because she's still in his blood. She roams around there and

89

that's why he feels strong palpitations in his heart. His body had never really felt things until after she died. His compañera *flowed in his veins. It's best to forget her, he told Ticha as soon as she could understand what he was saying. "Erase all traces of her," he told his daughter. Her memory seldom visited the hut. This time Eusebio had broken the pact. It was as if his friend had come to stay.*

"You shouldn't be alone, Emiliano."

"I can't . . ."

"You'll find somebody. . . ."

"Impossible—she never died."

The storm has abated. It is cold. Emiliano periodically feels the disturbance of his compañera's *presence. She's beside him as he sharpens his hog machete. A coyote howls in the distance. The sun begins to peek out from behind the clouds and hills.*

On one of his trips Pedro took both brothers. They went to help him sell pigs. The trip would take over a hundred miles and fifteen days and they would sell the pigs in villages along the way. They left in caravan, some carrying pots and *comals,* others feed bags, saddlebags, and sacks of millet. Pedro brought the grindstones and the pigs were tied to the cart's rear axle. At least the trip wouldn't be unpleasant, Pedro reasoned. So he said. He brought his brothers along to help him. "Manuel can help, but Jacinto is very young," thinks their mother.

"In my opinion it's all right if Manuel goes; Jacinto is too small," Grandfather says, agreeing with his daughter. Nevertheless, all three are going.

Ticha and Grandfather couldn't help laughing when they saw the pigs all lined up for the journey. Also, the cart was piled high with millet and hay for the animals as well as with grindstones.

"Don't forget to bring extra clothing, it's going to be a long trip," says Grandfather.

"Take these coins along, too, in case you see something you like," says Mother.

As they say good-bye, they wave their hands sadly, like dying birds taking flight; the last good-bye. There were even tears.

"You get used to the fact that male children leave home, even if it's forever," says Mother, as if she can tell the two oldest will leave for good.

Manuel is twelve; Jacinto has just turned ten. Emiliano and Ticha were concerned when Pedro told them he was taking all nine pigs, the entire family fortune.

"What if the animals get away?" Grandfather Emiliano asks.

"Don't even mention it, I'll get nervous," says Pedro.

"Goodness, what are you going to do with all those animals?" Mother says.

They got even more concerned when he said he planned to go as far as Usulután. Pedro assured them there wouldn't be any problems and that when they came back the family would be in better shape because with what they earned they could buy a cow or a calf. Or whatever they might be able to afford.

"If we want to stop being poor we've got to sell the pigs," Pedro says.

Everybody believed him. Confidence in the oldest son.

"How do you plan to keep the animals in line?" asks Mother.

That's when he got his bright idea: bring his brothers along. He presented his plan to Mother and Grandfather and they both said God is almighty and he knows what he's doing. They didn't have to ask the younger boys more than once if they wanted to go, because even though they had no idea what the trip entailed, it was something new. When they were little they had gone to the sea but they had no recollection of it, and now they were on their way to Usulután and maybe Jiquilisco, where there was also a sea, which Pedro mentioned to get them excited about the trip.

"They're not going to last on such a long journey," Mother laments.

"And there will be four hands less to work the family plot," says Grandfather.

"I promise the pigs will bring in more than we could possibly make as farm workers," says Pedro, defending himself.

"God be with you," Mother breaks in.

"Just wait and see," Pedro says enthusiastically.

"We'll be praying for you," promises Grandfather Emiliano.

"That goes without saying," says Mother.

Mother and Grandfather gave them their blessings while the younger boys laughed and the pigs' squealing made Pedro nervous.

"I have faith in him," says Grandfather, remembering that Pedro is very much the man of the house. "I'm already an old man," he thinks. "He's not even fourteen and already he's setting off on such an arduous journey." Times change.

The dogs at the hacienda bark in the distance.

Two months later, when the boys returned, they looked bigger. Their legs had grown and their faces bore the stamp of the days lived. They were thinner and sadder, poor things, and the eldest had no belly!

"I recognize the sound of Pedro's cart," says Mother. She can tell that her son is coming. She remains motionless with her eyes fixed on the wind. She hears the music of wheels rolling over stones.

"It's them, it's my sons," she tells Grandfather.

"So you say but I don't hear a thing." Grandfather turns his head looking for invisible grandsons.

"That's the sound I hear in my dreams," says Mother.

"Your ears must be consumptive," Grandfather jokes.

"I hear them with my heart," says Mother.

When she feels the beating in her breast, the palpitations of emotion foretold, she immediately runs out the door—it couldn't be anything else. She knows the sound of the cart on the road, especially when it returns unburdened at journey's end, because that's when it pierces her to the quick. It was them.

The minute she saw them she knew something had gone wrong, because she could see it in the younger boys' eyes as they ran ahead of the cart. In the vehicle at their backs she saw Pedro with his arm in a sling and his face covered with bruises.

"What happened?" Grandfather yells.

"I fucked up," says Pedro.

"You're a wreck," says Mother, who can't stop hugging the other two boys.

Manuel speaks:

"They tortured him, Mama."

Jacinto interrupts:

"It was the Guardia."

They don't even give them a chance to ask questions. Grandfather has run over to the cart, from which Pedro jumps out with difficulty to embrace him.

Grandfather touches the cast and Pedro goes over to his mother.

"You can barely walk," says Grandfather, giving him an arm to lean on.

"We fucked up," the son says again.

Pedro says he almost died. The younger boys want to break in, but Mother tells them to go inside and change because their clothes are filthy.

Pedro tells how when they got to the marketplace in Usulután they were offered a good price for the pigs but they decided to go down to Jiquilisco instead, where they could get an even better price for them. The only things they unloaded in Usulután were the grindstones. "I can't believe we dragged those fucking pigs another ten miles," he tells Grandfather, "when we could have left them in Usulután." He felt it served him right. They tell him to sit down, take it easy, have a gourd of coffee. Mother instructs Jacinto to light the fire. She is going to make tortillas. "They're starving."

"I've got to get this off my chest," Pedro says as he sits down and rubs the cast on his left arm.

Ticha looks at him as one looks at a son who isn't guilty of anything, who's not bad, who's wanted by the law. "Bad luck is bad luck," she thinks with a shrug of her shoulders.

"Come and sit down, Grandfather," says Pedro.

"I can hear you," says Grandfather, who is unloading some banana stalks from the cart.

Mother goes to stroke her son's head, and feels the stitches and fresh wounds. Pedro leaps out of his seat.

"You're hurt bad," says Mother with tears in her eyes.

"Maybe he'd better go lie down," Grandfather Emiliano tells Beatriz when he sees the way Pedro jumps after getting his head touched by his mother; Grandfather knew something was up when Pedro took off his sombrero and he saw the matted hair.

"You'd better rest and let Jacinto tell us," Emiliano urges his grandson.

"Right, let's stay calm; Jacinto is tending the fire and Manuel is unhitching the oxen—when he comes in we'll get him to tell us the whole story," Beatriz says, attempting to dispell the anxiety aroused by Pedro's mishap.

Manuel speaks:

See, the mayor of Jiquilisco—*don* Julio Cañas—passed a law forbidding pigs from roaming the streets—kind of like martial law for animals. This applied only to city pigs, since people used to let them run wild and then they'd get the streets dirty. The law couldn't have applied to our pigs because we never let them loose—we went straight to the marketplace to sell them. But we were resting under some almond trees in Barrio Honduras, which is where we decided to stay—it was close to the sea and we wanted the pigs to be able to get to the water since it's so hot in Jiquilisco and they could suffocate.

When the people in Barrio Honduras saw all these animals —we'd hooked up with a caravan of other people selling pigs —they told us to be careful not to let the pigs get loose, otherwise they'd come under martial law. Pedro asked how that worked. They explained that a pig loose in the street was a dead pig. Since everyone in the caravan was exhausted, we turned in early; we got our carts all set up because it was late—the sun was cooling down and it was low in the sky, about to drop into the ocean. Maybe that's why we weren't as careful as we should have been. We got under an almond tree. Pedro tied the pigs loosely and said he was going to play guitar for a while. He must have dozed off, I'm not sure. We said we were going to have something to eat; as we took the food out we heard squealing down the beach. Nobody figured that the pigs—not just ours but everybody's—would eat through the knots; in our exhaustion we completely forgot they might be hungry, too—it had been such a long day—we'd all been walking since early that morning and all we wanted to do was get there, eat, and sleep.

So that's what was happening when I guess Pedro was woken up by pig squealing—we didn't hear anything—and he yelled: "The pigs!" and the shock nearly made us fall flat on our faces —especially Jacinto, since he was right in back of Pedro. My crazy brother runs out into the street, then, telling us to stay right where we are, which was near the beach, in case they came from that direction, since we still had to keep an eye on the two pigs left tied to the almond tree.

We didn't even think about *don* Julio Cañas' martial law, though we were worried that it was getting dark and we could lose the animals. Jacinto took off up the street. We were frantic when a man in the caravan, concerned about the noise we were making, came up and told us to look over by the beach near a corner where some mudholes were and there we could see some pigs taking a mudbath, the brutes. Just as he said this we saw some men in uniform with rifles in their hands; I can't figure out how they managed to sniff out the pigs so soon—or maybe it was just in their nature to go looking for trouble wherever they could find it.

Or maybe it was just the bad luck that seems to hound us poor people.

We saw the men heading straight for the pigs, but you couldn't see them all that well because they were buried in mud, in a place where the city's dirty water drained through a culvert. So I told Jacinto to go look for Pedro but not to go too far because he could get lost. I went over to the culvert to see if I could get to the pigs before the men had time to do any damage. I ran as fast as I could. I thought maybe the men had already seen them. I'd only gone a few steps when I heard them cock their guns and surround the sluice, aiming their rifles. I shouted, Don't shoot. Maybe they couldn't hear or didn't care to. After I shouted there were other shouts. People were shouting, Jacinto was shouting as he came running up. That's when they opened fire. The animals in front fell instantly and the rest, frightened by the sound of gunfire, came out unharmed. I screamed, begging them not to shoot, but the sons of bitches laughed and ran behind the other pigs now headed for the beach.

They nailed them on the spot. There were four *guardias* armed with rifles that looked like long poles. And they wouldn't stop shooting. Foam and blood. Foam oozing out of the pigs' mouths mixed with seafoam and blood. The sea itself was blood-red as the sun set behind Conchagua volcano.

When Pedro came up he tried to tell them the pigs weren't from Jiquilisco and please don't kill them because he'd brought them a long way, and he tied them up but they got loose. The *guardias* laughed and got ready to fire another round into the pigs' corpses. We were all shouting. Finally Pedro went at the *guardias*. What more could they ask for? They started ramming their rifle butts into him and one of them even took a shot, which is how his arm got broken—lucky he got hit there because anywhere else would have killed him. The *guardias* dragged him to the hospital themselves. We followed them, running beside our brother.

Later we came back to the beach to cry.

The *guardias* only took him to the hospital because the people in Barrio Honduras knew who we were. They yelled that we were honest people and if they hadn't done that, Pedro might be dead now. The people in the caravan tried to cheer us up, telling us not to cry, everything would be all right, just stay here and look after your things, we're going to visit some villages nearby and we'll come and get you on our way back, after Pedro gets out of the hospital. So that's what happened.

We learned from our neighbors in Barrio Honduras that the *guardias* get paid for every pig they kill, which was what *don* Julio Cañas' law stipulated. That's why the *guardias* hovered like vultures in the streets, like dogs on the scent of pigs. We also learned Barrio Honduras had once been full of pigs but they had almost all been shot.

This is what the boy told his grandfather and his mother. His mother hardly paid attention since she was busy applying hot compresses to her oldest son.

"Good thing the beasts didn't kill you," says Grandfather.

"Thank God he's still here to tell the story," says Mother, overcome with sobbing. "We've got to call the tortilla woman and tell her to come quick," says Mother, referring to Lastenia, the village midwife and *tortillera.*

"Get going," Grandfather orders Jacinto. The boy flies out the door.

Pedro holds his sides, he holds his head, still feeling the *guardias'* blows and the bullet in his elbow.

"Blood was coming out of his mouth and his ears," says Manuel, his eyes still filled with the horror of seeing his brother on the ground in Barrio Honduras.

"They broke my ribs," Pedro adds.

"It's a miracle they didn't bash your head in," says Mother.

"We've only got two pigs left, the ones that didn't get loose," sobs Manuel.

"Luckily they didn't steal my money," says Pedro. "We still might have enough to buy a calf after all."

"We sold everything we brought with us for a good price," says Manuel. "If it wasn't for the pigs we'd be celebrating now."

"You must leave it up to the Lord," says Mother.

Emiliano thought they should forget about the pigs and how much it would cost to replace them—they should just stick to grindstones and salt. "We were just meant to be poor, that's all."

"We must have patience," Mother says to this strange outbreak of pessimism. "Where there is hunger, God provides."

"He does?" questions Grandfather.

"Any day now," says Jacinto, coming through the door with Lastenia.

"Be still, heretic child!" threatens Mother.

VII / JACINTO

1952

"CIVILIZATION COMES over the horizon," Emiliano tells Jacinto, his youngest grandson, several years later. Jacinto stands wide-eyed and filled with the wildness of a young boy before the sea. The sea foam blankets his bare feet. He scoops water into his hands and splashes his face: he has been baptized into the earthly paradise. A different kind of baptism invented by the Salvadoran collective imagination.

Not the same as the baptism performed by the missionaries; theirs was for the purpose of attaining a place for the poor in the heavenly paradise. These were the same missionaries that arrived in boats filled with mercenaries, guns, military hardware, horses, candles, fine silks, and perfume.

Today's baptism allowed him to enjoy and revel in his right to life, regardless of sickness and hunger. From now on the important thing is to have eyes to see and hands to work; a mouth to say words, to say mama, lover, I'm thirsty, thank you, God bless. To have a heart to warn him against losing his feelings and dreams, which are also a part of living. Jacinto sensed this.

To know the sea and die. Not now, but eventually. Struggle to survive and keep your loved ones from mourning you too soon. At twelve he had few ideas for such incommensurable dreams. Macario was the same age when he came to know the sea.

There was talk of being thrown out of the hacienda. The crisis of 1950 was making haciendas unprofitable. Children were no longer needed. The land barons had no more use for them. "What will become of the family when they fire me?" Jacinto wonders. "We'll just have to wait and see," answers Grandfather. "Are you going to teach me the trade?" he asks. "Yes, you and I will do it together," says Grandfather, referring to the grindstones. "Maybe we'll plant millet," says Jacinto. "Or a few beans," concludes Grandfather Emiliano.

From that moment on he would begin to reap the benefits of life. Concerning the problem of eternal bliss: he would leave that to work itself out once he was dead.

Once you know the sea, you start having the best thoughts, though some real dreams can fade away.

Too bad for Ticha. Macario dead. Eusebio gone. Her two oldest sons forced to join the military. That left Jacinto and her father Emiliano. "Between the three of us, we'll keep from starving," says Ticha. Jacinto carried on his brothers' business. Living off the family plot meant certain death. Conditions were rough. "But we're still here," says Jacinto, using the poor's favorite expression of hope in Cuzcatlán.

"Having a bit of land is slow death. There are no seeds, no fertilizer, no grass." Nothing but the awareness that you're poor and the will to live.

"Jacinto hardly spends any time in the village," the neighbors say. "He's got to go out and earn a few more *centavos,*" says Ticha. "Could it be that he doesn't like living in such a rundown shack?" the neighbors ask maliciously, hinting that the other sons left and never came back. "They didn't leave, they were abducted," Ticha says, defending them. "Necessity has the face of a dog," says Emiliano. "Now that he's gotten hold of that cart, he'll never let go," Mother says with admiration. Her son knows the world. Cuzcatlán is the world.

It's just a few miles from Apastepeque to the city of San Vicente. Jacinto likes to go beyond that. Sometimes he goes as far away as Usulután, and from there he goes down to Jiquilisco to look at the sea in passing. And to sell pigs.

"If you want to eat fish, you've got to get your ass wet," he says. Though he's only working to earn his tortillas and salt. And once a year a few new clothes. "The gringo fishermen who control the Jiquilisco coast eat lots of pork, pigs sell well there," says Jacinto.

Between the lagoon and the village of Apastepeque runs a highway that leads to all the cities in Cuzcatlán.

"You can get anywhere from Apastepeque; there are two routes that lead either up the highway or down the highway, including all the roads that branch off." The whole world within reach. All the villages and all the hamlets of Cuzcatlán in the wheels of his cart, all he has to do is decide where to go.

"Going to Jiquilisco is like descending the petticoat of the world," he says jauntily, since not many would cover the distance alone. It's nearly a twenty-day trip.

At first he only went as far as San Vicente, but when he ran out of buyers for his stones, he went farther. He had no choice.

"As long as nothing bad happens to him and he manages to sell the stones and pigs," sighs Mother.

"Good thing he has no vices," says Grandfather.

"If he uses his head and puts his trust in God, nothing will happen to him," Mother observes.

"He's a man," says Grandfather, proud of his grandson. He sticks out his ancient chest, displaying his feeble arms like flagpoles, from which hang a threadbare shirt as ancient as he is. Bone-thin from being worn out and malnourished.

———

Young Jacinto joined his grandfather and mother when they went to quarry stone. He was excited about his new profession. Stonecutting is a sacred occupation.

Every day there were fewer buyers for the stones because they lasted forever and you only bought one in a lifetime. In the absence of Pedro and Manuel there was no one but Jacinto to go out to the villages.

"We would starve to death on corn alone," says Grandfather.

"And now that the land won't produce, it's even worse," says Ticha.

"On top of that, the stones are worth less and less," Grandfather Emiliano laments. "Too bad I'm too old to go traveling anymore."

They decided to continue selling pigs. At first they sold them in their own village. Then Jacinto decided he could take them to the coast, where the Southern Sea beats. Trade the hogs for salt. They needed salt as a staple along with tortillas. Bring it back to Apastepeque, where there is no sea and salt is expensive. And not readily available.

"What would we do without salt?" muses Grandfather.

"Without tortillas, you mean," Mother corrects.

"Well both, actually," he assents.

Jacinto interrupts:

"If the stones aren't selling in Apastepeque, since everybody already owns one, then we've got to look someplace else; and if I can't get a good price for pigs in San Vicente, then I'll go to other villages."

"Too bad the grindstones last as long as most people's life story," Emiliano says to himself.

Grindstones are meant to last for all eternity, like true love.

No room for improvement. A grindstone is sold to a customer only once in his life.

The stone grinds the corn cooked every day.

Our daily bread.

You eat tortillas until you die. Salt, too, though it symbolizes sin. That's what the missionaries say.

"What do we eat, then?" Grandfather Emiliano wonders.

"Maybe that's why we're sinners," Mother reflects.

Emiliano remembers his brothers and his mother and going hungry:

"What are we going to eat now, Mama?"

"Chicken shit," Mother answered feebly, having run out of salt and with nothing but a hot tortilla to feed her children.

The children guessed what the matter was:

"No salt today, Mama?"

She just stood there thinking for a few minutes and said:

"When Macario comes home there will be more than enough salt." The hope and tenacity with which she awaited her com-pañero's return gave her the strength to go on.

Beatriz makes the tortillas. All mothers in Cuzcatlán make their own tortillas. Not always. Sometimes there's a tortilla maker in town, a *tortillera;* but generally each family makes its own. That's the way it's been for generations. The *tortillera* is for backup, just so no one goes without. When the woman of the family gets sick, when the mother has to go to the fields or do the wash by the river, it is the *tortillera* who supplies the daily bread. The village *tortillera* makes the bread of God. She is also the official suppliant, the masseuse, anesthetist, remover of worms from babies' stomachs, attendant at birth, teacher of the Christian faith, and the one who teaches children how to read and write. She knows the mysteries of herbs for curing sickness.

The *tortillera* is like a white witch: she does only good. Ancient Lastenia is the people's mourner.

The *tortillera* is the mama of all Salvadorans.

That's how it's been for centuries. She's the Virgin Mary of the poor.

He was alive and kicking. He was awake. Jacinto became aware of this, lost as he was in dreams, when he heard his mother shout. Be careful of the waves. Waves the size of a hut. He looked back to where the family was gathered, next to the cart under a *tihuilote* tree. Along with two oxen eating hay. Ever since his father Eusebio and his brothers Pedro and Manuel disappeared, he's considered not only his mother and Emiliano a part of the family, but the oxen, too.

Further along the black beach that stretches like a long plain sleeping beneath the sun, Grandfather Emiliano catches crabs, covering them with his hat, then tying their claws shut and tossing them in his knapsack.

Behind Jacinto lies the road back to Apastepeque. A yellow road carpeted with bellflowers and natural pastures; a road that climbs up into the mountains, scaling peaks, until it is lost in heaps of clouds. That's the only road they would take in their cart, loaded down with salt and dried fish. Climbing the whole way up to Ilobasco. Along the way they would trade their wares for necessities like clothing, strings of dried fruit, sugarloaves, a mirror for Sundays, sandals for Grandfather. In other words, whatever they could find to sell in Apastepeque. Salt for the poor; dried fish for the affluent to eat during Holy Week.

They had come down from up north two days ago, bringing grindstones, and they would return with dried fish and salt. They looked for other ways to live since there was no work. The country had even less use for their hands than before. The ships left with less coffee and came back loaded with industrial products. Ships filled with strange merchandise would leave again empty of raw materials. Warships also came on goodwill visits; however, this was something they failed to understand. The ships made sure the Americas were for Americans. For Grandfather, Mother, and her children—but they didn't understand, they didn't know what America was. They knew about their own Cuzcatlán, but they were unaware of their America, to say nothing of the reasons why the warships came to display their guns. This philosophy of death didn't put food in their mouths. Their survival and protection were in their own hands, in the small plot where they grew millet and sometimes corn or beans; and in the wildflowers—bellflowers and dandelions—which no one planted but which covered the ground with rainbows.

Jacinto was not able to put such complex problems into words at the age of twelve. This was the day he was baptized into the earthly paradise. With sea water, which is universal water because it bathes all the world's coasts.

See the sea and die. Contemplate the blue eyes of the sea, while the geography behind you rises tall and wide. You can touch the volcanoes with your hands.

They had come to Acajutla—Grandfather, Mother, and Jacinto. In her time, Mother's parents brought her, in more rugged times past, when there were only burro and mule trails. Grandfather had also known the sea at the proper age, brought here by his parents in an age that belongs now to the distant past. And his great-great-grandparents brought his great-grandparents.

Jacinto would also bring his children, and his *compañera*—

when it was time to have a *compañera*—to these beautiful, unowned waters. His brothers, Pedro and Manuel, had been brought in their time.

He would come to this place every year, many times in his life, in a future that at the age of twelve was a dream. And he would see newer and more modern ships. In that future he would come to know that he would not change, nor would the sea. Only the ships would change, bringing guided missiles, planes like lice on deck, and nightmares that he, at the age of twelve, and with a certain innocence, could not yet imagine.

He would not change as he grew older: skin darkened by perpetual malaria, eyes hollowed by a chronic and centenary malnutrition. Yes, he would reach forty and he would get to know his grandchildren, who will be like him when they are young: feet bitten by chiggers, bodies covered with horseflies; tortillas and salt their only diet. He doesn't think things will get any better in the foreseeable future.

Years afterward, Jacinto would bring his *compañera* to the ocean. He would also come with his children. And without realizing it, he would fill them with inspiration.

Jacinto can't imagine how long his life will be. But he would decide the day of his death, the exact day and hour, and character, of his death. He does not want to die in bed, but on his feet at the very least.

Watching Cuzcatlán from its blackened silver beaches; mountains and volcanoes covered with bellflowers, broom, dandelions, and boys and girls with guns in their hands.

It is a dream he has at twelve.

He will not be the same when he reaches old age, because he will have lived several lives, more lives than a cat or mountain lion; more lives than Mexica-Pipil poetry. Than the songs that invite him to sleep:

> *Hush little baby*
> *Pumpkin head*
> *Coyote will eat you*
> *If you don't go to bed*

His grandfather sang this song so he could sleep without being afraid. No one is the same after so much living, so many lives. Realized through his children, who would be lying among the mountain flowers. Fighting. In those mountains he looks at now, turning his back to the sea.

Mother tells him to get out of the sun, or he'll have kidney problems or headaches. Jacinto listens to the shout his mother emits beneath the *tihuilote* trees, which have been planted by birds for miles and miles along the coast. The birds eat the fruit and scatter the seeds throughout the land. At the age of twelve he has beautiful dreams. Mother tells him to get in the shade. There where they have made camp, waiting for the salt sellers and fishermen, who will sell them salt and dried fish.

At the age of forty he will come here with his children in search of salt and fish to take back to the village. It will only appear that he hasn't changed. He will have changed through his children. The inspiration with which he instills them. The fish and salt carried by his children will go first to Apastepeque and then up north by cart, toward Chalatenango, where the other boys and girls, the *muchachos,* are. The *muchachos* spread across the volcanoes and hills, holding guns. His children will have wrested the whip from their executioners' hands. They will pursue their executioners; they will be climbing those beautiful mountains, ascending peaks, scaling passes, hiding from the bombing. Full of inspiration that, like the tail of a comet, reaches into every heart and sets the spirit aflame.

At twelve, Jacinto is a full-grown man, ready to face all the deaths they heap upon him. That is what it means to live many lives: to confront the possibility of death many times.

Life and death. They were identical. To him, who had known the wide world of towns and villages in his eight-thousand-one-hundred-twenty-four-square-mile country, with lakes and mountains and landowners who had been his enemies; though Jacinto could not know this at the age of twelve, or twenty, or thirty—but at forty-four, when at the end of his particular history, storm clouds in his family life would gather overhead.

And now he stood astonished before the sea. And frightened at times to be submerged in it; maybe because that's where invasions always came from, and where the blood of the poor, like him, flowed. However, it was also a sea of hope. Its saltwater arms reached out to another world, to other brothers. Someday ships would come not laden with death and destruction.

A tendency to be left on their own. First it was Father who abandoned them to go to a gold mine, El Divisadero, in Morazán; next Great-Grandfather Macario died; and finally the older brothers left. Only Jacinto, Ticha, and Emiliano remained. Grandfather Emiliano would never leave them. Neither would Mother, who was the center of the household, the sun around which revolved the planets of poverty and hope. He took pig selling more seriously. He tied ten hogs to the axles of his cart. Two groups of them trailed behind. Under those conditions Jacinto drove carefully. He had just turned sixteen.

"Jacinto, listen, don't take a goad, because you don't want to take unnecessary risks and you could jab the poor things to death, son," says Mother.

"How can you say that?" says Jacinto, defending himself.

"It's just in case, son," Grandfather interjects. "You don't want to stab yourself in the hand while you're goading the oxen, because then it's good-bye pigs—they'll take off with the cart and you won't have beans," concludes Grandfather.

"I'm not that stupid," says Jacinto.

"You can be very stubborn," says Mother.

"You must take me for an idiot," says Jacinto. "It's our blood I'd be spilling." He says this seriously, as though seeing endless rivers of blood.

The first pigs had been bought with everyone's savings, the result of sales; therefore, they belong to everyone. Though the group left the decision-making up to Jacinto; he had earned that privilege. That's how Grandfather saw it. It was also his mother's opinion, though she wouldn't say so. Because she had faith in her son. She was with him in thought, alighting like butterflies on his head, fluttering all about, not leaving him be. Thoughts are guardian angels.

Eusebio was dead. They didn't like to think about it. Ticha had illusions. Besides tortillas and salt, the poor also live on dreams. "As he came, so he left." She came to love him very much; but he was like fire in the hills, brilliant and beautiful, immense, but once the columns of smoke rise and the fire dies, nothing is left but hot wind. Traces of incandescent stars that have passed this way. Nothing but signs, flashes. "Poor man!" He was being eaten alive by indigo. His legs were red, and the skin began to peel off. It was cancer from the indigo. "He liked to sing songs and play along on his guitar." Perhaps Eusebio was the last indigo victim. He started singing her love songs without the slightest intention of falling in love with her. "He never flirted with me and I didn't flirt with him either—it was just the opposite: we were serious to the point of saying enough is enough." He left his guitar as a souvenir; now it belongs to Jacinto, the youngest of his sons. He had also left her Pedro and Manuel, the older sons, whom she was beginning to forget. They didn't live at home anymore, they'd been taken to the garrison to go and make war. "I never found out where they went." Once your sons leave home, you've got to learn how to lose them forever. She didn't even know whether they were alive or dead. Same thing with Eusebio, her *compañero*, all she knew was he'd been driven away by cancer from the indigo and the desperation of being poor. "His corn crop was ruined by locusts, a plague of locusts that neither fire nor noise could drive away." Then he said he was going off to El Divisadero, a mine recently discovered by gringos. "It was as if he was going to the asshole of the world, but face it, what could we do for him?" He said it was best just to make the decision to go and when he'd saved up enough he'd come home and maybe if they bought a couple of oxen everything would turn out all right. "So he left for El Divisadero, in Morazán, and they say there wasn't even a road, he got there by mule trail." Rising out of poverty. "It's the dream of the poor." Poverty was responsible for a father leaving his village never to return. "Maybe the cancer got him." But Ticha remained faithful, beyond death. "Because first of all there is hope." Years and years would pass and she would carry that hope on her face, displaying it like a star nailed to the sad look in her eyes. "He began by touching my hands. I was talking to him, without looking at him, because I had a feeling in my heart." His warm fingers flew like the butterflies in her stomach. From that day on she thought Eusebio would be her *compañero*. "And I didn't want him to let go of me." The heat in his hands melted those of his *compañera* and made them inseparable, welding them together as one. "And I swear I never even batted an eyelash at him; it's one of those things that happens and you can't explain it." He left home and never returned. "Maybe he didn't want to disappoint us; after all, he did leave me with three sons, how could he come back empty-handed, the poor man!" That was her hope: "Someday he'll come home." The dream of the poor, the most legitimate, is rising out of poverty. They also have nightmares. This fucking life. "Someday things will be better for us." Whoever "us" is. Maybe it's the family unit. When will that day come, who will make things better? Anyway, she was happy with her father, Emiliano, and her youngest son. Her family was her world.

They had received spiritual aid from the missionaries who arrived in their area every three to five years. The missionaries had taught them that only through forbearance could they save their souls. That was the only thing that mattered. Because if they couldn't find happiness on earth, it was waiting for them in heaven, complete with fruit, rivers, flowers, and seed. Heaven was like Cuzcatlán: a land of gems. That's why they had to be bound to their huts. Be content with a couple of oxen, children, and a little piece of land lent them by the *patrón* in exchange for free labor and a percentage of what they produced. The hut was also part of their world. To each his own: if you must starve to death, starve; if you can work, work. Eusebio had committed a sin by leaving home, because that meant he wasn't content with his lot. If there's enough to eat, then fine. If there's not enough to eat, that's fine, too. God decides these things. Each person must pray to his saint. Resignation was the other dagger that drew their blood. Though the deepest wound came from the exploitation by the landowners, heirs to the slave owners and Spanish colonists who were granted Indians by royal decree.

Those in favor of resignation earned the favor of God and therefore an eternity of privileges in the hereafter. In bliss beyond this mortal earth. If life was an accumulation of misery, then death signified a voyage to eternal glory. On condition that one prostrate himself before reality.

Resignation is like hope; except that hope deals in concrete dreams: "Someday Papa will return," says Jacinto. He never returned. He died of tuberculosis or cancer. Or was crushed in the collapse of a mineshaft out of which rivers of gold flowed into ships anchored at sea. Then off to other worlds beyond the sea they knew so well.

If it wasn't for the guitar, Father would have been just another dream; yet when Jacinto plucked the strings, it was his father's hands that played. In a way the guitar was the living spirit of his father. "He sings the same way, the sound he makes with the guitar is the same; it's as if I'm hearing *him*, and those are the hands he rested on mine so we would be one forever.

He had caressed her gently. At that moment Ticha knew they would always be together in dreams and death. But she was afraid to look in his eyes; afraid to find herself together for the first time with the compañero *who would share her life with her. Afraid her hands would not respond with equal warmth to Eusebio's. Life taught her how to communicate with him.*

Memories are dreams seen from the other side.

People lived without thinking about it. Everybody.

"So many mouths to feed," Ticha complains. Though the burden of their expenses falls on Grandfather and Pedro, the oldest son. Ticha and the other two sons work but not enough to make a significant income, especially since the hacienda doesn't provide food for children under eight. Pedro does get a ration of tortillas, but not the two younger ones; the youngest, who is six years old, can barely fill the quota required by the gang bosses: fill a bag with beans and you get paid tortillas and salt. Anyway, Mother didn't go to the hacienda often. She looked after the millet or did laundry by the river. The grindstones did give some respite from their poverty; but that meant they had to go to the quarries on Sunday—Grandfather and Pedro as well as herself. Any other way would have made it difficult to survive. There was no extra spending money.

When the oldest boys were captured and taken to the city to perform their obligatory military service, both Mother and Grandfather felt they had run out of options for survival. Because if they were barely scraping by with the older sons around, what would become of them without their help?

"God will provide," says Mother.

"Two less mouths to feed," Grandfather sighs.

"But that's four less hands," notes Mother.

"And the hands are what count," Grandfather says more to himself.

"Jacinto is our only hope; he's finally earning a decent amount from clearing land, almost as much as we do," says Mother.

"He can do half a job in a day," says Grandfather.

"He doesn't have far to go before he does a full day's work," says Mother, thinking about the quota required by the gang bosses for adults, even though Jacinto is only eleven.

"Maybe if they put him with us he would earn more," says Grandfather, thinking Jacinto could work one day clearing land and the next in the stables, milking cows and giving them water. "Clearing pays better," Emiliano adds.

"Forget it," says Mother. "Eusebio left home to earn more."

"You're right, forget it," says Grandfather, agreeing with Mother and not disputing Eusebio's reason for leaving: the disease in his legs was spreading, and he was fleeing reality.

"Let's leave things the way they are," says Mother. "Or better yet, let him work one day and not work the next."

"I was thinking maybe it would be best if he just did the milking, it's less of a burden," says Grandfather.

"When he turns twelve," says mother, "he'll be like his brothers."

"Don't ask too much of them, though, or they'll say they've had enough and leave," says Grandfather, thinking about Pedro and Manuel.

"We can't complain about Pedro and Manuel," says Ticha, reading his thoughts.

"Some luck, eh?" Grandfather reflects.

"That's what I was saying," says Mother.

"What?" queries Grandfather.

"God is good," Mother affirms confidently.

"You're right," says Emiliano, although after fifty years of life, during which he has not been separated from his daughter, not even when she lived with Eusebio, he has never considered God to be good. "He keeps us alive, is all," grandfather says to himself.

"Being kept alive is all we need," says Mother, as though hearing her father's words, though they were inaudible.

Tortillas with salt is what they eat. Sometimes beans, but not very often. Once Jacinto switched to working every day at clearing, they were able to buy a cow. "We have milk," says Mother. And they made milk pudding which Ticha sold door to door; or to the laborers. Jacinto had to double his contribution to make up for the absence of his two older brothers.

"The family plot helps out, too," says Grandfather.

"It doesn't belong to us, but it's something," Mother sighs.

"Nobody knows whose land this is anymore," says Grandfather.

"When it comes time to collect their share of the harvest, the owners remember whose it is," says Mother, referring to the tribute they were charged.

"Do they really need what they take from us?" asks Grandfather.

"Who knows?" Mother replies.

As the soil began to give out, the proprietors of the land disappeared; they surfaced again during the corn or millet harvest to claim their percentage of whatever was produced. The land was being abandoned, fallow fields scratched the sky; nobody cleared or burned them. The property owners had emigrated to the south, to the volcanic regions where the coffee industry was booming. Three hundred years before the Cuzcatecs were driven off their lands and forced to populate the volcanoes. Now, with the demand for coffee, there were new evictions; the land barons went into the highlands to plant the coffee; they issued the proper decrees obliging the population to turn over their small holdings to the new coffee impresarios. The Guardia Nacional was created at that time to put the decrees into effect in the event of opposition. So the Cuzcatecs returned to the north, which they had left three hundred years before, to go back to lands exhausted and impoverished by three centuries of indigo cultivation. And if they weren't willing to return, a war would have to be waged against them so the laws and decrees intended to stimulate coffee production would be upheld. The war had been declared at the end of the previous century. The proprietary governments made great economic sacrifices to dislodge the Cuzcatecs, the Salvadorans, from their lands, to exterminate and eradicate the cancer of disobedience. If they wanted a plot of land they could return to Cabañas and Chalatenango, where the land was unoccupied. Or they could stay on the volcanoes as mere coffee pickers. If they wanted to live on the volcanoes, they could do so under trees, because nobody was allowed to build a hut, nobody was allowed to grow anything but the new grain. And only the coffee barons could do that. To ensure the effectiveness of this decision, the army was reinforced and the Guardia Nacional created; the former to defend against threats from the outside, which usually meant Guatemala, the former captaincy general; and the latter to combat insurrections in the fields. Like any occupying army.

So it had been easy for them to get a small plot of land, which had room enough for a hut; they had stones and sun. Brambles, reeds, and mimosas. Vultures and a variety of birds. They had been able to take possession of parcels in the poor zones of Chalate, Cabañas, and San Vicente. The family had settled in like a *conacaste* tree, full of leaves, butterflies, birds, and flowers. Roots dug deep into the earth. On vacant land near the Apastepeque lagoon.

"The land isn't ours," says Grandfather. "They lent it to us, but now they have forgotten about it," he tells Ticha. "The owners come only once a year to collect their tribute."

"At least we live in peace and tranquility," says Mother, her eyes like lamps, because at that moment the fire of the five o'clock sky shone through the door of the hut.

Grandfather's grandfather had begun the stone trade. But they weren't quite sure about that. That's how long they'd been sculpting stones, selling animals and eggs, planting millet, corn, and occasionally beans. Beans make the earth porous, where the soil is poor, and the cornstalk serves as a pole for the bean plant as it climbs the corn's golden frame, like a river running uphill.

"We're not too bad off—we're still alive, there's the proof," says Mother.

"The land dies like the people, that's why they don't give out cornfields or beanfields like they used to. Everything is anemic; the land is dying, it doesn't want to give anymore," says Grandfather.

"Ox poop will make the land come back to life," says Jacinto.

"And where are all the oxen to fill the parcel with poop?" asks Grandfather.

"It doesn't matter if it's just a little, the land will gradually revive; if the oxen poop twice a day, that's enough," says Mother. "And to be honest, all we've got is a sliver of land in the first place."

"We also need water—plenty of water—and in the last few years the rain has been stingy—a storm every now and then isn't enough; we need something besides grindstones to live on, we can't depend on millet and corn anymore, and the haciendas are closing down," the youngest son points out, his eyes riveted to a bunch of mangoes hanging from a tree framed by the door to the hut.

"Without the hacienda we'll starve," says Grandfather.

"Maybe we can work harder at selling stones," Mother reflects.

"Or we can sell pigs full-time," Jacinto proposes decisively.

"They're not worth anything around here," says Grandfather.

"Maybe in San Vicente it would be different," Mother suggests.

"That's pretty far away," Grandfather interjects.

"With a new cart I could go even farther than that, like my brothers Pedro, Manuel, and I did that time," says Jacinto.

"God save us," Mother says in a panic.

"God will save us," says Jacinto.

"Don't make fun," Grandfather protests.

"Leave him be. He probably won't have to go that far to sell or trade." Mother looks at the bunch of mangoes swinging like the hanging nest of an oriole.

He saw Juana for the first time as a little girl, when he was on his way out of Apastepeque. She was lost in the underbrush, hacking away at weeds, gasping for air as though she had just run a long way. And she had a laugh that said, "Hi, how are you," though she said nothing in words, and there were no introductions. She was still too young to be introduced; only older people get introduced.

He arrives and quickly opens the door, shouting if there are any mean dogs around; they answer no, come on in. So he did.

"Can you spare some room for my cart, so I can rest and give my oxen a chance to eat while I lie in my hammock?" He would rather pay for a place in town than stay out in the open fields because he didn't feel safe there and he'd have to sleep with one hand over his heart and the other on his moneybag, where he kept a few pennies for buying salt. There was the little girl—the daughter—and an older woman—the mother.

He also says, "Hi, how are you," as he takes a seat on a wooden log they've offered him. He feels he is speaking with his eyes alone: "Where did this girl with the face of an apparition come from, walking on air like a phantom?" He never thought her laughter was directed at him, since little girls don't laugh at anyone in particular—they just show their rabbit teeth so somebody looks at them. Nor did he ever imagine they would be *compañeros* years later.

He takes a deep breath and from far off comes the smell of the lagoon wafting over the hills. He knows it well. It is carried by the strong south wind. The lagoon is about three miles from there.

"This is my daughter," the woman says once they've made an arrangement about the siesta.

"So, you can stay here, no problem." He feels like they're saying: "Stay forever, you're not in the way, you're the kind of person we can trust."

"I come this way often," says Jacinto.

"We've never seen you before," says the young girl.

"I take another road; it used to be a good one, but now there's so many carriage ruts, even though it's farther to San Vicente going past your place, the road's better." He addresses the woman.

"Have you come a long way, *compa*?" the mother asks.

"Not really. But the thing is there are no houses from here to San Vicente. I come from the lagoon."

"Oh, is that all?" the woman says.

"And what do they call you?" the girl asks.

"My name is Jacinto; what's yours?" he says all at once.

"Juana," she answers in a smooth voice, as though speaking into a cave.

"And I'm Rosaura," the woman says.

"Does she belong to you?" he asks, looking at the girl.

"Yes, she's the oldest—the other kids and their father just left for town," Rosaura replies. "They always go for an outing on Sunday," she adds.

It seemed as though they had been friends before they were born. Something about the trust that came out, the looks they exchanged. You get to know people by the way they look at you.

"Also by the sound of their voices," the woman says.

"What was that?" Jacinto asks Rosaura.

"Nothing," she says. "You can stay, there's no problem, we trust you."

"Thank you."

Friends for centuries. That's what that feeling of intimacy indicates, despite the fact they just met. They've known each other for four hundred years. He can feel it. They are bound by the prayers they were taught with violence. The cross placed on their foreheads as someone might stab with a dagger. The law of the strongest came from heaven.

Now they are together for the first time. Under the same roof. This is your house, Juana has said. "She's pretty smart," Jacinto thinks. And suddenly some of the songs his grandfather Emiliano used to sing silently come to mind.

> *We are necklaces and we are* quetzal *birds*
> *I string your songs together like emeralds;*
> *That's also how we come together as friends on this earth.*

Another song comes to Juana's mind, a song girls sing when they haven't yet reached adolescence and they meet a stranger who attracts their attention:

> *Get out of here you ugly Injun*
> *Get out you lazybones*
> *You look like baked* garrobo
> *Cooked on a hot* comal

She laughs when she thinks of this song. Rosaura looks at her and asks, "Why are you laughing, girl?" "No reason." "People that laugh by themselves are remembering all the bad things they've done," her mother quotes. "Let her be, children always know what they're doing," says Jacinto, trying to defend her.

VIII / MICROBUS TO SAN SALVADOR

January 9, 1981

A GIRL STARTS talking to herself. She knows that no one can hear. She began whispering when she was little. Silence in the chapel. Silence as she passes the authorities. Silence as she picks coffee or cotton, as she pats tortillas. Her life is a whisper.

Silence when she listens to her mother say she should marry young, so she can become a serious person, so she can start having children. The girl hears her own voice, resonating within like a cavern filled with doves fluttering their wings and taking flight. She knows she should speak, even if it's to the lagoon near her house; the lagoon she knows as well as her own body; the spot where she goes to do the laundry with her mother and bathe with her sister. She likes to talk to herself, it's one way of living with her consciousness at the surface of her skin. The solitude of working over the stove or on the estates is crushing. She remembers when she made tortillas, rounding them with a magical movement of her hands, in a praying position, caressing them, giving them thickness and texture, with the love women have lavished on their food for centuries.

"Poor, poor people," she says listening to her voice deep inside. "Look how they arrive—armed with powerful rifles—how can we fight them if we must use our hands for working? Our life isn't ours anymore. Maybe it never was."

"Look what happened to my son, *comadre.*"

"Be still, *comadre,*" the girl says, choking on her words as she places her hands on her kinswoman's shoulders, hugging her so she won't get cold.

"He was the oldest, you know."

"Yes, *comadre.*"

"They took him from me: he wasn't a bad boy and they killed him like a dog. He was coming home from the estate; he always goes with his papa, but this time the old man stayed behind to help make a canopy for some new workers to sleep under. Maybe it was better that way, otherwise they both would have been killed."

"Our luck gets worse every day, the people we love are leaving."

"They were waiting for him near the ravine, you know, and he wasn't even fifteen yet—our oldest child, our pride and joy. What's going to happen when we've got no kids left? They hate kids once they get to a certain age. They say it's because they're future guerrillas. It's an outrage, they just automatically make assumptions."

"They don't want people to grow up, they're afraid of us, they want to exterminate us all."

"What ingratitude."

"Don't cry, *comadre,* God is almighty."

"Sometimes I doubt his might, *comadre,* and I hope my tongue doesn't get struck by a bolt of lightning for saying so."

"You won't get struck, because you mean no harm."

"Even if I do get hit by lightning, it's long past time to keep quiet and say amen to everything."

"If we talk they kill us, there's the rub."

"Someday they'll pay for it, *comadre,* of that I am sure. These injustices can't go on forever."

Being a peasant girl. Being a peasant girl, a *campesina*, in Cuzcatlán means that my parents, grandparents, and great-grandparents were peasants. Their great-great-grandparents were Masters of the Earth, they cultivated it and distributed its fruits equally amongst everyone. Later the Masters became slaves and the talents they had developed for poetry and combat were suppressed.

There is much of the poet in the Cuzcatec peasant. It has been passed down to us by former generations. When they ask for rain, they invoke it not only to make the plants and fruit grow but also because they consider rain the Goddess of Happiness here on earth, since she brings peace and food to men. Rain is cause for celebration. The force of the wind that precedes a storm tears birds and leaves out of trees. The sky is covered with birds. People are filled with inspiration.

That was the reason I went to contemplate the hill for one last time. Because I was going off to live with my godparents in Chalatenango. I wanted to leave some seeds planted, *ceiba* seeds, so when I came back to my hamlet of Apastepeque I would be received by broad-limbed trees where *garrobos* and leaves and birds dwell.

"I shall leave these *ceiba* seeds," she tells Juana. "I snatched them out of the sky when they were airborne." *Ceiba* seeds are carried by the wind. "And I'm going to mark them so I don't forget where they are." So I put stones from the river at the foot of the hill. "So the hill won't go bald." And so the orioles and *guacalchías* come and sing in the morning. "That is all I ask of you."

"Don't be silly, child, you know very well the *ceibas* don't need to be planted, they sprout all by themselves," my mama says.

The daughter disagrees: "They can't sprout all by themselves."

"The wind sows *ceiba* trees," says her mother, furrowing her brow because Lucía doesn't understand her.

That very afternoon I climbed the hill. So I could gaze in the distance, as far as the eye could see. To view other hills and highlands, the cordillera and the volcanoes way off, covered with steam or clouds. Volcanoes as blue as the eyes of sea gulls I once saw at the beach. See the sky-blue highlands and the purple cordillera; colors always changing depending on the distance and the angle of the sun. Look farther, where it is no longer Cuzcatlán but other neighboring countries: Honduras to the north; Guatemala to the west. The burning volcanoes of Nicaragua to the east; and the Pacific Ocean to the south. I love seeing the white thread of the sea, its foam tracing gulfs, inlets, and coves. My eyes can see beyond Cuzcatlán because my country is small, smaller than the breatdth of my gaze. Her eyes are like a net of light pulling in the surrounding lands.

"In winter it gets very dry. I want you to pour a drop or two of water over every stone, because a *ceiba* tree will grow next to each one," she tells her mother.

"Nice little job you've left for me," says Juana tongue-in-cheek, kidding around to add some levity to Lucía's imminent departure. Her face is covered with mist, either from a light rain borne on the breeze or her feelings getting the best of her.

"Don't worry, Mama, I'll write," says the daughter, trying to make her feel better; though her own voice is feeble, as though she doesn't take much stock in what she's saying.

"I'm not worried," her mother responds.

"Then what are those tears for?" Lucía asks.

"It's the breeze blowing rain from Honduras," says Juana wiping her face with a coarse cotton apron. "You learn to be prepared for times like this, so don't worry, I know you won't forget us."

"All right," Lucía sighs. Her eyes are still sky-blue from her contemplation of the hills, the volcanoes, the cordilleras, and her own Southern Sea.

"And of course I'll water the stones, the *ceiba* trees will grow and maybe we'll have some shade for hot, sunny days."

"And more rain," her daughter says. "Leaves attract water and wind." You can still see traces of the highlands and distances silhouetted in her eyes. These are things I will never forget, they are my hope and my strength.

"Listen, child," Jacinto had said that morning as he prepared to leave for the hacienda. "Your mama's going to take you to the bus stop; be very careful, because you're an inexperienced young girl; when you get to Chalate, stay in the bus station, because that's where your godmother will be." He speaks with the voice of wisdom. Suddenly he feels his mind has been enlightened. As he talks with his daughter he continues with his daily routine: he gets his machete, goes over to the beam where his sombrero is hung; he checks his pack of tortillas and bag of salt, puts his sandals on, breathes deep the pleasant smell of morning. "And if you've got a few *centavos* to spare, and learn to write well, send a letter to San Miguel, to your sister Toña, because family sticks together." He doesn't know why, but suddenly the memory of his brothers Manuel and Pedro strikes like a bolt from the blue; they might still be alive; maybe they became *guardias,* although he could never confirm it; besides it wasn't his place to find out; they knew the road home. "And you," he says to Juana, who is lighting the fire and putting a pot of water on for coffee, "Don't leave the highway until this little girl is on the bus, because I'm about to leave for the hacienda; you know how things are, you can't trust anybody." He says this only to give Juana support when she watches her child go away, as if he will be there in spirit, saying good-bye. "Did you hear me?" he asks when his *compañera* remains silent. He speaks quickly, intermittently; blurting out the words, firing them off in the hut the way he fires kernels of corn into furrows and hastily covers them with his bare feet. This time his phrases are buried by long intervening silences. "Oh, and make sure not to let the driver overcharge you," he adds, "because sometimes they try and fleece you if they figure you've never ridden a bus before." He brings up the economic problem only as a way to conceal the slight trembling in his body, of which he alone is aware, but thinks the women detect nevertheless; he doesn't want them to know how affected he is by Lucía's departure, so he hides behind petty details, like the fact that the driver might overcharge her.

"Give me your blessing, then," I say sadly.

"Wait a minute, *niña*, I'm not going just yet," Jacinto exclaims. "I'm just giving you some final advice."

"I thought you were in a hurry," I said, trying to justify myself.

Jacinto is relentless on the matter of bus fare:

"You should ask how much the trip costs," he tells Juana, "then give her the money." He feels the need to speak fast. He doesn't know whether it's because it's getting late or he wants to make these last few minutes in the hut with his daughter count. It wasn't like this when Antonia left home, perhaps because the presence of his younger daughter was a consolation; now there would only be his *compañera* Juana. His heart tells him he and his mate will be left in the dust while his daughters head toward a transformation whose dimension he can't possibly foresee. Though he can't form a picture with his mind, he can develop one intuitively with his heart.

"Don't let it get too late," says Juana, "or they'll fire you." The mother watches the red-and-orange splendor enter the cracks in the hut.

"The foreman knows I might be late," says Jacinto.

"You told him?" the mother says.

"Yes, I told him Lucía was going to Chalate," he says with genuine pride. His daughters are being transformed. This is what he has sensed.

"And what did he say?" the mother asks once again.

"He said it was too bad because there's a lot of work this summer since they're planning on cutting bushes instead of burning them and they'd miss Lucía's arms. 'Other than that I'm not saying there won't be any more work, just that people leave because that's their choice.' " Jacinto says the last bit in an exaggerated voice, mimicking the gang boss.

"He can eat shit," Mama says.

"Oh, and another thing," says Jacinto, returning to the matter at hand. "Be careful about sleeping on the bus—they say the bouncing makes you sleepy, and they let all kinds of pests and vermin ride those beasts. Before you know it they'll steal the shirt off your back—so keep your eyes open wide." Somehow Jacinto has managed to get his things together and he's ready to leave for the hacienda.

Juana breaks in:

"Coffee's ready." She serves it in a calabash gourd on a makeshift table made of pine. The gourd rests in a thatched headband—a *yagual*—made of tulle. I'm aware it is the last gourd of coffee we will share.

"I hope the things I've told you don't go in one ear and out the other," Jacinto says solemnly as I reach for the coffee that steams like the mouth of a volcano.

———

One day they got a telegram from their *compadres* asking if they would send their younger daughter to Chalate to take her sister's place in the cooperative, now that Antonia had moved on to San Miguel. They thought maybe it would be all right, their girl would go to night school and be educated properly. They held on to the telegram like it was a treasure; it was the first time they had ever received such a message. The telegram had been brought to the village by messenger from Apastepeque. At first they weren't going to let her go, but it happened that a few days later the cow died. Juana went to tell their daughter the bad news. The girl was coming down the road with a sprig of mignonette in her hair, her body lean, hips wide, laughing like a new woman who would soon meet someone and have a few children of her own. She carried a calabash at her waist filled with cottage cheese and pudding to sell. Then Juana noticed her daughter was crying. "What will become of us now?" Lucia asked as she walked down the road with her mother.

Juana showed her the telegram from her godmother. "When we get home we'll discuss it with Jacinto," her mother says. "I didn't want to wait until you got home to tell you these things." So she went out to meet her on the road. "You take the good with the bad," she thinks anxiously.

"What do you think, Juana?" asks Jacinto.

"Same as you," she answers, trying to avoid a concrete answer. "And don't talk so loud, the girl might not be asleep yet."

"So I guess she can go," says Jacinto.

Lucía is listening. She starts to tremble beneath the *nance* tree.

"God's will be done," says Juana as she goes to snuff out the *ocotillo* torch that bathes the hut in gold.

The girl in the microbus remembers what it was like when her sister left for Chalatenango:

It was all I could think about and then I started to cry the kind of tears that give you away and embarrass you. Because Toña says she's leaving. I say: You're digging your own grave. No one can prevent her. She has a right. Godmother says she'll be responsible for Toña. She'll take care of her. Papa says we women are like young sparrow hawks: once we learn to fly there's no stopping us. Papa is strong but when he found out Toña wanted to leave he asked Mama if she was going to let her. He says it like it's a challenge. He's the only one who can decide whether or not she'll go, because my papa is different, he speaks with conviction. "No matter how much it hurts me, I can't stand in her way," says Mama. Maybe if she could get a job at the hacienda we could convince her not to leave. "That's the most difficult age for kids, when they want to try their wings and take off on their own," says Mama. As she says this, a flock of doves, startled by a thunderclap, takes flight, as if to illustrate what Mama said. I say *Ave Maria Purisima*, because the sound frightened me. Mama responds: "Conceived without sin." And then I feel sad all over again. I just want to huddle with my new dog in the corner, so I don't feel so lonely. But I better not, because I could get fleas or even sick. His name is Tepezcuintle because he has a big snout like a *tepezcuintle,* or paca. I better let him sleep, because if I go over there he'll wake up and start barking, then no one will be able to shut him up—maybe that's why we got him when he was full-grown. He's crazy, it's a miracle he's still asleep at this hour. So I don't go over. I stay with my papa while he polishes a stone. Mama says put it down, it's dark already and you could ruin it. Toña goes to get water from the well, but the evening has caught her by surprise and all she'll get is a bucketful of stars.

129

———

"Are you sure our *compadres* in Chalate are on the side of the poor?" Mama asks Papa. I pretend I'm not listening as I clean the stove, sweeping out the ashes so it will be clean at night. They say if there are too many ashes the Cipitio, son of the Siguanaba, will come and play in the stove and he won't let you sleep because he'll tickle your feet. And since it's been a week that we haven't cleaned the cooking area, I tell Toña that I can't help her draw water from the well. I want to sweep out the ashes. So she says, "Fine." I'm listening to my parents' woes and it hurts me to hear them recount their misfortunes.

"If nothing can be done, then God help her," says Mama as she brings her apron up to her face to wipe away her resignation or a sob that suddenly escapes. I tell them enough, don't wallow in bitterness. And as if awoken from a nightmare they both simultaneously say don't meddle in the affairs of your elders. They should be thanking me for waking them, but who can say why we poor like to drown in our sorrows and, instead of casting them aside and forgetting about them, dwell on them until finally something gives? This time that something is our feelings over losing a daughter and a sister. That's why Mama cries. And my daddy says all right already, the girl isn't dead after all, you're only supposed to cry for the dead. And that's because you have to, so the other souls welcome them—that's why people cry for the departed.

"We can go see Toña if we make an effort," he says.

So it turns out my papa's more optimistic. But maybe not. He concludes the sentence with: "Everyone makes his ass a drum, I guess."

"Don't say that," Mama tells him, because Toña doesn't even know what she's doing. And that saying about making your ass a drum refers to stupid people who insist on making trouble.

"Toña's doing it to help us out, that's the worst of it," my mother says.

"You're right," says Papa; but you get a tough hide from so much hard luck and suffering, and the worst thing is not having enough work. "That's why a person doesn't know what he's saying half the time." And when my papa is done talking, Toña appears, her eyes like fireflies or the eyes of a puma. She's just bathed in well water. She's so lovely she appears to be a queen of the night. A flirt. It's the way she moves her waist. People say it's the age. And my time will come soon enough. I hope the only thing that happens is that I feel like putting flowers in my hair; though you get kind of tired of the smell of mignonette, myrtle, and spikenard. Besides, flowers sometimes smell like death.

When I reach that age I hope I'm just the same as I am now. Just a clean body. Smelling like a river, that's all. Like well water.

She also remembers her mother, Juana, and how her voice sounded in those days. This time it was me leaving home.

Lucía has suffered a lot. When she was eleven, they took her for eight, which meant they wouldn't feed her, because that's how those bastard gang bosses are, they make any excuse to withhold a tortilla; how do they expect us to prove she's older than eight? The least they could do is give her some salt; but there's no convincing those beasts. She started to develop a few months ago and she's gotten very pretty—her coccyx stretched, her breasts grew: she was becoming a woman. And that's just the time her godmother came and got her all worked up about going to live in Chalate. Certainly it's better for her to stop suffering this wretchedness and find new surroundings so she can improve her life; after all, men aren't the only ones who have the right to want to change. Women do, too.

131

What makes me sad is that now that she's old enough to be admitted to the hacienda to earn a few *centavos* including meals, she gets it in her head to leave us. This thing young people have about leaving the house of their birth! She's helped out so much with cutting—even if they didn't give her anything to eat, she was always with us, doing the work of an adult. How can I stand in her way, why should only males have the right to leave?

And when she passes thirteen she's considered a woman. Her godmother says she's going to bring her to Chalate to take her sister's place. Because her sister has gone to San Miguel. Lucía's place at the cooperative was assured. "So many dangerous things can happen to a woman," is the only thing I can think of to say to her godmother. "What do you mean? Each person takes care of herself and does what she wants—if she doesn't want something she doesn't want it and she doesn't get herself into trouble," Lucía's godmother responds.

I'm afraid they'll cheat her, they won't pay her well; she'll start wanting to let loose and that will lead to babies and she'll wind up poor again. Jacinto's aunt, the girls' godmother, tells us not to worry, the girls need to develop themselves, to have opportunities.

How can I fight progress, when all we have for light is *ocotillo* branches—we can't even afford a candle. We poor must endure these things. So finally I said, when the godmother was out of earshot: "Well, my child, if you want to go, then go—we can't tie you down."

That's the way things go in this life.

The girl in the microbus continues reflecting, things that happened years ago, but which she remembers as clearly as last night's dreams:

Toña has been getting her stuff together. I come up and hear her say she won't forget us the way her two uncles and Grandfather Eusebio did. And we're reminded of them all over again. We've always had to suffer the disappearance of those we love in silence. As if they never existed.

You're leaving us all alone, I tell her. And she says: Bodies leave but hearts remain. Or something like that. Maybe she doesn't say anything and I hear her in my imagination. She's unable to speak, I know that. Because she's holding back an avalanche of tears and doesn't want to let them go. Her tongue is tied and she's got a lump in her throat, so she doesn't say a word. She knows if she starts to speak her heart will break and it will hurt. We're all embarrassed to cry. Something happens to us. We're ashamed of our misfortunes.

She's tying up the knapsack, where all her things are, and she's looking for somewhere to attach her *tambache,* her food pouch, so it won't fall off. Finally she says: "Don't look so worried, the world hasn't ended, yet." And my mama says these are the things that are hard to take, they're worse than hunger or disease. Toña says, You're exaggerating.

That morning my papa said, "I'm going to the quarry," just to avoid having to be there when she left. So he went to quarry rocks. All he did was put his arm around her, touch her braids, arrange them to make her look prettier, and admired the way her hair went down to her waist. And he says we won't be seeing you again. And she: "Maybe not." Meanwhile Mama walks in circles, tossing Tepezcuintle a shred of tortilla. Even the dog is sad, but that's how animals are.

Mama keeps pacing in circles; maybe she's nervous. She puts some water out for the chickens. She wants to keep busy, distract herself. After a while she comes back with Tepezcuintle stuck to her like a shadow. Papa says, "Why did they make us of stone and wood instead of clay?" Thinking perhaps clay is more fragile, it breaks easily. I believe that is the significance of his words. They also made us of corn. He talks to himself even though he knows we can hear him. We hear you, Papa. "It began a while ago," he says. He pretends he's talking to Tepezcuintle. He talks to himself. He says the word *Eusebio.* Invoking the name of the grandfather who went off to the El Divisadero mines.

I heard my daughters, Lucía and Toña, talking in the yard. Juana and I just stared at each other. Suddenly we feel all alone in the world; fortunately, though, we're beginning to understand what life is about. Toña's smile is not her usual carefree smile, but one that says I'm sorry. When there's nothing to be sorry for, she hasn't hurt me.

I remove a sprig of mignonette and throw it on the granary. And I tell Toña to cut me a bunch of flowers and I'll help her tie up her knapsack. So she goes into the yard followed by Tepezcuintle. After a while they come back, she with a bouquet of mignonettes, trailed by the dog.

My mama just looks at us, without saying anything. Then she asks Toña if she wants to take some milk pudding to eat. She says no. I ask if she wants my mignonettes, just for something to say. She says yes. I arrange them in her hair. She looks more lovely than before, like a lady. I'll look like that when I'm her age, which won't be long since we're only two years apart. Mama tells her, You'll need a blessing. All right, says Toña humbly. There were long stretches of time when I couldn't hear her voice. The soft voice of a turtledove. Maybe I always compare her to beautiful things because I love her so much.

And Mama gives her blessings.

IX / JUANA, TOÑA, LUCÍA

1960

WE WEREN'T LUCKY with the first three children. They all died. Our luck changed with the fourth. She was a girl. Still, we were happy. I went into town to have a few drinks with my friends. Her face was the same as Juana's, the same dimples. "I don't care if she doesn't look like me—she looks like my *compañera* Juana," said Jacinto. People made a big thing about girls looking like their fathers and boys like their mothers.

When he saw it was a little girl, he said it didn't matter, they're all the same after all. "The days when only men counted are gone, that's bullshit now." Sometimes parents really want males for their strength, though females are strong, too. Anyway, after the death of three sons, you learn to be more accepting. We looked after her as if she was made of glass. During the first days we didn't let anybody see her; the best thing is to protect newborn babies from people's stares. We only let people come in contact with her after forty days. Our friends understood. They said: "She's the spitting image of Jacinto." It makes a father feel good. Then he starts getting a big head, like he made the baby by himself. Nobody paid any attention to Juana, who ordered a bed of straw made up in anticipation of the baby's birth. She was proud of her daughter and her straw bed. She had always slept on a wooden cot. Within a month the excitement died down.

Jacinto barely had time to look at her, for he left very early to go to the cutting fields, and came home after dark, when the baby had already gone to bed. I don't want to disturb her, Jacinto thought, I should let her sleep.

"Nothing will happen if you just look at her," said Juana.

"It's just that after working so hard my sight must be very powerful and it could wake her."

"If you don't make too much noise you won't wake her," says Juana.

"All right, I'll just take a little peek so the power of my sight doesn't wake her," says Jacinto.

"You wouldn't even if you were a hawk," says Juana.

"You never know, I really don't want to bother her," Jacinto says, defending himself.

Two years after our first baby girl, Toña, was born, the second one came along. "Maybe God is favoring us with females," I thought. When I saw she could barely open her eyes—more undernourished than a kitten she was—I was very worried, because that's the first thing kids die from: malnutrition. But once again we were lucky, because even though she was so tiny and all, she managed to resist getting sick until she was old enough to be out of danger. We named her Lucía because she had the eyes of a saint. That was her most noticeable feature, those big, round eyes.

We didn't raise any males, that's true; but we had no regrets —females work right beside you, there's very little difference.

"You're right, we shouldn't resent the fact God didn't let us keep any males," Juana agrees with her *compañero*.

"I never had any resentment," Jacinto protests.

Father and daughters, clearing the fields:

"Let's take a break," Jacinto says to himself. He feels his face with one hand as he takes off his sombrero with the other and fans himself. "Let's get in the shade, this sun is hotter than a sonofabitch." This time Jacinto addresses his daughters.

"You two can rest if you want, I've got to finish this row," answers Toña.

It's six in the evening by the time they return from the cornfield. They can tell day is done when the tree fills with birds; that's when they gather their belongings together: a knapsack for tortillas, a long knife called a *cuma,* and a wooden club called a *macana;* two *tecomate* gourd bowls, and the ox yoke. Juana was waiting for them with hot tortillas and beans. They don't need plates because they put the beans on top of the tortillas. The three of them feel like a gigantic family that has existed for over a thousand years. It's the way they sit on the log, the way they hold their heads, the way their looks pierce the ruddy yellow light given off by the lamp.

The mountain howls in a night full of crickets and mice and *masacuata* snakes and nocturnal birds.

"This will be a good year," says Lucía, thinking about their cornfield.

"How do you know, baby?" asks her father.

"Because of the kites heading north."

Kites fly hundreds of feet above the earth, and ducks never touch ground, they just fly by, waving farewell with gray handkerchiefs, perforating and shattering the blue sky. Winter's abundance depends on how many kites there are. This is common knowledge. But first you must see them, so you can tell how many there are. Lucía has been watching them as she rests under the mango tree at the edge of the cornfield.

"You're still young, Lucía, you should rest for ten minutes after you eat while I pull up some of these weeds robbing energy from the corn," says Jacinto, speaking about the family cornfield.

"All right," Lucía assents. And she watches kites crossing overhead.

"I haven't had time to watch them this year," says Juana. "But I'll take your word for it and hope we get a lot of good rain for the beans and corn."

Beans and corn grow together. The bean plants twist around the cornstalks. Beans fertilize the ground for the corn. That's why you plant them together. They help each other. And then tortillas and salt aren't the only things you have to eat.

"Things have gotten better lately," Toña reflects.

"That's right—now we can eat beans with our tortillas," says Jacinto.

"God is good," affirms Lucía.

The chickens are asleep. They, too, should be in bed. They're tired. May is a frantic month for the people in the village. Once the Mayflower Festival and the Festival of the Cross have passed, they have to break the ground with a *huizote,* a type of pike, if the land is on a slope, or with a plow when it's flat.

Then they wait for the *atole* parties. Every year during the festivities in May *atole,* a cornmeal drink, is made from the first tender shoots of corn, which are cut back to provide for a second harvest, allowing the corn to get bigger and dry out on the stalk; this is the corn that will be saved until the following year. Prior to the *atole* parties the villagers celebrate the festivals of the Cross and Flowers, all in the month of May.

"Of course, you can't trust in God alone," Juana points out.

"You've also got to bust your ass," agrees Jacinto.

"That's right," says Lucía. "If we don't work we don't eat."

"There are also times when we work but don't eat," Toña notes pessimistically.

"Something is better than nothing," says their father, thinking about tortillas and salt.

Of the five children he had with Juana, only two survived: Antonia, or Toña; and Lucía. The other three, all males, barely made it past a year. "There wasn't even time to baptize them properly, all we could do was sprinkle some holy water on them." Lastenia, ancient by now, was given the task of sprinkling the water. "I thought God was going to leave me helpless, childless, because of our luck with the first three." She had them one after another, and one after another they died.

"When Toña was born she was so chubby and full of life, I knew right away she wouldn't be allowed to die, that all we had to do was be extra careful about even the slightest diarrhea. So Lastenia was always nearby. She had brought me and my brothers Pedro and Manuel into the world. She was part of the family; an old woman loved by all."

Whenever Toña had the least little fever, old Lastenia was there. It was the same with Lucía. Juana attended them constantly, following the ancient woman's instructions. "When I prescribe an herb it's because the baby needs it, but you people think all you have to do to cure somebody is pray to their saint; you have to know how to combine the two," says Lastenia.

"When we saw that both baby girls were going to be all right, we were very happy. Once they get beyond a certain age, it's hard to make them die, because with us Salvadorans, if you let us live, if you give us even half a chance, we can fight off any disease. Past three, there's a strong possibility we'll live."

When Toña turned four, and Lucía two, they decided to have them baptized as God ordains. They started looking for godparents.

"We chose an aunt of Jacinto's and her husband in Chalate. She had always helped us out with little things like buying stones and reselling them, for example. And since godparents take the place of parents when they're gone, we thought our daughters should have a secure family that would at least provide for their survival, should they be orphaned. You've got to be prepared for everything."

Jacinto's aunt and her husband agreed to serve as the girls' godparents. Jacinto made the trip to Chalate to ask them himself.

They invited all the neighbors. At the beginning of the party little children arrived wearing paper hats and white cotton clothing. Barefoot but very clean. The parents had taken great care to have their children look their best for Toña and Lucía's baptism. "We had *horchata* to drink and some sweets we bought in San Vicente. The godparents gave each of their goddaughters a pretty dress. I remember that was the first time I saw Lucía with a sprig of mignonette in her hair. Her godmother put it there and arranged it very nicely. Meanwhile Toña, who was already four, fixed her own hair, which Juana had recently cut. In those days little girls liked to decorate their hair with fancy combs and colored ribbons. Lucía always preferred a sprig of mignonette."

At six, Lucía helps out by selling things out of a basket; she takes cottage cheese and milk pudding to sell in town. She almost always goes alone, though sometimes her older sister Antonia goes with her. She walked down the road like a grown woman; though she was only six. Her mother, some time later:

"I felt awful when my baby girls grew up and decided to leave."

"At first Juana would not give her consent. Since I was the man, I had to be firm, too. Toña was the first to go; she stayed with her godparents and helped them around the house as a way to earn her keep. These same godparents sent for her so she could learn to read and write. They would also find her a job in a cooperative; that's how they could help out financially in case of emergency. I never asked anything of my children, you understand; all I need are my arms in order to live."

In Chalate Antonia met her *compañero,* who brought her to San Miguel; every once in a while she sent word to her parents through the bus driver, who left packages and letters at the Apastepeque bus stop.

Three years after Toña left, the godmother sent for Lucía. Her godparents worked in a crafts cooperative, making cornhusk flowers, corncob dolls and pipes, and other knickknacks that some nuns from San Salvador had taught them to make. The same nuns helped them sell their crafts in the capital. In addition they worked for the church, people said it was a new church for the poor. And it would be better for Lucía not to be stuck back in the hills for the rest of her life.

"You want progress for your children. For God's will to be done. The godparents never once complained. They were catechists themselves and they worked with Christian groups. So my daughter would be in good hands, since they had the protection of the groups organized there in Chalate, so they could advance in their studies and learn a trade in order to make a living."

Later, Lucía also left Chalate and continued her nursing studies in San Miguel. With the same Christian groups.

Though we were unfortunate with our three sons, it was just the other way with our little girls because we were able to watch them grow and develop.

"My sons died. That happens with boys: they die easily—you could have ten of them and more than half would die. It's our only diversion: having children. But it's also our greatest sorrow, since we have to watch our babies die and we can't do a thing about it. Maybe that's why it's impossible to have too many children—that way at least we always have something. I wasn't so lucky."

"I remember the first time Padre Ventura came to the village. He came on a visit for water, he asked if we had any cold water in a pitcher. I tell him, Of course; it's an honor to have a padre in your own hut, almost a miracle. Then he starts asking if I'm with God with respect to Juana. I say, Could be—since God has always been good to me: up till now we haven't starved. And actually, this visit is a blessing from the Most High. But Padre Ventura tells me being with God means being married. I ask him how he expects me to buy that. Pardon? the padre asks. About being married, I say, without being able to repress a snigger, because his question really caught me off guard. These things should not be taken lightly, my child, he says. I only ask how I'm supposed to buy that because around here people aren't in the habit of getting married, I explain. That is because you have been abandoned by the laws of God and man, he says. Well, go on then, explain yourself, I say.

"And Padre Ventura tells me that to have God's favor you must be married—that is to say, have the sacrament of the Church, something the Church dispenses by means of a ceremony which will only cost you a few *centavos,* he says. And he's only waiting to get several couples together so he can marry them all at once and then it won't cost so much money.

"I tell him no one ever explained that law to me before and I've always been fine with Juana, but if he says so, we can try to find the money and by the way how much does it cost to get married. He tells me not to worry about the money, I can pay him with one of my animals, whatever I think best, he says. All right, I tell him, just let me know.

"So one tenth of May, on Mother's Day, the Vicar Ventura arrived with all his trappings for saying mass, looking like a king, and got us all together in the plaza. We made an altar the way he told us to and bought some special clothing. We spent a lot, but we needed to be right with God if we wanted him to favor us with better luck. Everyone was pleased; you don't lose anything by doing it and the party was nice.

"In the six years that Juana and I have been *compañeros* we have achieved something, why deny it; they rented us a parcel of land where we planted a cornfield, millet, and a pumpkin patch. We paid our annual tribute to the owner of the land and still had enough to eat. Sometimes we even had a few pennies left over, and we held on to them like they were glass—you know, look but don't touch—because in an emergency you always have to have something to fall back on. It's difficult, but we manage, precisely because we are in God's favor. That's how we were able to have a little celebration on the day of our church wedding; all the couples chipped in and bought party supplies. Like a marimba and some chicken tamales. I was sorry it cost me two chickens, but Padre Ventura told me we had to make sacrifices if we wanted to earn God's favor. I think we were all in the same boat; nevertheless, everybody made the sacrifice. After all, we had to pay the padre. With whatever we had to offer: a bunch of beans, some corn, a chicken, and someone even gave a pig. We had to take them out to the highway and put them in a cart so the padre could carry all our gifts away.

"I know it's hard to believe, but things never got worse after that. I'm not saying we won the lottery or anything, but at least we weren't struck by any disaster. Of course, we were just scraping by, as usual, but you don't earn God's favor if you don't sweat for it. There's always a lot to do once May is over, you know; even before, actually: you weed at the end of February —you've got to pull up every inch of brush and every weed, then you've got to make a circle and burn everything you've pulled up in the middle of it. You have to dig the circle so the fire doesn't spread. You dig a trench around your whole property, or else you just clear it and make sure you haven't left any straw lying around that could catch fire. Then you have the actual plowing, which happens in May. Everybody has to help: Juana, Lucía, Antonia, and myself. Sometimes you have to push real hard to help the oxen, especially if there hasn't been much rain. So you're not expecting a flood or anything, but then just as you start plowing down comes rain and you've got to clench your teeth to get the water to stay in the furrows. You're not done yet, though, because then, just as the sprouts start to appear, the birds start pestering you; then you've got some birding to do— that's Lucía's job. She has to spend several hours a day in the fields scaring the birds with either a switch or a slingshot.

"I think our first reversal was when Mama Ticha's land was flooded and she had to move to the north side of the lagoon. The thing is, we had always lived on the south shore when we were little. I'm certain this simple change resulted in one of our worst tragedies, which had to do with my grandfather Emiliano's death and later my mother's. But it's best not to speak about it."

Sometimes troubles rain down on you. And you can't avoid them. It hadn't even been six months since Toña left for Chalate. I came this close to turning up my toes.

"My problem was with a rattlesnake. And all because I mistook it for a *masacuata*. It nipped me and I paid no attention; I did think it was odd, because the *masacuata* doesn't usually get so pissed off that it will bite. Imagine my surprise when I heard the rattle as the snake shook its tail. Listen, I wouldn't wish that on my worst enemy; the minute I heard that rattling coming from its tail I said to myself: Feet don't fail me now— the last thing I wanted was to pass out before I got to the hut, just lying there by the side of the road with no way to get help. I got home with great effort and by that time my leg had swollen.

"Hurry, Lucía—as fast as you can, Jacinto is dying," says Juana.

"I'm on my way, just let me get a towel on my head so I don't catch cold," Lucía replies.

"Forget the towel and get out of here—and don't stop, for anything, do you understand?" Juana says, letting down her skirt, smoothing it from nerves; she wanted to spread her slip like wings and fly away. "I hope she has an antidote."

"Were you able to kill it?" Juana asks Jacinto.

"No, child, it got away," says Jacinto nearly fainting.

"Why didn't you at least bite it so the venom wouldn't get you?" Juana exclaims.

"I thought it was a *masacuata*," Jacinto explains, "so I kept on going and didn't track it down; I was petrified when I heard the rattle, but by then it was too late, the snake was lost in the mountain."

Juana put a knife in the fire.

"What are you doing?" Jacinto asks.

"It's to cauterize you," she says. "Lastenia taught me that in emergencies like this you have to cut the wound, make it bigger and burn the flesh with the knife. Here's a stick to bite so you can take the pain," says Juana.

"We'd better wait for Lastenia," Jacinto says.

"Forget it, you'll be dead by then."

How I screamed! But there was no other choice—I'm alive to

tell the story. By the time the medicine woman arrived I had passed out from the pain, Juana had applied some *floripondio* plaster to relax my body. I was like that for more than a month, I couldn't walk because my ankle was so swollen. The medicine woman told me I had been saved by a whisker. This was unheard of because rattlesnake bites are fatal, so I figure the sonofabitch didn't really get his teeth into me and didn't get a chance to empty all his venom.

Lucía had to work double the whole time I was sick, because Juana had to spend all her time looking after me—applying tobacco and *floripondio* plasters every hour, at least in the beginning when I couldn't do it myself. That's how it was for more than a month, until I finally got the feeling back in my leg. Every day I'd watch my little girl go out with her *cuma* or *huizote* to turn the earth. All she brought with her was a sack of tortillas and beans and a calabash full of water. Sometimes she came home and ate with us instead of staying in the field. But the minute she finished her tortilla she was off again, taking a shortcut through the scrub. Sometimes I saw her wrapped in a cloud of smoke at noon, a dust devil at the witching hour. And it was as though she were flying. Actually, she's so skinny it's a wonder she doesn't take off and float right away.

In a few days it will be Lucía's birthday. She'll be eleven, she's growing up. Juana would have liked to watch her growth more closely, but it was impossible—in those days Lucía went to the cornfield and Juana stayed at home to make tortillas and plant annatto trees.

The girl would come home for lunch, but not every day, because the cornfield was some distance away and it was more convenient to eat lunch there. However, once Jacinto's snakebite began to heal, Lucía decided to work only in the mornings. That way she could come home at midday, particularly in the summer, when the sun is high; the poor girl's head ached from being exposed to too much sun at such an early age.

Juana, the mother, thinks: "Not having many children is a big disadvantage. Now that Toña isn't around anymore, Lucía works more than her share. It's true—if there isn't another hand to help there isn't enough food to go around. The cornfields are anemic in these parts. Maybe because the soil is so poor all that's left is gravel; pretty soon we'll only be able to till with a *huizote* —now that you've got to dig holes for planting with your bare hands. I hope that day never comes. That's why it's good to spread fertilizer on the ground—but if you don't have it, where does that leave you?

"Poor Lucía's had a rough life. No fun, no frills, nothing but work and more work, like a grown man. That's the way it is for all the girls around here but at least in families with a lot of children you get a break every once in a while. That was our disadvantage. Jacinto gets no rest, either, except when he's sick and that doesn't happen too often, only when St. John points the finger. Lucky thing, because no one likes having sick people around, though that's the only time the poor man takes a day off, it doesn't matter whether it's in his own cornfield or when he has to go to the estates to pick coffee or cotton."

"Lucía is my pride and joy, the apple of my eye. When she suffers, my blood chills. Fortunately, I never get sick, nor do I ever have moments of weakness, so I end up being the nursemaid in the house, always looking after the two of them, always bringing them their hot tortillas, their coffee when we have it, their hot beans. So they have something hot in their stomachs—I never serve cold food because it makes the insides bloat. I hope she finds someone like Jacinto someday. May it please God."

———

Both girls are pretty and poor. Walking like delicate, frivolous birds. Hair falling in dark rivers around their shoulders. Eyes black and shiny like the beaches of the Southern Sea. Golden skin, ceramic skin fired in wood kilns. Indigenous noses. And a look that comes down from distant and fairer centuries.

Both girls are unwashed and good-looking. Lucía has just turned eight, so she has the eyes of a woman about to take flight and touch the volcanoes with her wings. A fledgling's head. An indecisive walk, a crystalline bird that often breaks into a thousand colors in the afternoons of Cuzcatlán. Toña is ten.

Both girls have the bodies of wild plants, figures of broom: supple and filled with white and yellow flowers, trembling in a gust of wind, swaying in the northern breeze. The voices of turtledoves. Timid bellflowers that close at the first light of day only to open again another day, radiant, colorful, dazzling.

All girls are equal among themselves. All the girls of Cuzcatlán carry traces of their ancient poetic lineage, wise and overflowing with wealth. That's why it was called Cuzcatlán—this is the land of lakes and volcanoes, where the Southern Sea beats, the land of rivers and fruit, land of riches, jewels, and gems. That is the meaning of Cuzcatlán. The conquistadors changed its name more in keeping with their own ambitions and tribulations: El Salvador, the Savior. Because in the eyes of the conquistadors, the country's riches had been plundered and it had become a region of misery and rebellion. The difficulties they encountered with the indigenous peoples compelled them to invoke Christ the Savior, *Cristo salvador.* And that motivated the name change.

———

Lucía, the younger sister, pastures the two oxen and the cow. She speaks to the wind, the mountains, the sun, the bellflowers that close at break of day, her animals, and the trees. Ever since she was little she has enjoyed talking to herself. Or dreaming:

It's always been my job, I take a switch and my cotton petticoat gets caught in the brush; my job is to look for fresh pasture for grazing, a hard thing to do when there hasn't been much rain. Then we go to the river so they can drink fresh water—which is better than well water because river water has nutrients and tastes of fish and water lilies. Animals grow healthy if they drink running water from a river or spring. That's what I do all day —herd and carry a knapsack of tortillas and beans. We children eat beans, grown-ups eat salt. Tortillas and beans or tortillas and salt. I don't get very thirsty, because I stay out of the sun. It's different when I'm in the cutting fields or clearing land, because then I need water every half hour, or often, anyway; you've got to fill your stomach with water so your body doesn't dehydrate, and so the sun doesn't cause nightmares or hallucinations.

Quietly I look at the *maculis* trees off in the distance, or lie in the shade of a *conacaste* tree and watch birds sing and kiss, lost in its heavy branches.

I don't lie under just any tree.

There are poisonous fruit trees. Tiny red droplets fall from them and if they drip on your head they can seep in and then you've got your toes curled. People call these droplets coral water or coral drops. You can't even touch the water or you faint dead away, no matter how good a Christian you are. They say the coral snake, which is a poisonous viper—*very* poisonous— eats the flowers of certain trees and sometimes all he has to do is kiss a flower and leave his venom; then the flower cries and the viper's spit falls like tears.

When I pasture the animals I rest a lot. Let my eyes roam.

But I also keep them peeled in case the cattle decide to wander off. For the most part, they take care of themselves, they look for food: purslane, mint, mulberry, *chipilín,* chayote, bindweed shoots—in other words, all the same things we like to eat. When you look at it like that we're not that different from animals. Except animals eat their food raw, and Christians cook it. We don't always eat herbs and plants, but sometimes we need to, or we feel like making some mountain soup. I like *chipilín* leaves a lot, so does my papa; the problem is if you eat them by themselves in hot water they're so bitter you can't swallow them, so you add an egg to kill the taste; but there's no way we can convince Mama to spare an egg—only once in a great while does she consent, when things are going well or when Daddy craves them—then Mama doesn't say no, she always wants to keep my papa happy. It's a sin to eat an egg. We have some little chickens that lay every now and then but God help us if we ever eat an egg—we always trade them for salt or brown sugarloaf, sometimes even a couple of cigars. My papa likes to chew tobacco, he doesn't smoke it much—he loves walking around with a huge wad bulging out of his cheek and then spitting the juice as far as he can. I've never seen Mama chew tobacco, though, she only smokes it, especially at dusk. She claims she's never gotten malaria because she's been smoking since she was young and the smoke scares away the mosquitoes and evil spirits, microbes and imps. I've never tried tobacco, I'm still too young—maybe later. Cigars frighten away sadness and melancholy. But I like eating flowers. The ones I like best are broom—they're sweet and taste like honey. I don't eat bellflowers, they're too bitter! But they're pretty and even if they were sweet I wouldn't eat them. Besides, there are so many broom flowers that you could eat thousands of them and the mountain would still be yellow and white. Cottage cheese made from the milk of a cow that has eaten flowers tastes better than any other kind. That's why I take the animals to broom fields. You can use a whole broom plant as a broom, just pull it up by the roots and you've got your broom —you can sweep the yard or the hut with it. We make cottage cheese and a sweet milk pudding. It's my job to sell them. Sometimes Toña helps me, but she's usually out picking with Papa and Mama. I sell the cottage cheese right here in the village. But not the pudding; I have to go to San Vicente to sell that. I go with Mama to San Vicente—she does her shopping and I sell whatever I've got to sell. I go from house to house. I have to shout in the street. People in San Vicente love milk pudding. It's a luxury we can't afford in my village, that's why I go to the city.

Depending on the time of year they let Toña, who's older than me, work as a pruner on the estates. I'm not allowed because they say I'm too young and the gang bosses don't want to have to feed me. So it's better I earn my daily bread taking care of the milk cow, because you make cottage cheese out of the milk and then I go out and sell it. We also make blancmange, milk pudding. That's how I earn my meals and do my share.

The gang bosses don't like to feed children. "Come on, give me just a little more salt for my little girl." Parents beg to see if they can't get the men to have a heart; or they might say, "Just another tortilla for my daughter." But nothing, the gang bosses have to answer to the owner and their hearts don't easily soften, maybe that's how they got to be gang bosses. If somebody complains too much, their hearts get harder. "Shit, that's annoying—shout like that again and I'll let you have it." "Then sell me a tortilla." "Where's the money?" "I've got it, I'll pay you later." "Cash in the hand, ass in the dirt," says the gang boss, who doesn't trust anybody. "One *centavo* for a pinch of salt," he says. "As if it was yours to sell," people mutter. "They're worse than the owners," others proclaim. "You're not going to sponge off me, leeches," the gang boss says when one person starts to plead with him. "Eat shit, shepherds, Easter's over," he says as he puts the leftover salt away, without so much as a pinch for the younger children. "Salt is for those who really put their backs into it," he says, "not for babies who come out to do a little weeding."

The gang bosses say children have small stomachs, so they can share with their parents; they can eat the leftovers. What leftovers? There's no way—if parents share with their children, then we're all left with a burning in our stomachs, so better the parents eat, because they give their lives for you.

We have to quench the burning with water, big gourdsful of water to extinguish the hunger that rages like a fire in our bodies and souls.

Water is holy, all water is holy—the water that runs in rivers, and underground; the water that falls from the sky and collects in bellflower blossoms. Water in puddles is good too if you have nothing else to drink; the water in ravines and water that comes down cold from the mountain above. It isn't only the water in churches that's holy. It is a blessing to us—up until now it hasn't occurred to anybody to sell it, or forbid it. Up until now no one has died from drinking a gourdful of water as far as I know; it's a sin to deny it, it's a sin to sell it. Water is almost like the tortilla, except that you have to earn the tortilla by the sweat of your brow, while God made water for everyone, so no one would be without, even if they were poor. Even if they didn't have a *petate* to drop dead on.

And air is like water too, except you don't eat air. If you could eat air this would be paradise, because then nobody would go without. But things are the way they are and not the way you wish they were. This whole mountain of air, which stirs the trees and shakes the mangoes and hog plums loose, is immense and has no end—just as the water in the ocean, so is the air boundless. Too bad you can't eat or drink seawater. Sometimes we're very hungry and we wish everything was good for something— good to eat, in other words. When you're hungry, strange ideas pop into your head. At least that's what happens to me. When the sun is high at noon and you get hungry you have these thoughts; you start thinking about sin; because if you're unhappy with the way God brought you into the world and you think about things as they aren't, you're sinning. Maybe it's because the sun is beating down on your head. That's when my insides start to shriek.

And then I think about my tortilla with salt. And I toss some flowers in my mouth to hold me until I get home, which is far away. Where the dogs are barking. Maybe they're hungry, too, because they really make a racket at this time of day.

I'm hungry. God will provide. Won't he?

I harness the cow and the two oxen and head in the direction of the barking dogs. The sun beats down. I carry a stalk of flowers in my hand and pick them one by one with my mouth, until only the shrieking is left, because I even eat the leaves.

Juana's thoughts are like rain, they fall and fall until the sky is blue, clear; that's what her memory is like, a storm that has come and washed away all the tears and dirt. An afternoon squall that always leaves it sunnier than it was before the wind and lightning appeared.

Juana herself is the rain. When she thinks:

The gang bosses say we have no control over our children,

that we let them leave home when they start complaining about how hard the work is. "Injun eats, then he hits the streets," they say; so that's why they don't feed them. Kids don't produce. "We don't need any shit-ass kids for work today," they say. Shit-asses are those who haven't turned eight yet. After we get to the hacienda in caravans, they decide what age the kids are —meaning which are the shit-asses. And so many kids are undernourished that you can't tell what age they are; they look like infants because even their eyes are dim, or their bones break because they're so thin, the poor things. Even though they might be older, the gang bosses decide what age a kid is. It's just an excuse to hoard another tortilla at lunchtime. They know very well that no matter how weak we all are—not just the kids —we all make an effort to produce, we don't cheat the *patrón*, we don't even stop to catch our breath. If we had to stop moving our hands to take a breath I'm sure the gang bosses would forbid it. That's why Jacinto calls them sons of bitches. I'd rather hold my tongue. Even if they are sons of bitches.

"Shit-asses over to one side," they say. And they start counting off, using the riding crops they always carry in their hands, and if they see there are a lot that day, they start exaggerating and arbitrarily make kids move to one side: this one yes, that one no; this one, not that one. He says he's not going to let us leeches sponge off him when we protest that we've come a long way and the kids are a big help. "They just come to eat the food other people work for," he says. It's been like this ever since they cut back corn production, because they didn't use to give us such a hard time, with an attitude like 'don't tempt me,' looking down their noses at the hired hands. But now they say the *patrones* are getting poor; corn doesn't sell well overseas. And the smart thing to do would be to move to the coast and grow cotton. Then you'd see, you couldn't live without them; all you people do is complain, they say, and you don't realize that without their land, without their money, you're nothing. That's what they say to us.

I get furious when they don't take Lucía, nobody works as hard as she does. And all because they don't want to give her a scrap of tortilla, and here we've walked all this way to get to the hacienda to do some planting. She can't just stand around and do nothing, and she tells them she'll work without eating, but once the gang bosses make up their minds, that's that. So she has to go home. Sometimes it's several miles away, depending on where we are that day. You walk and walk and still you're not there, which is not how it used to be. We must sacrifice Toña so Lucía doesn't have to go home alone; even though they're both young, it's harder to trick two people than one. We don't want some satyr coming after her—there are all kinds in the Lord's vineyard. Usually we avoid the problem by not bringing Lucía to the fields; anyway there's plenty of work at home. You can never have too many people in the hut. There's always something to do. "Get ten pails of water from the well," I tell her. "Don't let the pigs out of the pen." Lately we've kept two pigs. Jacinto made a pigsty so they could dig holes whenever they felt like it and so they'll stay out of the corn. "Give them a few beans," when there are beans. "Light the fire at four and heat up the *comal*," assuming we'll be home at four. "Go and collect some firewood." So many chores and she never complains. I only give her all these instructions when she has to be alone, because if Toña goes with her I don't need to tell her all these things, because she's more experienced and knows what has to be done. "And if there's time, let the cow out to graze." Not the oxen because Jacinto's got them—actually they've got him, pulling him in the cart. That's life.

"Oh, and don't forget to give the chickens some water so they don't die of thirst." I say all this as she gets ready to go back to the hut. "God be with you," as I watch her walk down the road. Toña stays with us because we can't spare her today, anyway the hut isn't too far away. Lucía says she's not afraid to go back by herself.

We're sorry because she was really counting on earning a few *centavos*. Sorry because she has to go off alone, and lonely too because we should all be together at times like these.

I watch her cross the road; she goes fast, as if carried by the wind. That's how she walks, like she's flying. Like a little dove.

Jacinto is made of volcanic rock, like the basalt of the grindstones. That's why he is hard. No one has ever seen him shed a tear. At his age his body is still erect, in spite of spending most of his life stooped over, clearing land, sowing in rows, finishing stones. You can only tell how old he is by his hesitating walk, weary but firm; and his hawk eyes, something he's never lost— rather, he's known to possess a look that never grows old. After eating his tortilla with salt, he takes out a cigar and, in the few minutes allowed by the gang boss, he smokes half of it. He thinks. Or maybe he talks to himself. Who knows, the wind blows and his words fly off like birds escaping their cage.

Maybe he thinks. No one knows. Or else he talks to the birds:

That's how our life is: if we're not at home, we're at the hacienda. Nothing to complain about. If you fall on hard times, tough luck. It's no one's fault. There's bad luck and there's disease. Bad luck could be getting bit by a snake, large or small. It might come from getting hurt from mishandling a machete— just starting to hack away after working all day. I was almost killed by a rattlesnake. I don't know how in hell I survived.

Disease is the worst because you don't know where it comes

from and it just sneaks up on you; a Christian can fall prey to anything from malaria to mortal plagues like whooping cough or typhoid fever. You just sit there waiting to die. Tiny children are the most common targets, very few survive. We old people tend to die of old age.

In that sense we walk with God.

We shouldn't complain about how God treats us. When you complain too much, disease rains down on you. Troubles, too.

It's better to bear your burdens patiently; as long as you don't die of starvation. As long as you're not wanting for water or work. Salt and tortillas come by themselves.

That's how it is around here. We shuttle back and forth, here to there, hacienda to hacienda, looking for work.

We've been lucky because we have a cow and two oxen and they give us a little protection. What about those who don't even own a *petate* to drop dead on? With a cow, we've got milk in the house, except nobody drinks it. They say it gives you stomachaches. Never in my catholic and miserable life have I ever tasted a gourd of milk. Neither have my daughters or *compañera*. It gives you nausea and diarrhea. People have always said that. And we all believe it. So when we work tending the cows, the gang boss doesn't have to keep an eye on us because he knows we won't steal any milk. He doesn't need to as long as we think raw milk is poison. We prefer to make things with the milk we get. With a little sugar, a few slivers of cinnamon, and some fire, you've got milk pudding, *conserva de leche.* Or we make cottage cheese. Lucía and Toña are in charge of selling pudding or cottage cheese. With the *centavos* we get from it we get by when there's no other work, when the season is through and there's no other way to make ends meet. That's what savings are for, when the lean times come round, when there's nothing to harvest and nothing to prune because now they've introduced burning and the fire takes away our chance to work. That's where the milk comes in handy. The cow is a blessing. The girls go from house to house offering cottage cheese and pudding. If you want luxury you've got to pay; you want heaven, there's no time to play. Over there they like spending their money on luxuries. But there are always people of means, especially bachelors. They can eat cottage cheese or invite their girlfriends over to have milk pudding. At first we didn't have the heart to sell to our neighbors; we were embarrassed, all we did was trade with them. That's how it went with eggs. I wasn't born to sell. The girls were; Juana, too. They have youthful spirits. I used to go from marketplace to marketplace selling stones and hogs. These days my daughters go to San Vicente to sell the cheese and pudding. We all work on the assumption that we've got to save money for the times when there isn't any work at the haciendas. That's why we went back to pigs. Except that now we don't have very many of them, just a pair and once they have a litter we immediately sell them. It's better to get rid of them when they're young because raising pigs is a thankless task; they shit anywhere they please; they dig holes where water collects and mosquitoes breed; they fill the yard with chiggers; and since we all go barefoot, the chiggers are relentless when they get into our feet. The bites keep us awake at night.

Saturdays and Sundays we add the grindstones. People know it's our family's business, though we only do it on weekends. But we've run out of clients in the village. That's the problem with the stones. They're eternal. We have to find customers elsewhere. That's where our vocation as merchants came from. I used to travel in the cart a lot. Not anymore. I'm a farm worker.

If we don't keep at it, if we just sit back and fold our arms, death will come quickly. Death will come anyway, slowly but surely. Sometimes I wonder if this life isn't a kind of slow death.

Who knows. Though I do know that thinking about these things is a mortal sin.

Lucía is about to turn fourteen. It's starting to show in her happy little eyes. The little wildcat fixes her hair before she goes out to sell. It is clean and nice, like wildflowers. It smells like myrtle and mignonette. She gathers looks as she walks along, like someone collecting fruit in a basket. The looks used to drive her crazy. She didn't see that they saw her. Now the boys along the road have grown up, as she has. A butterfly collector, she keeps all the good-byes, the nice words she hears, the affectionate laughs, whispers, sighs, and heavy breathing locked away in her breast. Butterfly collector, she captures the smallest gestures. Life has become full and illuminating. With a sprig of mignonette adorning her hair she enters the road as though entering a new life. She would like to fly, she feels she's sprouting wings.

Lucía entertains herself with her thoughts on lonely stretches of road. She dreams:

They say you can do well in Chalate, you can improve your life just by cleaning and taking care of children. That's what my godmother said when she came for a visit. I heard her tell my parents that things were going well for Toña in Chalate; there was work for her in a cooperative. Here in Apastepeque you could get lost, do nothing but raise children in poverty. All my mama said was: God keep you! At least that's all I heard. But later I heard my papa say that males aren't a problem, because they make the world. Their danger lies in bad habits, but everyone does what he wants. Females face other dangers. That's what he said.

Suddenly I remembered my uncles who had disappeared.

We're forbidden to speak about them, but not to think about them. Every now and then they come to mind. But when my godmother came to the house and spoke of the possibility of my going to Chalate, then everyone thought of my uncles. Pedro and Manuel. It's a story my papa used to tell.

My brothers were tied up and taken to the barracks. From that moment on they forgot the family. The truth is, they could even be dead. Around fifteen boys were taken from the town. And only three returned; they didn't notice what had become of my brothers, they had been taken to different barracks. The younger one was crying; when the guardias *asked him why he was crying, wasn't he a man, he told them he was crying because the rope was too tight, that he had a cut there where they had bound him. So he hid his tears though we knew he was crying from fear of the unknown, they were being taken to war, to a garrison. To fight a war against Communists. That's what they said. They were only going to do a year of military service, the country needed them. We got used to not having them around—after all, we usually lose our males when they reach majority. I was saved because I knew how to read. They didn't take literates to the barracks.*

My mama and papa say we've always been at war. Or even if we weren't at war you could be sure that every year they would come and round up the young men in town and take them away tied like *garrobos;* the older men hid up in the mountains in caves.

It was a very sad year. The Guardia Nacional and the patrols arrived at midnight, when people were asleep and weren't expecting them; they surrounded the town and started taking people out of their houses. We're sorry, they would say, but it was the only way to find them all, the boys, in their homes. Making fun of us, ridiculing our misfortunes. And what could you do? If you make a move to run for it they start shooting. No one could run that night, maybe because the boys were still half asleep. I don't know.

They are only going for a year, the members of the patrol would say to make us feel better, and they'll be more civilized when we send them back. This is what their leader would say as he waved his rifle in the air, tossing it from one hand to the other. In the barracks they learn to read and mind their manners, they went on, without looking at anyone, addressing the stones which were us. The year was up but they never came back. No one comes back. It wasn't until two years later the three boys returned and when they were questioned by everybody else they knew nothing, each was in a different barracks. What was there to know. Later we found out they were alive and had become guardias. *That was just a rumor, though, no one could confirm it. If they did become* guardias *that was even worse, it would be difficult to see them because they never go on missions in the areas they come from. Because of their work they'll never come around again. And they never did. All it would have taken is the desire and they could have visited us whenever they felt like it.*

Mama made me swear that if I went to Chalatenango I would never turn my back on the family, because it is sacred. I didn't want to make Mama cry or worry Papa. I know Papa is different from everyone else. He's hard and nothing bothers him, though he's a dedicated family man; but he lets us do what we want, as long as he feels it isn't wrong. Mama doesn't see anything wrong with me going to Chalate either. Though I know she will suffer. Up until now we've never in our lives been separated. I would miss her, too, and if there's any reason I wouldn't go it would be because I don't want to leave her all by herself. If I do go, I hope I can see her soon. "Don't forget us, Lucía," she says.

We poor always end up leaving home. Maybe it's because we're fleeing poverty. Looking for better roads. Sometimes it's dangerous because of the temptations in big cities. I think my mama will be all right if she knows I'll always be with my godmother. A person's godmother is like another mother.

Maybe I'll go to Chalate. When I think about it I get kind of cold. All right. That's where we follow God's path.

X / JACINTO

1979

"IT'S A MIRACLE to be alive, that's for sure," says Jacinto.

"Love keeps us alive," Juana reflects.

This time Jacinto is telling his compañera *about his second encounter with the* guardia—*the first time had been in Jiquilisco, when he and his brothers were selling pigs.*

The second time I was older and maybe that's why the beating I got was fit for a man, it was the kind that changes you forever —they're just dying to grab you like a sack of corn and thrash away, they really get into it. That's what happened to me; good thing I didn't end up consumptive or with breathing problems.

So the guardia *was tormenting a drunk. Then I notice the drunk is my friend. They were whacking him with the flat of their machetes; you should have heard the blades whistling in the air as they came down on the poor man's shoulder.*

Like I was saying, I know the guy and it's hard to keep my mouth shut—no matter who it was, it would be hard, not to mention a harmless bum. I had just gotten off work—the sweat hadn't even dried yet, and this is what I see. So I tell the guardias *to lay off, I know him and he likes to drink, is all; then I see the reason they're beating him is that he's carrying all his worldly possessions with him. They pay me no attention, maybe they can't even hear what I'm saying over the sound of machetes whistling through the air and the man's shouts. Still, I stay where I am and keep my distance, watching until I can't stand it anymore and shout: "Leave him alone, he can't even feel the blows anymore." That was all they wanted. The* guardias *were already so fired up from working the bum over it was easy for them to switch victims; besides, they have no idea who they're hitting half the time, and they could care less. So they started in on me like there was no tomorrow. "Who the hell are you, sticking your nose where it don't belong, bastard?" they say. The man is senseless, I tell them. That was it, they left my bagman friend and came at me, machetes in hand. I didn't even move. I figured I couldn't leave my friend alone. Besides, if I had run they would have plugged me with a bullet, they were so eager. I could see the hate in their eyes. The angrier they got the more their hate surfaced. I wondered then what I was in for. What's left to tell? Half an hour later, after the* guardias *had left, a few people got up the courage to come over to where we lay in the dirt. Try and imagine, blood was coming out my pores; I don't know if you know what that means, Mama, to have blood coming out your pores. Bruises are one thing, they're painful and leave scars, but it's different when you get hit with the flat side of a machete—it doesn't just raise welts, the blade actually penetrates your flesh and when it meets resistance and can't go in any further, the pores open and blood starts gushing out. You sweat blood. You're covered with blood without even being cut. To get in one last dig the* guardias *told some people, See those two drunks over there? They're so shitfaced they're half dead. Do something with them. Of course the people knew they were lying—they know the* guardia *too well for that; besides, they saw them walk off swinging their machetes, looking for their next victim.*

A little while later some people came and took me to San Vicente in a hammock. I was unconscious for more than twelve hours—more on that side than this. The bagman died three days later. The coroner said the cause of death was a hangover, not the machete blows. They took advantage of the man's weakness to justify his murder. Hell, what do you expect when you're in their hands. Someday we'll make the laws and there won't be any objection when those laws favor us and punish all those assholes who've been shitting on the poor for centuries. We won't be bastards like them because you have to have the soul of a common criminal for that, but we will be strict and severe, there's no doubt about that. When that day comes they better not complain they've always been the guardian angels of the law. It's just that your blood boils and you can't forget what they've done so quick. I know I should forget and we shouldn't be out for revenge; but hell, I'm human and I have my faults. We'll never be bastards. I swear to God we won't.

They had almost always lived in fear. The poor. Always the hard times, never finding the good. For the poor there is suffering and that is all. Jacinto is sitting on the log he uses as a seat, in the shed where he always kept his cart, which is nothing but a skeleton now. He talks to himself or a group of friends which are the imaginary product of his thirst for companionship.

"For example, as far as we're concerned there are no laws, only when they round men up and drag them off like animals to do their military service. The law exists when a cow or ox disappears; that's when the *guardia* appears searching houses or hillsides to find the cow's remains; and if they come up with a suspect they tie him up, take him away, and beat him. The law is always upheld through beating and brutality."

Jacinto says this softly, to no one in particular, just the phantoms of the night.

"Or when they come on Sunday to keep the peace; they wander up and down on the lookout for anyone who steps out of line. If you're having a saint's day or birthday celebration, they smell it from a mile away."

Whenever the populace wants to have some fun, the authorities are there. In search of anything out of the ordinary.

"An ounce of prevention, they say; they're tired of battling us peasants, we've got to disappear from the map."

Gunshots can be heard in the distance. Jacinto doesn't bat an eye. Gunshots are like rain; all you can do is listen, you can't pay any particular attention to them.

"Sometimes they're in a good mood, cracking jokes and clowning around. When they've got money, after they've been paid by the hacienda or garrison, they're congenial. When they say the poor ought to be wiped off the face of the map, they say it jokingly, because they can't just come right out with it. Of course, you can't trust them. You never know. I wonder: If they're poor, why do they attack the poor with such vengeance?"

He thinks a long time, trying to come up with an answer, but he gives up.

"They don't commit atrocities at the end of the month or on weekends because they've got money in their pockets. They say money buys happiness. I don't know; we barely get to see it change hands—one day you get paid, the next it's gone, even deer aren't that elusive. We get no more than the scent of it, most of it comes in the form of credit and discounts at the company store. They say money makes people happy. To me, seeing is not believing."

And his voice is the wind, blowing through the hut's open door; wind that smells of the sea when it blows out of the south; from the north it carries the scent of liquidambar and pine.

"The *guardias* haul people off just for looking at them cross-eyed. When the devil gets into them they're dangerous and we have to shuffle our feet and take care not to get too close to them for fear our luck will turn and we'll get clubbed with the butt of a gun just for the hell of it—we poor bear the brunt of it."

He moves his cigar from side to side, smoking heavily to chase away the mosquitoes. He takes a deep breath, getting ready to fly to another more beautiful and human reality.

"That's been the law since we were born. You can say there are other laws, but we never heard of them."

Some of the evening stars have suspended themselves from his eyelashes and drop lightly into the dark river of his eyes. Meanwhile, Juana lights the *ocotillo* torches.

"At the beginning of March, for example, the provincial patrol comes looking for young people to do their hitch—meaning, to do their obligatory military service, as they call it. The kids have to hide because it's sad when they take them away and leave you even more poor than you were before."

The hut shines with the orange glow of the torches. Way off a coyote howls. A shot is heard.

"You know this thing about going to the city and walking around in uniform is no picnic. I was lucky to be spared; I don't know how; we all know how hard it is. Can you imagine? They've never had a war, why do they need soldiers? For no other reason than to shit on you. They send people from here all the way over there, and they send people from there over here. That way, nobody knows anybody else and they can treat their fellow men like enemies. They don't train soldiers to fight, but to make sure Salvadorans don't make any attempts on private property—can you imagine? With all this misery, private property is always in danger. 'The righteous will halt before an open vault' especially when they're hungry."

———

The most miraculous thing that ever happened was when Jacinto was hit by lightning. He was young and they left him alone in the hut, husking corn. When the whole family was working at home. This is what they were doing when a storm was sent from Heaven itself.

"You were barely thirteen, and your brothers had just been taken. I can't imagine losing you at that age, God forbid."

"I don't even know how old I was, I only know I was young."

When the lightning started striking he burned oregano leaves to scare it away. It was hitting pretty close and getting closer. He got in his hammock to keep calm. He didn't want to be shucking corn while the lightning struck because the rubbing action could attract it. Even the dog tried to get in the hammock with him; but he pushed her to the ground: "Get out of here, don't mess with me." Good thing. Because dog hair also attracts lightning. Lightning goes for anything that shines. The worst part is the dog howls every time it strikes. "I was scared."

Grandfather Emiliano had taught him that when lightning strikes you've got to get your feet off the ground because if you don't you become a lightning rod. So he got in his hammock to get his feet off the ground and huddle against the cold. Rain brings cold air.

The dog lay under the hammock whimpering in fear.

Suddenly Jacinto saw a jagged green line above him. His eyes lit up and he felt as though the dark sky had become clear. The jagged lance came through the roof, making an unearthly noise. At that instant he thought about the dog under the hammock. And the entire hut fell down on top of him, grass, logs, poles, and all. He remembers nothing after that.

"My God, what happened?" shouted Emiliano, who came running home once he got the news.

"The hut is on fire," someone said.

"Jacinto's in there!" screamed Ticha, arriving moments after Emiliano.

"Forget it, *niña*. If he's inside he's already dead. The fire won't last long, the rain will put it out."

Luckily the rain came down thicker and nothing but smoke poured from the hut as the flames were quickly extinguished.

"I'll go in and take a look," Emiliano shouted.

He runs over and starts making his way through sticks and straw, gasping for air. Others gathered around.

"I heard a moan," says Emiliano.

"The dog is in there too," says Ticha, starting to cry.

"It sounds like a person moaning. Quick, help me get this grass off of here," he says to his neighbors in the village.

And there under the hut's thatched roof lay Jacinto on the floor, his clothing scorched, his hair singed and his skin blackened by smoke. When Emiliano saw him he thought Jacinto had turned to charcoal because of the black color of his skin. Jacinto was in a state of shock when he came to. The first thing he did was ask about the dog that had been under the hammock. "Where's my dog?"

"Are you alive?" Emiliano asks without giving his grandson an answer.

"I guess so," Jacinto answers, rubbing his body and howling in pain.

"He's alive," Emiliano shouts to the neighbors.

"Thank God," says Beatriz.

The rain has begun to taper off. People tell Emiliano they can take the boy to the nearest hut. Several offer to let them spend the night in their homes.

"What happened?" Beatriz asks a little while later as she gives him some mint tea; they are guests at a neighboring hut.

"I don't know, I was lying in the hammock when the lightning struck," Jacinto answers. "But what happened to the dog?" he asks.

"The poor thing died, son," Beatriz laments.

"She was under the hammock," Jacinto explains.

"The lightning must have passed right over you."

"Miraculous," exclaims Emiliano.

"And they say God isn't good."

"That he doesn't perform miracles anymore."

"That it isn't worth believing in God when you're down and out."

"And then I saw a big flash, the sky turned blue above me," continues Jacinto.

"Will you look at that, so young and he survived a lightning bolt," someone says.

"When I saw his charred body I thought he was dead," says Emiliano.

"I fell on top of the dog and was scared out of my wits when I felt the poor thing's singed flesh—except I didn't think it was real since the dog was under me—if I made it, the dog must have made it, too—I thought I must be dreaming," says Jacinto.

"Imagine, you're saying the lightning passed right by you and hit the dog," interrupts Beatriz.

"That's exactly what I'm saying," replies Jacinto. "That's why I couldn't believe it when you said the dog was dead. I had just been stroking her, rubbing her fur when I saw the bolt above," Jacinto goes on, shaken by the accident that almost cost him his life.

"There's no doubt God was watching over you. To me this is nothing short of a miracle," says Emiliano.

"Cat luck, I say," declares Beatriz.

"Both," Emiliano interjects. "Cat luck comes from the fact

that my grandson has entrusted himself to the hands of divine providence, as he should."

"Except that I thought it was divine justice that had sent the thunderbolt," says Jacinto trying to explain the phenomenon to himself. "Because you realize that out of all the huts and trees around here, it hit right here, directly above the hammock."

"It's also because dog hair attracts electricity," says Emiliano, trying to find another explanation.

"That's right," says Beatriz, backing him up. "And since you were in the hammock with your body in midair, the electricity didn't get you, but if you had had your feet on the ground, it would have been all over." She suddenly hears what she's saying and tries to take it back. "God help me! I better touch wood," and she raps her knuckles on the new centerpost of the recently reconstructed hut.

"We're lucky our friends helped us resurrect the hut."

"They're good people," says Beatriz.

"In March you see people strung out along the hills with their arms tied together, many of them beaten and crying because this might be the first time they've ever left their mothers and fathers, and they've never been to the city before—it's not because they're cowards; it's because they get taken when they're still young, they're only little boys."

His cigar goes out and he gets up to light the end on one of the torches.

"It used to be you were in for a year, now they say you have to do two years and it might go up to five because they claim people in places like this are getting too uppity, they won't settle for being poor anymore. Imagine, how can a family go and see their young ones if it's almost the same as losing them? Who's

171

got the money to pay train fare and pay for a place to stay in the city? Just thinking about it is enough to scare you; people aren't used to leaving home. At least I had some experience when I was young, but even so, when they took my brothers to the barracks, we didn't even know whether they'd been killed or if they had decided to become city people—we knew nothing. You must understand that that is the reason being in the service is as hard on the families as it is on the kids. To say nothing of the fact that their training consists of kicking and insults; they get locked in dungeons without light or air for the least little infraction."

The red embers of the tobacco contrast with the green stars in his eyelashes. Jacinto reaches for the cigar. The red star of the cigar makes a coral circle. Only Jacinto interrupts the soft harmony built over silences and swaying trees by the pillars of night. A quaking dog rises from his corner and growls inaudibly so as not to alter the harmonic structure of the world around him.

"The young soldiers must obey orders, they must enter houses and take things without asking, to earn respect, they're told, but the only thing they earn is hatred. You get tired of being good, that's for sure. And patient."

Another shot in the night. Each shot on the mountain is without doubt another death. Jacinto thinks about the person just killed by the shot.

"They come into the district and ask for food—what food? I wonder, since they're used to eating something besides tortillas and salt. And still they get mad when that's what you offer them, and they make fun of you."

Some things he says from his own experience, others from what his friends have told him. Jacinto has also had to flee into the mountains, sleep in caves, and climb trees to escape from the regional patrols that capture young people for mandatory military service. He was spared because those who knew how to read were exempt.

"Of course, it is a sin to deny your fellow man a bite of food, but you can't give what you don't have. If tortilla with salt is all I have, that is what I offer; but these people come and ask if we can make them some chicken, if you can imagine. So, you have to kill a chicken. The sergeants in charge are like *gambusia* fish —the minute you deny them anything they immediately order you to hand it over; what can we do? Might as well hand it over for your own sake and save your own life. Besides, if you get them riled, they'll destroy all your chickens. For being stingy, they'll say. Then you're further up the creek than you were before. They want tortillas, so you make tortillas; they want coffee and though you barely have enough for yourself the next morning, you give it to them. They have their own laws which derive from the guns they carry. Might is what makes people respect the law; without guns there wouldn't be any laws, they say. And life, though it must be cared for in poverty, must be lived; it is beautiful to be alive. So why give them an excuse to fill you full of holes?"

"Imagine the disgrace of being killed by them, beginning with the funeral costs, even if all you can afford are some slabs of pine and a little wreath of flowers. There's no point in working all your life if you don't even have enough wood for a coffin. I don't want them rolling me up in some old *petate.* I don't know anybody who would, but around here most people make do with a *petate,* the oldest one they've got so they don't waste a good one—that's where they got the saying 'One hole for a dead man, another for the man who's still alive.' That's the most pitiful kind of poverty there is. I refuse to die simply to spare my people the aggravation. There's the money to consider, naturally; you have to have a wake, a coffin, and flowers. Regardless of his poverty, a Christian should die like a Christian. I do know that death is no consolation for the poor. Death means trouble for those who are still alive and know you."

Nobody refutes a thing. All Jacinto does is open his mouth, sometimes to talk, other times to change the position of his cigar.

"The law used to cause a lot of dread; in the last few years it's caused death. It leaves us childless, homeless, and without animals. The government vents its wrath on us simply because they claim subversives from the city come to this area. We tell them it isn't our fault if strangers pass this way, why would we cut off our nose to spite our face? And you know what happened? One night the *guardia* came; though it was dark, I recognized some of those who had been to our hut asking for chicken soup. They came and woke us up. Have the subversives been here? I said no, I hadn't seen the *muchachos* in the last few months, they'd only come once and no one knew where they went after that. They start telling us we're lying. One *guardia* told us we had a duty to our country and we shouldn't lie. They took all the men out of our huts and threatened us with their rifles, saying we were a bunch of dumb fucks, that's why we were there. They took us all out to the football field to insult us. Only the sick can stay in their huts, they said, everyone out to the football field, we're going to read a proclamation that will tell you how to behave in front of the subversives; and then they scold us like little children. And since we didn't respond to their little pep talk and just sat there playing dumb, they changed their tone, taking us into their confidence, saying everything they did was for our own good, they didn't wish us any harm. They shined searchlights in our eyes the whole time. Don't be afraid, they said, the searchlights are to see you better. That's what life is like these days."

Complete darkness fell over Jacinto. Night and sounds. Weighing down the eyes, body, and soul. He's comforted by the fact that sometimes he can be happy with the greatest ease; that it's his nature, given the exaggerated material limitations, to be able to express the good as well as the bad, with simplicity and even tenderness. As a man resistant to disease, starvation, and pain, he has reason to feel strong and immortal; under no circumstances does he think he must die someday, despite confronting death every day, either his own or those close to him. His words contain no bitterness, nor do they emphasize the difficult stretches. The nuances of his expression can only be detected when he changes the position of the tobacco in his mouth. His own inhalation has put the red ember out, leaving only a wheel of white ash where once there was fire.

"There's no doubt about it, you've got cat luck," Juana tells her *compañero*.

"That's nothing," brags Jacinto. "I haven't told you about the time I got bit by a rabid dog. You know, the only way to cure rabies is to kill the dog." And I didn't kill it. Though now they say that's not true, about killing the dog; now they give you shots, which they didn't have before. Though around here, we'll freeze in hell before we see any of these new things.

There I was, acting like hot stuff. I went to buy some cigars at Lastenia's and just to show off and keep my hands free, I got the bright idea to leave my machete at home; it was a short walk, so it didn't seem to matter if I left it—you know, a machete is like a girlfriend, you don't want to let it out of your sight. Suddenly a dog comes up. I have no idea where he came from, because I know all the dogs in the village; though sometimes avocado pickers come around looking for avocados on the estates —maybe it belonged to one of them. No one had ever seen the dog before. It lunged at me from some underbrush where it was hiding and I saw it coming; so I took a swipe at him with my bare hands. I thought there's no way I'm going to let him go without a fight; but shit. There weren't even any rocks in sight. He leapt on top of me and took a chunk out of my left arm, since I was protecting my right like a baby—I earn a living with that one. I was so stupid. Because of the blessed habit of always having a machete at my side, I took another swipe, this time with my right. That was all he needed. He latched onto my arm and would not let go, he shook his head from side to side like he wanted to take another big hunk out of me; the more I tried to pry him loose, the harder the bastard gripped. Then I got another bright idea. You see how God works. War requires thought. Since there was no other way to defend myself, I figured maybe he'd let go if I bit him back. So that's what I did. First I bit his paw. Did he let go? Let go, you sonofabitch, I yell, then I sink my teeth into his ear. I knew I was getting somewhere then because he let out his first yelp and had to let go; I kept on biting; but ears are soft, and before I knew it there I was with a piece of ear hanging out of my mouth. That dog lit out of there like the devil himself was on his tail. Some people saw both my arms bleeding and asked what happened so I told them and they gave me lemon juice and brown sugar because the dog had rabies, they said, he'd been hanging around for days, hiding out in the brush, maybe to die in peace. It was my bum luck to walk by. To make a long story short, I'll just say that I had a wicked fever, and waited for the rabies to take me. On the fifth day they came from Lastenia's and said they'd found the dog, he'd died, and maybe that's what saved me; funny thing is he died from having a piece of his ear bit off, or maybe it was the rabies after all, I thought. Impossible, someone said, because if the dog dies of rabies, you die of rabies, too.

People who saw the dog said his ear was infected. Maybe I did bite the bastard to death after all. What more can I say? I got famous for possessing the *chinchintora* viper's amulet, because nothing bad ever happened to me. Not only that but I killed a rabid dog without getting rabies myself, even though he took a chunk out of me. People believe in these things. Others said maybe I had a thunderstone from the lightning bolt; I've been lucky ever since I was little and got hit by lightning so maybe that's where I got the amulet. All I know is I've never seen this amulet they're always talking about, the most I ever saw were lights in my head that day as a child when I watched the sky crash in on me. Anyway, I'm not convinced I'm all that lucky—it would be nice to think so! So many bad things happened, maybe that meant I wasn't so lucky; or maybe my luck came from having all those things happen to me—how twisted —I must have been quite a guy at one time to have had all that luck. The only good luck is what we poor in this region have: enough work to keep us from starving and that's how we get by. I'm convinced if they raffled off a *guardia,* I'd be the one to win.

So I have just the opposite opinion: I'm jinxed and that's why these things happen to me. Something in my blood attracts these kind of disasters. I'm not complaining about my life, either. But that's something else. Giving an account of my poverty isn't the same as complaining about the way God treats me. Instead it's a conscious attempt to stop accepting things the way they are. To give myself some hope and encouragement. Because one thing is certain: the poor live on hope, though not everyone believes in it, and maybe that's why their misfortunes are greater. You know I don't like to complain about my life, but

I do like to protest in silence the things that happen to us, because when I do it makes the blood go to my head and ideas start to flow and then I'm no longer at the mercy of trouble and misfortune. It's simply a matter of learning how to adapt to the hard life, of learning how to survive, and it's also a matter of seeking out those little points of light that many times enlighten you.

XI / MICROBUS TO
SAN SALVADOR

January 9, 1981

I CLEARLY UNDERSTOOD the message when my *compa* made me touch the weapon under his shirt. I was surprised that he was armed. But these things should come as no surprise. I had to pretend, with even more conviction, that we were two separate people without any connection whatsoever. Too bad for me. What would happen if they found the weapon? I didn't even want to think about it. It's a real case of being face-to-face with death. Two minutes away, five, ten. You don't know. We looked at one another for no more than a few seconds. Asking each other things only the two of us could understand. A small group of *guardias* approached the microbus, pointing their automatic rifles, telling us to get off the bus and leave our things behind. Women on one side, men on the other.

They talked to the driver. They had a "mazinger" hidden under a *tihuilote* tree. Luckily they didn't search us. I can see my *compa* is nervous, watching the hills nearby. A weapon in a case like this means they won't take you alive. After a while the driver comes back and says the *guardias* want us to walk in front of the "mazinger." The people from the bus protest. The *guardias* say the guerrillas are about a mile and a half down the road. We can't do that, someone said, we'll all be killed. We'll get caught in the crossfire. The driver defends himself. That's what I told them but the *guardias* won't listen to reason, you know that as well as I. Why don't you wait for the guerrillas to leave before you go on? the driver had insisted. The officer: We can't, we have to get to San Salvador today. All the more reason to protest: Why don't *you* go in front, it's *your* duty. Everyone responds affirmatively, out loud, so the officer, who has remained next to the "mazinger," hears our protests. The women shout. The men don't because they run the risk of being shot. The officer also raises his voice and tells us if the subversives see a microbus with passengers they won't shoot. He stays where he is. And how are they going to know there are passengers aboard? a woman asks. They'll shoot no matter what, the driver yells to the officer. None of the *guardias* have moved from the "mazinger." Suddenly we see a sergeant coming toward us aiming his rifle. My captain says they won't shoot because the subversives are observing us. See that hill over there? he asks. You can see everything from there. So if you lead the way they won't shoot. The women continue to protest: You want to use us as cannon fodder. The sergeant speaks: We'll give you a few minutes to think about it, because neither we nor they can pass and they will decide what is to be done without consulting us. It's a threat. I know if the guerrillas are on the hill, the *guardias* wouldn't dare shoot us. We have the choice to go to one side of the road and wait for the crisis to pass or for the authorities to resolve it. The driver comes over to the group of women, because we are the only ones who have raised our voices. I'm scared, he says. There are four "mazinger" trucks hidden under some branches. He could see them when he went over to the captain. They're on the dirt path. We can see the path, covered with some heavy foliage. It's swarming with *guardias.* He says. Even the leaves are moving, like it was the wind.

What will happen if they shoot us? I ask just to say something, to make believe the situation isn't that serious. The sergeant can't help boasting: Too bad for them. So it was an ambush and they were using us as bait, it didn't matter if we were sacrificed. They wanted to use us as a shield, to shoot at the hill and when the *muchachos* fired back they would surround them with the troops hidden on the path. I tried to see through the green depths of the foliage, where the "mazingers" were; finally I could make them out: large trucks, armored and camouflaged, like walls of steel. I had seen them on the streets of San Miguel. So it wasn't only the one "mazinger" and the *guardias* under the *tihuilote* tree. The very leaves on the bushes shook, there was a swarm of men whose breathing stirred the branches. That's why they hadn't searched us. They weren't interested in that. They had another mission. Look sergeant, if you will vouch for the life of the passengers I will be on my way. He said no, we'd better stay right here and sleep on the road. Yes, the women repeated. The men were also working up their courage. We'd rather wait, says an old man. I look at my *compa*. I can tell he wants to talk to me, to come near, but it's impossible because they've separated us. There's no chance to talk; nothing to do but look at each other and say hello with our eyes. Are you all right? How lucky they didn't search us, I tell him with a look. Though we don't know how we'll get out of this. Either you go willingly or by force, the sergeant says. And he brags: We've learned a thing or two from them, we haven't slept a wink all night. They had taken their position the night before. We've been here since last night, he says. This is what he means when he says they've learned from the *muchachos*. They are preparing an ambush and that's why they want to use us. The "mazinger" that stopped us has been following us since San Miguel; then it overtook us. They stopped us in the exact spot where the other "mazinger" trucks were hidden.

"My captain says ten minutes are up and you'd better get back on the microbus," the sergeant says. The use of the word *better* is an implied threat; however, the officer doesn't appear impatient.

We are having doubts about obeying the sergeant's suggestion. Now I've had a chance to look at the hill in more detail, and I'm filled with a mixture of confidence and dread. I know the *guardias* can't strike us as long as the *muchachos* are watching from the hill. If indeed they are watching us, as the sergeant claims.

Various vehicles have been detained behind us, but they are kept at a distance. From what it looks like, the *guardias* have boarded them as well. Up ahead we hear whistling, birdcalls carried by the wind from the hills.

"It's them," the sergeant says to our unspoken doubts. "Those are the subversives' signals." He puts on a cynical face. He knows the success of the ambush depends upon us and so he must pressure us, though he would prefer to persuade rather than force the action so the operation goes as planned.

"Have some understanding, sergeant," says the old man who has been speaking.

The *guardia* once again adopts his paternal tone:

"No cause for alarm. When the microbus starts moving the caravan of cars behind us will follow." With the barrel of his rifle he indicates the line of cars pulled to the side of the road.

"They're not stupid enough to follow us," one woman says.

"If they see us move, they'll follow," the sergeant replies.

"How do you know?" I dare to ask. Ever since they pulled us over I've worried about my *compañero,* especially about his weapon. He's been driving himself crazy over in the men's group. He hasn't had a chance to hide it. Unless he left it on the bus. Though I think that's impossible. I don't see as much uncertainty in his face now; so I figure he's solved the pistol problem. I see a glimmer of hope. It's like being at death's door.

The key to not having the guerrillas shoot is the microbus with its passengers. First they must convince us. And the driver. It's nothing to be taken lightly.

"Twelve minutes have passed," shouts the captain.

"Come on," says the sergeant. "Make up your mind, they'll fuck me over for being so lenient with you."

We women who had approached the truck to talk to the sergeant start walking towards the microbus.

Up ahead, from behind the hill, a shot is heard.

More vacillation on our part. The sergeant hits the ground. Some do as he does, others remain standing. The captain yells at his subordinate. Get up, asshole, the shooting's coming from the other side.

The sergeant gets up and says it's nothing, the best thing would be to keep on going. You can't go on stalling forever. And once again he wears his cynical look. He is trying to cover up his moment of weakness when he mistakenly hit the dirt: Too bad there's not enough *guardias* to give those assholes up ahead in the hills a run for their money. He tries to deceive us about the number of men he's got. It's ten o'clock, he says. Soon the sun will be beating down.

We head towards the group of men. I look at my *compa*. He looks at me. He can tell. Or maybe my eyes gave it away. We're decoys for an ambush. I doubt he can see the horde hidden in the bushes or the other "mazingers" on the path. I feel we've got to get on the microbus. Or maybe I want to head for my *compa* since we're already walking in the direction of the men. The sergeant follows, more cautious after having heard the shot.

He hasn't lowered his weapon once. He talks and gestures with it as if it were another finger on his hand.

Another shout from the captain that I can't make out; but I see him leaning back against the steel-plated truck, nonchalantly toying with his beret. Maybe it's just his way of acting like he's not anxious about the prospect of carrying out a successful operation. We haven't slept a wink all night. That's what he said. We make sacrifices but we must use the same tactics as the subversives. In other words, this is the first time they've ever had to make sacrifices in this war. These assholes keep getting stronger and more arrogant. That's what I overheard when he was talking to the sergeant. He had allowed the group of women to come up to him just for show, to make it look good to the *muchachos* who, according to him, were watching from the hilltop that lay ahead further down the road.

Suddenly I turn around, just to make sure my *compa* is back there. To see him and get a little of his strength, the same strength I've come to know throughout our life together. I can just make out his hair, sticking out above the heads of the men's group approaching us. While I look back, I turn my head further to see the "mazinger." I see the captain open the vehicle's door and I see *guardias* climbing over the rear of the vehicle. As my head comes back to its original position I look straight into my *compañero*'s face. It's less than a second, but I try to burn it into my memory as though that instant were the last in our lives. Actually, any expression or gesture can be a last farewell to someone we will never see again. As I finish that thought I hear a short burst behind me. It sounds close. Someone shouts: "Hit the dirt." I don't have time to look back, but instead of falling to the ground I hurl myself violently against the bus. I see the sergeant, who is down and wounded. Another round, stronger and more sustained, comes from the "mazinger"; and the *guardias* rush out as the officer shouts: "Kill him." In the seconds that elapse, I see my *compa* jump the wall of volcanic rock at the highway's edge, his body horizontal, as though flying. The last burst of gunfire was directed at him, after he took out his pistol and shot the sergeant, catching him off guard. He disappears over the wall, which serves as a parapet. The volcanic rock flies like sparks, destroyed by the shots. Maybe five minutes have passed, and they equal a lifetime. The sergeant is quivering on the ground and howling. Another burst of fire. And another. The *guardias* hiding in the underbrush come out in force. The captain continues shouting orders at his subordinates. He's started the motor of the "mazinger" and heads for the highway, trying to cut off my *compañero*'s retreat. I see he has a two-way radio. Then I hear women shouting, confused by the deafening dry rattle of the automatic rifles. They can't figure out what's going on. I haven't even had time to notice that I am on the brink of an overwhelming sadness. Shots come from the nearby hill. The captain abandons his forward push and begins to retreat in our direction again. Nearly all the *guardias* have left their hiding places and take positions. Some watch from the top of the wall and others hide behind trees.

I have no idea how many seconds or minutes have passed and anguish creeps up on me. I try to concentrate as though these were the final moments of my life. This is all a dream, I tell myself, or else it is the beginning of a loneliness I have never known before. I keep repeating: This is all a dream, this is all a dream. Then I turn my attention once again to the sergeant, who has stopped shouting or moving. Several *guardias* drag themselves over to him. New burst of fire from far off and the sound of lead hitting the steel of the now visible "mazinger." Then I realize this is all very real; I will keep on leaning up against the microbus for who knows how many months and years. Then I slowly start to crouch, more out of weakness than to protect myself from the shooting. But not physical weakness. Something more inexpressible, as though all moral strength has run out. Or as though the landscape were gradually being obliterated—the hills up ahead, the green trees that moments ago were stirred by the wind and the soldiers' hidden breathing; as though this hot air that makes you sweat inside—sweat blood —had begun to turn into a flock of hawks coming to prey upon you and devour you with their beaks. It is like going to your extinction, the way small sand dunes are beaten back by the sea; suddenly they are both there and not there, they disappear but you know it is just the shifting of the sand. Nevertheless, you are no longer there. When suddenly you hear helicopters and that, too, is real. The helicopters were standing by waiting for the captain's orders to come in and support the ambush. Now they come to seek out the person who flew like a bird over the stone wall. The furious din of the helicopters. Hungry coyotes. I haven't crouched all the way down yet; it is happening with a slowness I want to last a lifetime. Finally I feel the heat of my thighs touch the heat in my calves and I have almost reached the ground. My eyes fill with a strange turmoil. Again the helicopters. This time they come close, filling the hills with noise and furies. Once again I wake to reality. There is nothing more real than those steel lobsters that exhale fire and spit death. Once I feel my eyes start to fill with tears I realize I can't stay in the dream. The noise is too intense for sleeping. And I am the only one who can say this reality is my reality. And not run away from it, and there's only one way I can put it: it is mine; I earned it, and I owe it to no one. Others can keep their dreams. I'll keep my reality. I have earned the right to express it and share it. And whoever decides to join me in this quest will not be hit by any of the bullets that begin to pulverize the wall of volcanic rock—the same rock my grandparents used to make grindstones. Just thinking about them transmits their durability and smoothness to you. I don't know how long I've been squatting like a tired little girl. This is the way we used to rest after long days spent in the country clearing weeds, planting corn, or picking cotton. I feel an enormous rage as I come back to myself and realize there's someone I love and respect who might not be able to keep on sharing these real events with me. As I raise my head, which I had covered with my hands to protect myself from the bullets fired by the helicopters, I see my traveling companions scarcely daring to look in the direction of the sound made by the criminal lobsters. And I see their dirty faces, covered with earth, as though they had been mingling with their own origins their whole life long. Ashes to ashes, dust to dust. And I want to laugh, seeing them there dirty, in rags, wallowing in the dust. I know it is not the time to laugh so I try to repress it, hold it in, grind it and tear it up with my rabbit's teeth. But then again, I wouldn't want them to be in my situation of anguish and desperate doubt, either. Nor in that of the sergeant, whom no one has had time to attend because everyone is doing what he must beneath the hail of bullets. Then I remember I have a wristwatch and it says three in the afternoon. It seems a short while ago someone said it was ten. Then there is a great silence as bodies begin to move. Military uniforms can be seen once again. Someone breaks the silence by saying: "We found him, captain. He was like a bird on a hilltop when the helicopters spotted him; they're bringing him in now for identification." I have continued gnawing on my newfound emotions. I reflect: It might be possible to love all those still lying on the ground the way I loved my *compañero.* I remember my two small sons. And I wonder when it will be possible not to confuse dreams with reality.

XII / EMILIANO, JUANA

October 1980

"I KEEP STILL, watching people on the road go by, while the children sleep on some cornstalks. And I tell Ticha to go and take some ears of green corn to Jacinto. It's hard for me to leave you here by yourself, she says. What do you mean? I ask. You know how things are. Can they be any worse than what we've already gone through? So many people in the family dead, so many friends. Everything is resolved in death. If we're hungry, death takes the hunger away; or else they kill you if you say you're hungry. If you demand your rights, they kill you. They always respond to our protests with death; but we go on protesting, we can't quit demanding things. Our own teachers and priests have told us not to keep quiet. And you see the struggle that follows. Threats do no good. If it isn't here, then it's over there—people are always struggling. What happens when they tire of struggling with words alone and having the authorities show up for the sole purpose of wreaking havoc with their guns? Who wouldn't get tired of it? They always win. That's why they've started talking about treating us humanely—from now on they will only burn our houses; they have orders not to shoot civilians except in emergency situations or when a crazy captain like the one that shot at us this morning comes along. Then suddenly you've got helicopters flying back and forth overhead. Imagine, all those helicopters and they still can't get the *mucha-*

chos out of the zone. People say higher up they spend all day shooting cannons, then they send the soldiers in and think everything's secure because they've obliterated the hill with shelling, then—though they're not rabbits or gophers—the *muchachos* reappear from underground. The authorities say it will be over when they've leveled every hill and left them balder than bald from fire and shelling, and when they've finished off all the 'Salvadicks'—short for Salvadoran hicks, which is what they call us. We don't want to die. I don't think anyone would choose death. You'd want to live a full life just to be able to do all the things you couldn't do in my time, because you know in my day there were different problems—they tormented us but we never raised a hand to them, we were too good, too passive and patient. Now the *muchachos* stand up for us old geezers, those of us who have fertilized these lands, these estates, with our blood so others can live the high life. At least we know that if we go to our deaths it's because we have done something useful in life, we weren't born for the sake of being born. It's different with the *muchachos,* they know what their best years are for and that there's no other way to end the injustices. Certainly many people die, but that is the price of rebelling against so much injustice. Tell me it isn't right for them to go into the mountains. The authorities used to go around chasing them in their homes, you had to sleep outside and put up with the separations they caused. And though it's true we hung our heads, we were also learning, every blow taught us something. Now, of course, it's completely different, you know; you can see it every day. We used to see soldiers come running by saying it was better for them to escape because there were so many guerrillas fighting just a handful of soldiers. We knew they were making it up; because, look— around here it took only two *guardias* to keep the population under control; they put fear in us—since they had the guns, two

189

guardias was all it took. And we were inert. I've lived a long time but my grandchildren have barely had a taste of life. Should they die like all the other children we know around here have died? I don't think so; they should hope for a better life, different from the life we had. In the past only the strongest among us, or those favored by God, were spared; but that's not right, no one should have to die abandoned. Children should not be allowed to die. Something must be done to save them. I think that when the war is over and we have the rights we have won, people will be shocked to see zones like these and find out how cast down we are and how much injustice we allowed ourselves to endure. We will want them to study us, so we don't get fooled again. They say education helps you get out of the dark—well, fine, when the war is over we are going to want to see schools in these places, we're going to want at least a nurse to come and rid us of our parasites. And we should be given a piece of land, seeds to plant and fertilizer, because the land no longer wants to produce on its own. In other words, we want them to give us a means to live and not a means to die like they do now.

"This year has been bad for us, because we've been left homeless more than once and had to build one hut after another from scratch. Some planes came by and dropped a bomb. Then soldiers came and asked us where we had hidden the subversives. There's no one here. 'Mangoes!' he said. 'Don't think you can play games with us.' There's nothing you can do to make them believe you. We can't swear before God, because it's a sin. And we can't start begging them not to mistreat us either, because that makes them worse; even the little ones know not to cry when they come. It's no use because being hard is a way of life for them and if they see you're soft, it makes them want to be even more cruel. We've seen ample proof of that. 'You're not going to tell us you don't see them when they come down from the hills,' the corporal said. 'We see people but we don't ask who they are,' we replied. How the hell should we know where they were hiding or which direction they took. They wanted to find them, though. But the worst thing is that on that particular day not a single *muchacho* had come around. Sometimes they come out to buy tortillas or a few pounds of corn. Imagine! Where the hell do we get the corn to sell them if we don't have enough ourselves? The *guardias* unjustly accused those of us living near the hill. They just want to fuck around with you. So they came and burned the hut for the first time. They threatened to come back if we misbehaved, if we sold things to the *muchachos.* The second time it was the same thing. First came the planes; they dropped a few bombs about half a mile from here, we could tell because the hut shook and our ears were ringing. Then the *guardias* appeared. They're always accompanied by airplanes, some in front, some behind. They never go alone, always acting like the great bullfighter, stirring up a cloud of dust. All for nothing, you understand, because being who we are, we've never seen all these people that merit so many bombs and so many soldiers—in other words, we've never seen groups of *muchachos,* no more than two or three come down at a time to buy things. We know they're nearby but they don't allow themselves to be seen. We can't say how many there are. Nor do we sell them much corn. Of course, they buy a little here and a little there—no one around here has enough to sell more than a minimal amount. And anyway, we don't know how much they need since we don't know how many there are. Maybe that's why they never let you see them."

Juana is like a river when she speaks and like a lagoon when she is quiet. Between silence, laughter, and interruptions, her voice carries on:

Since I was turning sixteen and didn't like men much, they began to be worried at home that no one would take an interest in me, and that's not right for a woman, especially since her main mission is to bear children as God commands. That's why they were worried. Not me, though. I was truly a happy girl. I went to the dances they held in the common hall, and I was what you call a flirt because I made eyes at the boys; also, I liked getting all dressed up—I had my two changes of nahuilla *when I was young. I wore* nahuilla *even though it was a thin material, but we wore slips so they couldn't see our skin. In other words, our clothing consisted of wrapping the* nahuilla *three times around from the waist down. With that we had our slip, or skirt, that is; meanwhile the shirts or blouses we wore were made of cotton coarser than* nahuilla.

I used to like going to the river with my mama. I helped her do the wash, since she took in other people's wash too—they sought her out every now and then; even if they were just rags, people liked to be clean, especially on Sundays, which are days of rest and celebration for us; except the men do most of the celebrating —they had a good old time, shooting dice and going to the edge of town to have a few drinks on the sly. The women would go out for a stroll on the main street; we rarely left the village. One time I was in the city of San Vicente, where we went to buy things or really just to get out and have a ride in the cart; though the more rugged of us walked—it wasn't an easy journey, it took more than two hours to get there; we had to spend the night in the city, outside the gates. We would leave at four in the morning to avoid the midday sun, a fierce sun, and we would return the following afternoon.

So my family was worried because I hadn't found a mate for life, a compañero. *It got to the point where one day my mother said: "Look, Juana, you flirt too much. It's not good to peck around so* much." *Like a greedy hen. Maybe that's why men don't pay any attention, because they don't trust fickle women, the kind that put flowers in their hair and wear too much powder—in those days they sold scented powder to put on your face to accentuate the yellow highlights, so you didn't look splotchy. In that respect my daughter Lucía turned out just like me.*

I told Rosaura, my mama, that practically all the men were losers and good-for-nothings anyway and so it was better to stay single. She answered by saying since I wasn't serious they paid no attention to me, and men are the only ones allowed to pick and choose, women should act differently. Then I asked her if by chance she had ever flirted with anyone, or if she had ever worn flowers in her hair. She was appalled. "God forbid!" as though it was a sin. That's how we got along, always at odds. I thought the way I was was perfectly natural and I had no intention of changing, since you are the way you are and not the way your mother would like you to be. About that time she got the idea to pray to a saint to get me a boyfriend.

"You're coming with us." And off they went. No one knew if it was for good. And the women and men that were left at home are expected to sleep at night without knowing where the person has been taken. "We're taking this one," they said as they pointed their guns. And they push them off in the dark. They take them out to the main road. There's no time or strength to say good-bye. At moments like that you don't even think about saying good-bye. You don't have the strength to cry out or protest. Someday it will be different. Not now. Imagine what it feels like, once you realize you might never see your loved one again. You think: "Maybe one day he'll show up, maybe they'll let him go." Hope, we've got plenty of that. You can tell someone's being taken when you can hear dogs barking. They use the main road and leave a trail of barking dogs all the way up the mountain.

Miracles don't happen anymore, you know, because the next day they show up hanging from a barbed-wire fence, with their hands cut off and their head severed from their body. You have to put the pieces of their body together. Whose head is this? This body looks like my son's, I recognize these pants. This was my papa. That's my *compañero,* my mate for life. You get used to making do with just a part of the person's body. Something is better than nothing. In order to give it a Christian burial. Even if all they leave us is an arm; even if it's only a finger. We collect all the pieces and bury them where we find them, since you can't carry body parts into the village. Transporting the dead is prohibited; their remains are buried wherever you find them. We put a cross on the site so their souls don't wander about in pain.

And what are we going to tell the kids, the tiny ones? How can you make them understand death? How can you tell them a person has died for spreading the word of God or for working in organizations asking for improvements for poor people like us! How can they understand? Better tell them their papa or their brother has gone away forever, that they'll never see him again. They can understand that. And they won't go around asking questions anymore.

The worst part is you can't cry, because the men in the *guardia* start talking big and getting tougher. Frailty provides them with the courage they need to kill and commit atrocities. So it's best not to show weakness of character. Sometimes we do go into the mountains to cry, where our children can't see us and where the *guardia* can't see us. While we work in the sun we cry, our tears mix with sweat and nobody is the wiser. You don't have to make explanations. Just wipe your brow and your eyes so the tears fall away like sweat, so they'll go away and leave you alone.

If God takes one of your children, it's no problem; but if men do it, then it is a problem, it's a wound that will never heal. So it should come as no surprise if in the future we remember what happened and demand that their deaths be paid for. The blood of the poor has a price, about that there can be no doubt. And that price will be paid; so shed no crocodile tears because you must pay what you owe.

We didn't want our children to grow up and have birthdays, because the older they got the bigger a target they became for the authorities.

Look how my father Macario died. He struggled to live for so many years. How it cost him to grow old! And for what? I ask myself. Why reach eighty if you're only going to suffer? What good is life, then? Is it just for eating, working, sleeping, and dying? Some people say you rest when you die. Death is a blessing. I think life is a blessing if you spend your life doing different things so you're not a mere bearer of pain. That's why I get incensed at the way Macario died, thinking there was nothing he could do. It's a disgrace. So I ask myself: Did God give us life so he could bestow his blessings upon everything, so he could give his blessings to suffering and injustice? Look how Macario died, my old man. How we loved him! But we let him starve to death. This makes it all the more disgraceful. If only death served to open our eyes and make us reflect! The tragedy is that you look at everything as though it were perfectly normal. You get used to the injustices and the fact that they treat you like a dog. Those who don't die of some known disease die of starvation. We could barely help Macario by feeding him *garrobo* broth. What a shame! One broth of *garrobo* per week. One soup made of leaves every two days. But that's what you do until a person starts to die. Until he sees death coming for good. My poor pappy! He grew old bending over the volcanic stones; he was always sculpting *metate,* to make the blessed grindstones. What for? Who appreciates it? I think you should work, if not to make money, at least to gain some appreciation. We were even ungrateful to him! He kept to himself in a corner of the hut. He never stopped working. One day he told us he was tired, can you imagine—first time in eighty-odd years he complained of being tired! Go and rest, papa, Ticha told him. Maybe I'm going to die, he said. Don't be silly, papa. And then he really did go lay down to die. He himself felt death approaching. He lay like that for two days. He never once complained. Then we went to get a priest in San Vicente. In emergencies like this they attend you because they want to try and save your soul. And the priest arrived to give him confession. But Macario could hardly recognize us, much less a priest. So when the padre touched the crucifix to his forehead, Macario could barely manage to mumble something that sounded like "roast." We and the padre were equally surprised to hear him speak; once again the padre touched the crucifix to his lips; then we heard him say very distinctly: "This roast is given for you." And he breathed his last.

In other words, he imagined he was Christ. The poor man died of starvation. He never knew what it was to have meat in his stomach. Not even small mountain game. That's one of our problems: when it comes to edible animals, we have plenty; but all you can think about is selling them unless you manage to catch a rabbit or coati. He went to heaven hungry. That's terrible. His last wish was to eat, so he asked for roast crucifix. That's what hunger does, it can even make you blaspheme. It's just the sort of thing you can never explain. And all because you reach old age and don't open your eyes. For example, I now feel that even though my old lamps are giving out on me, people should open their eyes, so we don't become spiritually blind.

I said let's see if the saint pays any attention to you, because I'm always going to be this way, and if you like me as I am, fine, and if you don't, you can jump in the mud. She started telling me not to say things like that, or God would punish me. Well, this went on for a year until June arrived—that's when we celebrate St. Anthony's Day. My mama promised him she would say three rosaries and light a firecracker after each rosary, three in all; also she would hold a dance in his honor since St. Anthony was one of the few saints partial to dancing. How could she fail if she was willing to do her part to help the saint perform his miracle?

All the families in the district were invited to occasions like these; in other words, young and old alike attended the dance. And not to press the issue, but even dogs were invited to dances—that is, no one minded if your dog tagged along. I'm sure you know how loyal these animals are and you can't get them to leave your side unless you're very firm with them. So, when it came to fiestas like these, no one made the dogs go home; instead they became useful companions since the dances often ended after sundown when the shades of night came out; and in a case like that a dog is the best protection from zombies, enchanted wagons or the Siguanaba.

For the big party my mother made marquesote *cakes to eat and* horchata *to drink. In those days there was plenty of work and things were less expensive, so you could have a few special items for your party; though for the Fiesta of San Antonio everyone pitched in, bringing eggs for the* marquesote *or fruit for the little ones; and more than one person brought a bottle of* guaro *because men can't seem to have a good time unless there's something to drink. And if there was music provided by a* marimba *or* chanchona, *all the*

197

guests contributed—they passed a hat and counted up the change until there was enough to pay the musicians, which wasn't all that much because many times they were content to take their payment in the form of whatever food was available at the party.

The actual service was conducted inside the hut and then we moved outside under the mango tree to keep out of the sun. Of course, this time it rained so we couldn't dance in the yard; but my mother said that was all right, we could just say a few more rosaries, though there weren't enough firecrackers to light after each one. As you know, people are very pious and since it was raining, that meant that the Old Man Upstairs didn't want us to dance, and whoever deprived St. Anthony of his rosaries deprived us of water. The storms on that saint's day are legendary; luckily, there was no storm this time, just a steady, slight rain, which was getting to be annoying because it never actually out-and-out rained, it just got on your nerves. My mama was worried because she couldn't have the dance—you can't hold a service for St. Anthony if you can't dance and can't light firecrackers and the latter hadn't been lit on account of the water coming down. Well, people got tired of saying so many rosaries so they decided to go out into the yard anyway to see if they could dance under the mango tree, despite the possibility of getting wet. The marimba was also brought out into the rain. Actually it was just a sprinkle and we weren't making much of a sacrifice for the saint. Soon the first firecracker was thrown into the air and everyone was glad to hear the double crack! as it exploded near the clouds; they were also glad to hear the pulum-pulum of the marimba playing pretty songs. And since most of us went barefoot it was all right to dance in the puddles, and if God was willing, the rain would let up and the puddles would dry out quickly because the water gets absorbed into the porous earth and the hot air makes it evaporate.

One time, when Jacinto stopped by on his way from the lagoon,

I saw him in a different light; every now and then he would stop by the house, but I never took any notice of him. He had a reputation for being pious and he wasn't even good-looking—more like ugly, or at least that's how he looked to me, because young girls are very presumptuous, wanting to meet only people with saints' noses—naturally all our noses are flat; people with the noses of saints are generally considered good-looking, though you find only one in a hundred like that and he turns out to be stupider than guaro. *You shouldn't go around looking for pretty faces, because there can be just as much charm in things besides noses and eyes. I'm not sticking up for Jacinto, though nobody ever says anything bad about his hut, even if it is on the verge of collapsing; but why should I lie—few people were as famous as he was for being hardworking and serious. That mattered to me because when you're young you tend to be interested only in the obvious things. Imagine, I didn't like Jacinto because his nose was flat and his hair was kinky—when it's the person's other qualities that count, right? Well, before we knew it, there we were having a little dance together, though it made me laugh to see him so serious when he asked permission to dance.*

The "mazingers" came to the hamlet by the lagoon. At first the *guardias* did not show their teeth as they inspected the fields. "Trust us," they said.

"How do they expect you to trust them with those hideous trucks?"

"No one believes anything they say, anyway, but you have to listen—maybe someday they'll behave like human beings, because up until now, they've been acting like animals."

"And do you know what they did? Look at what they did! While we've been outside, after they forced us out of our huts, they started burning them! It has taken us all our lives to make our little homes; even if there's only a hammock inside, it's worth something. You've also got your corn and all your little odds and ends. All our miserable things were burned."

"The roofs are thatched, all it takes is the toss of a match and it all goes up in flames."

"And you want to know something? No one cares—the suffering, the feeling in your heart when your world goes up in flames: they could give a damn."

The people from the village are talking as they stand in lines on the football field. There are no laments. At times a child's question falls like a whisper. The authorities tell them that if they're not ashamed then what's the point in asking why they support the subversives? After a period of impatience and scolding the smaller children cry. The blazing huts and spotlights upset them. Or maybe it's because they're shivering with cold because it begins to freeze at that hour, and many of them came out naked: there wasn't time to dress, since they had already been put to bed; the adults came out running with their children by the hand before the authorities broke down the doors.

"And they say vulgar things to us because they see it doesn't affect us, our bodies don't tremble despite the cold. They ask why we don't blush."

"It's best to turn a deaf ear."

"Look, in here, what you're feeling can't be expressed, there are no words for it."

"A raging inside. There are no words to describe it."

"We're not made of stone but we do resist."

"We protect ourselves by turning to stone, because what they want is for us to start complaining so they can insult us and make fun of us; dammit! I'd rather have them say we're made of stone."

"What's going to happen to these sons of bitches? They act so brave now, but we'll see how brave they are once we start pulling triggers. That's what they want."

"The saddest thing is when they kill dogs."

"Dogs are like people, they're everybody's children."

"They mean no harm to anyone, they protect the house, they're affectionate with the children."

"I wonder why they kill them, then?"

"To get to us. They know how we suffer when they kill our dogs."

"They shoot them in the head, and if the bullet doesn't hit the right spot, the dogs go howling up the mountain, poor things, like souls in torment."

The little ones cry while the people talk.

And they ask us about our young people. We tell them they've gone off, they've headed for the hills because it's getting to be very dangerous for them. Sometimes what they're talking about are very young kids, but they are big for their ages and so the authorities are after them. They never know at what moment they'll have to hide, it's a lucky thing when they don't get caught. The best thing is for anyone who can walk or crawl just to leave. That's why we don't want them to get past the age of seven, so they don't get too near the age of death. They run less risk when they're just babes, guileless, their only pastime picking flowers or chasing butterflies.

May they stay forever young and not get killed, even if that means not having their help in the fields. We'd rather sacrifice their help than see them die.

We don't know when this will end, but we know it is going to end; evil is not eternal, only love.

Sometimes people pass this way and ask if we're organized and if not they say they can be trusted and we say we don't know what you're talking about; there's no organization around here, the only organized body around here are the authorities who say they come to punish us, as if they were the keepers of God's law, and they burn our huts and kill our men. They say anyone who isn't attached to a security unit or doing military service is under suspicion of being the enemy.

And to discourage us from assisting the *muchachos* fighting in the mountains, they bring us out here without coats, they burn our huts, they shit on our poverty; after all that, now they're burning the hills so we have nowhere to hide, they set the forests on fire—whenever they see a patch of green in the hills, they burn it. They don't want us to have herbs. Most people depend on herbs, either as medicine or for herb soup with eggs. We also need firewood for the stove, and they burn that. Everything is consumed and turns to ashes; we now have ashes on all sides. They also leave us without water, because the fire chases away the rain, and the dryness of the earth also scares the moisture off. There's so much burning that every month seems like summer and it's so dry even the rivers stop flowing. Nature goes against us when it won't give us water, when the rivers dry up. *They* change nature. *They* want to change everything. Leave us with nothing because we're in their way and they want us to disappear from the face of the earth. At this point, no matter what we do, the corn won't even sprout, it's afraid to come out, afraid it'll get burned. Corn is sacred and we're taught not to squander it; not one scrap of tortilla goes to waste, and you shouldn't cut corn with a knife because when you do you are mistreating the Lord's body.

No matter how much we implore San Isidro, patron saint of laborers, to bring water and take away the sun, the water won't come; the smoke from the hills frightens the rain, rain is afraid of fire. Fire is the worst thing for these lands. That's why we would rather clear the brush with a machete and then burn it off to one side, in a cave so the earth isn't frightened, so the clouds don't take off for other parts.

We've always had corn. Now the sprouts are stunted and the stalks barely flower and then they droop, like they're melancholy, and they stop growing. When we go to check the tender ears, we see a scrawny yellow creature, like a newborn baby wrapped in a husk. That's as far as it goes; you can't see any kernels, it doesn't have the energy to thicken. Since corn is sacred, what it's doing is rebelling. It prefers to die of melancholy, and so the only parts we can use are the leaves for feeding livestock—sell it to people who need food for their cattle.

For some time now, everything has turned to flame. I wonder what we'll live on if they don't allow the corn to grow. Just salt, I guess, but salt without tortillas is nothing; there's no way you can fool your stomach with a few pinches of salt, your stomach shrinks. And at this point, beans have gotten so expensive we can't even afford to make a pot a week. What little we pick, we have to sell.

"Please don't burn our corn," we said to see if they were at all concerned.

"You don't need this corn because you plant more than you need and sell it to the subversives fighting in the hills."

And we said:

"Look, the corn doesn't even want to grow, at least wait and see if it has the strength to come out; and we don't sell it, we barely get enough to last three months."

"You don't need that much. Let us see if we can't get some

corn for you so you don't always think of us as the bad guys," is what they said.

"You're lying, you never bring what you say you will."

"You have to buy the corn at the store in the nearest village. It will be very cheap; we've brought it from another country so if you complain, it's because nothing's ever right for you people, you're not on good terms with either God or the devil."

"Foreign corn isn't nourishing, captain. We want *our* corn, the kind we grow ourselves. Buying it at the store isn't a good idea for us, we have no money."

The captain orders everything burned, he gives us almost no time to speak with him, he says we should thank God that they've gotten this corn for us from the United States. The officer isn't used to listening to people, only giving orders; now, we protest at least, but of course he pays no attention, but that doesn't matter; it's a way to pluck up your courage and not let them always roll right over you. Of course, their guns decide everything. And there they've got us at a disadvantage. The *muchachos* are a different story, but they're almost never around, they're further north. At least that's what people say, because that's where the shooting comes from at night and sometimes bombing during the day.

"The only reason you don't like the corn is because it comes from the United States and we know you people are Communists or at least sympathizers and that's why you are the way you are, and someday you're going to pay for it," the captain threatens.

"What do you mean?"

"You're all a bunch of Communists," the military man reiterates.

At that moment you can hear the song of the *torogós*.

"You must pay close attention, even to the sounds of the

birds." "Anything that moves is suspicious." These are the new things they've learned from the advisers.

"Listen, the subversives are nearby," he says, referring to the birds.

"They are *torogoses,* captain. There aren't any subversives around here."

"Like hell there aren't." And he makes like he's going to give the peasant a blow to the head.

"If you hit an old man like me your hand will wither, captain."

"You people have lost your respect for authority and then you whine that we're too rough with you."

"We have a right to protest, captain."

"Who the fuck taught you to say that? We're not through with you yet; that's the kind of shit the subversives put in your heads, they're brainwashing you."

"What are you talking about, *Señor* captain?"

"I ask you about subversives and you start spewing this crap about rights. What rights? You wanna see your rights? Here's your rights." And he holds up the automatic he's carrying. "I don't want to hear any more talk about rights or I'll have to take action." To himself: "These Indians are pushing it, they make me lose my patience—I come out here with good intentions to treat them like human beings and this is what I get."

"We already told you the subversives aren't anywhere near here."

"Then where did you pick up that shit about rights?"

"That's in the Bible."

"We're in bad shape if besides guerrillas we have to put up with subversion from faggot priests. They've come up with a new Bible just to deceive you; the sonofabitch priests have turned the Bible into a Communist tract."

"Cross yourself, *Señor* captain."

"I'll cross you with my .45 right where it counts."

"Go ahead, *Señor* captain, if you want to be damned," he says in a low voice as though he doesn't want to be heard.

"Speak up, asswipe. They haven't taught you to shut up in front of the authorities, have they?"

At that moment Corporal Martínez arrives, pointing his rifle and saying he's set fire to the cornfields and they'll burn fast because the plants and the earth are so dry.

So Jacinto asks me if we could move over a little because the ground was very muddy and he wanted to find a drier place. I told him everything was pretty much soaked and the driest spot around was under the mango tree. He insists you can't dance too close to people, because then when you hop around you splatter your neighbor's pants with mud. I smell something fishy. He's up to something; maybe he wants to hold me closer. In those days, you see, you danced far apart in order to avoid sinful thoughts. I still can't believe it but just when we were having the best time dancing he brings his face up and gives me a kiss on the cheek. I told him to cut it out, halfheartedly, and wondered how he'd gotten so bold. Then I remembered the invocation to St. Anthony—this is how the miracle would arrive. We took these things seriously, you realize. Oh no, I thought, just my luck, please don't let the miracle happen like this. Like I say, I thought he was ugly and right then it never would have occurred to me to like him. But the thing is, all it took was a touch and a kiss and he started looking good to me. Actually, nothing else happened that day. But I did start to take notice of him. And we developed a wonderful friendship. But I never flirted with Jacinto. It was pure friendship, because he wasn't pushy; maybe he was even a bit tongue-tied, because we spent an awful long

206

time just as friends. I could tell he liked me and that's when I realized I was fond of him, too. For instance, on Sundays he would sometimes come to our house if he wasn't away from the village—many times he went to different places with his cart; but he claimed he was visiting my mother, the skunk! My mother was just an excuse, because the one he looked at was me and coincidentally every time he looked my way, I'd be looking at him, as if we had some kind of deal worked out. Mama was happy as could be thinking her invocation to St. Anthony had resulted in a miracle, but it wasn't clear, because Jacinto was so bashful he hadn't even held my hand since the day of the dance, and six months had gone by!

"Look at you," she said. "All you've done is make friends with Jacinto, which is all right, since he's a decent person and all, but I'm afraid it's not going anywhere, child, so I think it's time to cut your losses." And I said how could you do that to him, he's my friend, I don't want to hurt him. "Fine," she said. "But I don't have much hope for him." You get a lot of crazy ideas when you're a mother. She could see I was still his friend; he came over to the house and no one wanted to be unkind to him, but my mama didn't like the fact I hung all over him, because I was giving Jacinto the wrong idea before he'd even made his move, as they say.

Then one day she said, "It's been thirteen months now and there's nothing to show for it, you're just leading him on, let's invite him to the party on the Day of the Cross." She was intending to kill two birds with one stone by celebrating the Cross, because we had never honored it before and it was a good chance to ask the Cross for a good growing season and a good harvest; a good growing season for the patrones *so we'd have food and work; and a good harvest for us because we'd planted some corn and beans out back of the hut that year.*

It was my job to make the jiote-wood *cross—I'd been working on it since the second of May; to make it come out right, I made it with red* jiote *wood and put it under the mango tree so that on the third of May the sun would rise on the coco-palm streamers I made the night before. My mother started talking the Cross up the week before, saying there would be a lot of fruit; because almost everybody made a cross, the competition was fierce—even though people went to all the parties and spent a little time at each house. Naturally, Jacinto accepted the invitation. My mother went door-to-door inviting people, saying since this was the first time she was holding a celebration, she intended to have every fruit available.*

The cross was adorned with coco-palm streamers, cohune palms, and cohune palm flowers. I don't mean to exaggerate, since I made it, but I think my cross was the prettiest one around. It also had red nances *and watermelon, which is hard to find at that time of year; but my mother was so determined that she sent all the way to the Lempa for them, since they always have watermelon there—it's the place to go if you want the biggest, reddest watermelons.*

There were also a lot of different kinds of fruit, I remember nothing was missing. There were cohune nuts, coconuts, these lovely guineo *bananas, apple blossoms, cucumbers,* paternas, *sapodillas, medlar, mameys, custard apples, ripe and green mangoes, muskmelon, papaya, crab apples, pear-apples, and peaches. In other words, anything you could buy in San Vicente, especially fruit that doesn't usually grow around here. We thought the Cross was a great party.*

"Let's see if they learn anything from this," says the officer in charge of the military unit.

"They'll either respond on their own or we'll have to make them," the corporal says menacingly.

"Let's start with you," the officer says to an old man who is watching the intensity with which the nearest slope catches fire. "Would you sell corn to a guerrilla?"

"How can I tell when a man is a guerrilla?" the old man responds.

"Don't give me that. How can you possibly not recognize them when they've always got a rifle in their hand?"

"If he has a kind face, maybe I would sell him some—you can't deny corn to your fellow man."

"No guerrilla has a kind face," the officer retorts. "Besides, they're not your fellow men; those of us who defend law and order are your fellow men."

"How can we tell who they are if they look the same as us?" says the old man, defending himself.

"You can tell them by the malicious look on their faces," replies the officer, suddenly realizing he's come up with the perfect way to describe a guerrilla.

"Some of them are good people, captain," the old man says.

"What makes you think they're so good?" questions the officer.

"Because they're poor like us, and we harm no one."

"Fuck you, bastard, that's another line they've fed you," the captain replies, losing his patience. "They hand you that garbage because you're such morons."

"We are not morons."

The corporal nearest the officer interrupts:

"Listen, captain, he's not giving you the proper respect." Then facing the old man: "Don't you know you're supposed to say 'captain' when you address this man? You people are getting very disrespectful, the guerrillas have encouraged this behavior in you." He walks up to the old man and threatens to hit him with the butt of his rifle.

The captain raises a hand indicating he should restrain himself, and shakes his head.

"Leave him alone, Corporal Martínez. We have to put up with the abuse these ill-behaved bastards give us so they don't go crying to some human-rights group and stop the gringos from sending us any more money for weapons."

"But no one will know, captain."

"Let him blow off a little steam, he's out of a home now and I'm sure he'll think twice before he sells any more corn to the subversives." The captain's tone is persuasive; he endeavors to teach a political lesson to his subordinate and the soldiers surrounding him.

The old man has backed off from the group of soldiers and makes a gesture like he's frightening a chicken. He realizes he narrowly escaped being hit by a rifle butt. The official takes advantage of the chance to be alone with his men and continues with his lesson. He addresses the corporal:

"Instead of getting pissed off, what you must do is make note of everything the old man says; this is the new technique recommended by the Yankee advisers—file a report, that's the new strategy. These advisers and their bullshit psychology."

"They don't understand us—you know as well as I that a swift butt with the gun would set the record straight."

"Yes, but don't forget: a ship has only one captain, and the advisers are the ones handing out the weapons. Where would we be without the gringos! So don't lose your head, just write everything down on paper."

"I'll keep it all in my head, captain," says the corporal. "Besides, I can hardly read my own writing."

"I'm not saying you're dense, but do you want the advisers to put a hole in my head? When we get back to the base I'm going to ask you to tell me word for word what went on." Then, adopting the tough stance one should expect in situations like this, in accordance with the guidelines set down in recent months, he addresses the noncommissioned officer: "Take notes from now on, prick. I don't want to have to say it again."

The corporal takes out a pad and pencil; he starts writing, holding the pad in his left hand. He's upset, but orders are orders, even if you don't understand them.

The captain looks up and takes a deep breath, wanting to fill his lungs with the fire all around him. The flames of the cornfield burning up.

The corporal has calmed down somewhat. The act of writing allows the blood to return to his veins—moments before it had all risen to his head. He was itching to shoot or hit something. This is what he was taught to do during their daily training; and now, out in the field, the captain was using that fucking psychology bullshit invented by faggots. "The Yankees don't understand us, that's what it is; they think things will work out all by themselves, and meanwhile people around here are used to brute force; that's the way I am, because I come from this stock. The only thing we understand is getting kicked in the crotch or having the shit beaten out of us—that's the way it's always been and that's the way it will always be: my great-grandfather Macario used to tell me how they got whipped and flogged at the indigo mill. I worked in indigo, too, when I was young: I'm doomed to belong to a condemned race."

The captain says you have to win people over, that's the cornerstone of the advisers' plan: shoot only when you have to, burn everything that serves the guerrillas' purposes; but don't mistreat people, don't give the human-rights advocates the chance to spoil a scientifically developed political strategy. You must learn self-control.

211

"They've always despised us," thinks the corporal. They create chaos. "The poorer people are, the more they hate us—as though it's our fault they're poor." The corporal is encouraged by his reflections because he wants to show the advisers that people like him can also arrive at the correct conclusions, that he's not dense, as his captain insinuates. But the orders state you should note everything you see and hear—no private speculations.

Every day they understand less about the war. They had been taught to kill, not be contemplative, and now they even tell you to get a grip on yourself. "What will they think of us? That we're ass-lickers and queers." It was better when just the NCOs and troops of the Guardia Nacional went out. There were never any problems. "The only thing we'll win is the poor's loss of respect—give them an inch and they'll take a mile." He put the tip of his pencil to his mouth.

Crazy mother. We were just putting the finishing touches on the horchata *when the guests started to arrive: aunts, cousins, nephews, neighbors. We had put up blankets so people could get in out of the sun—even though it was May and the sun wasn't too bad, but you always had to have blankets to lend more prestige to your Cross. Little children arrived with stilts and benches and the older boys and girls sat on the roots of the mango tree; also, we set up a big log for people who didn't bring their own seats and wanted to enjoy their fruit in comfort. In one sense, the Cross is the festival of fruit and friendship. Old people prefer to sit on their haunches and make holes in the ground with their machetes. This is what the most unsociable among them do, because they can't have a conversation unless they've got a machete in their hand and look at the ground; making holes in the ground is a way to avoid eye contact. Most of the girls brought towels to shade themselves from the sun, and also*

*to cause a little stir, because the towels were always very colorful.
More than one older woman wore a black shawl; all shawls are
black except those with white or blue flowers on them, but you don't
see that kind in our village. This time, instead of a marimba, there
was a* chanchon, *which is a five-man musical group whose most
notable feature is a double-bass, which everybody calls a* chanchona, *hence the name of the orchestra.*

We also had guaro *with coconut for the adults. We started eating
fruit at three in the afternoon and that's also when the* chanchona
started playing its tumblimbi-tumblimbi. *Let the dancing begin,
someone said.*

And the air turns yellow. The cornstalks roar, quickly catching fire. Smoke rises from the hill like a serpent ready to gobble
up trees, underbrush, people. Nobody says a word. The old man
embraces his woman. Children hang on the woman's skirt and
cry. Only the captain is aware he is waging a humane war,
though this does not mean he understands it. Under other circumstances he would have taken more drastic measures, which
would have made better use of his professional skills; but he was
restricted by the incomprehensible scope of the new gringo
regulations. You could be dying of rage and still have to put up
with all this bullshit. Tolerate the poor. Who the hell gave birth
to them? Why had they come into the world? He blamed part
of the frustrations impeding the normal exercise of his profession on the problems of the poor. Within the context of ideas
acquired throughout his career, he felt the solution was a simple
one: exterminate the poor; surgically remove them as you would
a cancerous organ. This is where he heartily agreed with the
NCOs and privates; of course, he was the one who had taught
them. Why waste time contemplating, he wondered.

"And your older sons, where are they?" the corporal asks the old-timer.

"I have only one daughter and she's not young anymore," says the old man.

"Doesn't she deliver messages to the subversives?" the corporal asks.

"She doesn't do things like that," the old-timer says.

"The older you people get, the dumber you get," shouts the corporal.

"It's the roads that are old, son, and the animals that are dumb."

The old man's reply confuses the corporal, as though he'd heard it before, here in Apastepeque. His grandfather. Meanwhile the captain goes on. He watches the fire covering the hill in a sea of flames in a matter of minutes. By the time they reach his face, the light and heat have soothed his spirits. The captain has ordered them not to lay a hand on the peasants. Burn everything to the ground, but don't beat people up, because that's now considered a violation of human rights. Upon this depend his salary increases, his bonuses, and better equipment that will command greater respect among the poor and a greater willingness to obey his commands. For the first time in his long career with the Guardia Nacional he can see that the poor are not as they once were: they protest, they question, they cloak their pretensions in false humility. You don't know what they're up to anymore. That's why, like his superiors, he was sure the tactics of the foreign advisers were bound to fail. He was nothing but a lowly civil servant whose opinion was rarely taken into account; why question the gringos whose training and money had given him security and created an enviable way of life for him, afforded him the opportunity to earn a much higher salary than his previous salary, which was barely adequate for his family to live in minimal comfort. Somehow he knew that his future depended upon obeying the advisers, though he might not agree with them; besides, those were the rules of his profession. He and his superiors could go beyond the new agreements and training up to a certain point, since they weren't being supervised. The advisers had no direct control over them if they wanted to act on their convictions. However, he knew his advisers would go crazy if they found out he'd overstepped his boundaries. In spite of his misgivings, he ordered the corporal only to interrogate:

"Do many strangers pass this way?"

"On occasion," the old man replies.

"And how do you know they're not subversives?"

"Because they're not malicious."

"So you think of the subversives as malicious?"

"That's what they say."

"And how do you know the people that come this way aren't malicious?"

"They don't burn down our houses or shout at us," says a woman nearby.

"They don't shout because they're faggots," says the corporal. Then, because she's a woman, he reconsiders.

"Who told you it was your turn to speak, bitch? Now, get lost before I bash your head in."

"Leave her alone, corporal. Women should be treated with respect," the old man chides.

"And who gave you permission to butt in?"

"Around here, we don't ask for permission to speak," the woman insists.

"You'd better get educated, pig, because a poor education could cost you your life," the corporal tells her.

"That's just great. Now we're not allowed to speak even though you're burning our houses down," she retorts.

"You'd better keep quiet," says the old man. "And keep an eye on the kids. Can't you see the corporal could get mad?"

" 'Get mad'? I'm already furious," the corporal says with irritation.

When the captain returns he finds the corporal with his eyes aflame. A glare that comes from the fire on the hill. The same fire has been etched into the captain's gaze as well.

Without corn we are nothing. We're living corpses. Corn is our light and life. That's why they came to burn our cornfields. The authorities say the corn we plant isn't meant for us but for the subversives. No matter how many times we deny it they refuse to believe us. As though we didn't need to eat! The *guardias* don't even check to make sure we've got a bit of corn left for our daily meal. They take all our grain. And if we need corn, they tell us we should buy it at the government stores; it's good corn, it comes from overseas, and they give it to the government to distribute to the poor. Listen, it sells for the same price as the corn we produce. It seems a shame that you can't plant your own if you've got the land. That means the land lies fallow. You can plant annatto or tomatoes, they say. We can only eke out enough from these little slivers of land to feed our families. Naturally, if one of our fellow men came and asked for a tortilla we wouldn't withhold it from him. Or anybody. It's a sin to withhold corn. All our life we've planted the cornfield. We try to plant enough to last the summer, in the months when things are scarce. They don't believe us. They'd rather burn it all down. Maybe a bullet would be better than this nightmare. This is what our life is like. We don't know how long we can go on like this. It turns out that now, not only are we accountable to our Maker, but to the Guardia Nacional as well. There's no way out. If they get it in their heads to put you in a truck and throw you over the nearest cliff, decapitated or with a bullet through your skull, then that's what they do. In these times we have to walk with lead in our feet, because if we don't we fall prey to an ungrateful round of ammunition. Every day people have less patience. Maybe it would be better if they just killed us outright and that would put an end to it. Because the way it is now, we have to wander all over the place looking for food, and when there's no work there are roots and leaves from the hog-plum and tamarind trees, and flowers from the bladder senna, pumpkin, broom, and *madrecacao*. But we can't keep living on flowers alone. And if you go to the city it's worse. That's for the young people, because they have an ability to adapt to new things. Even so, they end up stealing, begging, or pimping. Sometimes they get the idea to go to Honduras, where people say there are huge tracts of land without any owners and all you've got to do is bounce over to the other side of the mountain and you've got yourself a cornfield. It's not that easy to pull up stakes and hit the road. Because you've got to put up with the same abuses in a foreign country, only many times it's worse, because there's no one to turn to, no one to pray for you when you keel over, and then your soul wanders in eternal torment. We're going to plant in secret. So whenever we find any seeds, instead of eating them we'll save them, and when the rains come, we'll open a few furrows and plant, and if we're lucky they won't come until the corn is golden. It's a question of doing something instead of standing around with your arms folded. You must have faith in God, but at the same time you can't wait for manna to fall from heaven. Fire might fall instead for being so ignorant. The key is to look for new ways to survive. That's how it's always been and we're still here. The race is strong. I think even if it rains fire there will always be a seed left and the very ashes will serve as fertilizer, if only for flowers, and medicinal and edible herbs.

The impassive captain interrogates other speakers. He's not pleased with the task of setting fires and taking notes. He thought war was a matter of shooting bullets, saving the country from degenerating into scum. Think of how many of these people he could wipe out with a single order! These useless beings have brought nothing but trouble. All these impoverished pieces of shit care about is having babies and causing problems; they increase the population and cause greater poverty and greater ills. He didn't understand why he should treat them with such consideration. The poor were his enemies. And they had been since 1932, when they had risen up in arms. From then on poverty was communism. This country had been one of the most Communist countries in the Americas, according to the history he was taught in the military academy. These people had been Communists since the turn of the century. These bastards had come up in the world, he thought. They create so many problems. If it weren't for the poor, this country would be paradise.

A few steps away from the officer, the corporal continues his interrogation of the old man.

"Tell me your name and the names of your sons."

"I already told you I have no sons; and those kids over there are my great-great-grandsons. I'm too old to have sons. I can't even see anymore, *Señor* corporal."

Once again they hear *torogoses*. The corporal lifts his head and looks in the direction of the birds' melody.

"Are those the signals of the subversives?"

"No, *Señor* sergeant, it's a *torogós.*"

"How can you tell? And don't give me that bull. I'm a corporal, not a sergeant."

"You can tell because the sound of the *torogós* cannot be imitated, *Señor* corporal."

The corporal isn't convinced and writes that at that moment the song of a *torogós* was heard and that perhaps it was a signal from the guerrillas. Then, hoping to catch his informant off guard, he asks:

"Do you know any subversives?"

"No, *Señor* corporal, they know not to come around here; maybe they're further up the lagoon, beyond the hill."

"And do you know anybody living on the south side of the lagoon? There used to be a few huts there."

"It's been a long time since anybody has lived there, because it was flooded; they took the land over to plant rice; we all came to this side of the hill. The authorities kicked us out, they needed the land."

"And when was this?" questions the corporal, paying close attention.

"Hmm." The old man thinks a long time. "Years and years ago." And his eyes, turned inward to see the light, nevertheless reflect the past, like a lazy river. There is a radiance about his eyes, coming not from the fire on the hillside but the expression of a long life.

The song of the *torogós* had interrupted the corporal's routine line of questioning. As though a void that spanned twenty-five years had suddenly been opened.

Then, snapping back to reality, he once again looks at his pad. "I asked for your name."

"Pardon?"

"Your name, what is it?"

A stream of sweat pours out from under the corporal's steel helmet and runs down his face. The heat is intense. His face is like bronze. He must be about forty-five. He has had to pay dearly for even a minimal promotion. Nonetheless, he is privileged, with the authority over life and death, which gives him an unyielding personality. Or so it would seem—his bearing, his voice, his look. Everything seems to indicate a man belonging to the category of the invincibles. He has been educated in the school where men don't cry. They're not allowed to, they must not be weak. That is his crowning glory; those are the qualities that have helped him ascend to the rank of corporal in the Guardia. Not an easy task for someone who had risen out of great poverty. As he had.

"The day I shed a single tear I will be through as both a man and soldier." He considers himself a person for whom only the present exists, and it is also his past and future. Looking at it from that vantage point, his power becomes confused with eternity. And eternity is the moment he pulls the trigger and watches someone fall down in front of him. If it was any other way his life would be without purpose or meaning. It has taken twenty-five years of continual education and great hardship to transform his life and become different from all the other human beings with whom he daily comes in contact as a uniformed professional. That eternal present causes his conduct as a strong man to become immutable. He even confuses the sounds made by his rifle mechanisms with his own heartbeat.

Great economic and moral investments have gone into making him different. His country and his sense of humanity have been mortgaged. It makes no difference if the man and the country are one and the same; after all, there must be a reason for giving him the instruction and skill necessary to take less than a second to pull the trigger of his automatic rifle in defense of his own specific individuality. The rifle represents a wall of defense and the law. The future. Which is to say the present, vested with power. As far as he's concerned, everyone is free to do what he wants, as long as it is in defense of the interests of the individual. And he is that individual, who must rise above everyone else and be in conflict with everyone else. To each his own, his grandfather used to say.

"A soldier should have no compassion." He remembers his adviser's voice. After being in uniform for twenty-five years, he didn't need to hear it again. "Otherwise, you might as well be a monk or a schoolteacher." What was new in the advisers' training was that now a war was won not only with bullets but also through public works. He thinks: "This bullshit gringo psychology is really fucking us up."

Suddenly he noticed he wasn't taking notes anymore. He still hadn't gotten the name of the old man after asking twice.

The old geezer answered:

"My name is Emiliano."

The corporal wiped the sweat from his face as though wanting to blot it out. And in a voice lacking all the arrogance he had previously displayed, he asks:

"Emiliano what?"

"Emiliano Martínez."

The corporal started to shudder. An earthquake directly beneath his feet would not have caused such trembling in his body. He feels betrayed by his spirit, he wants to fling himself on the old man, not to hurt him but to hug him. However, in less than a second his entire twenty-five-year career flashed before him: the gringos, the punishment, the humiliation, the daily training, and the irreproachable conduct of his commanding officers. He thinks he can't let it all go to waste, because all those years of suffering and sacrifice had led him to a position of privilege—

in spite of his impoverished background he felt he had risen above other men because of his Prussian uniform and ultramodern automatic rifle. "How could I not have recognized him?" he wonders, alarmed.

He can hardly mumble a few words, but to him they sound like a shout echoing from the nearby hills, reaching the captain's ears a few feet away.

"I'm Pedro Martínez," he whispers, reluctant to unveil the life of poverty he had always denied and tried to forget. Everything his memory wished to conceal was crashing in on him. His reflections hindered an immediate reaction when the old man lunged for him and said: "God damn you!" Or perhaps it was just a scream. The corporal retreated a step and fell on his back. The captain turned at the scream in time to see the old-timer go for his subordinate. And he saw the chance to vent all his pent-up energy. The nine-millimeter bullet made the old man jump, as though he'd been given a push to make him fly. Like a wisp of straw, he was so light. He fell on his grandson, still on the ground.

Corporal Martínez rolled the body off of him.

"Did I get him?" the captain asks.

"I don't know," answers Pedro Martínez. And he thinks: "They moved from the south of the lagoon to the north, at the foot of the hill." He senses it is too late.

"These bastards don't even bleed," the captain says.

Still holding his rifle and looking foolish there on the ground, Corporal Martínez sees the captain and then the body of his grandfather out of the corner of his eye. His steel helmet has come off and hangs around his neck, exposing the corporal's pale and sweaty face. He realizes he is sitting on the fence between life and death and he must choose.

"What's the matter?" asks the captain. "You're not going to tell me the gunshot scared you, are you?"

"You killed him, captain," he says, but he is prevented from continuing by a group of peasants and two young boys who heard the shot.

"What's with you, bastard?" the officer asks a second time; however, his question will never be answered.

In a split second he realizes he is unquestionably Corporal Martínez, who has undergone a life of misery and degradation in defense of his individuality. His liberty. His honor. His God. He doesn't even notice the two small boys, who share his blood, standing in front of the old-timer's corpse; nor does he heed the people who protest Emiliano's death. He can hear nothing but the sparks crackling on the hillside.

"There's nothing wrong, captain." He takes a second to collect himself, then nearly stutters: "That's what they want, that's what they'll get, the sons of bitches."

But he doesn't know why a great wave of panic washes over him, a novel experience for Corporal Martínez. He starts to cry. First time in forty-odd years. There's no backing out now, though. And he thinks: "What will become of Corporal Martínez now?"

So I stood watching the people dancing. I hoped Jacinto would ask me to dance and then I saw him coming my way, and I thought maybe he was mad at me, but he had the sweetest smile; I'd been watching him for a long time drinking guaro *with coconut under the blankets we'd put up. I didn't have much of a crush on him, because we had been such good friends, and he'd never said so much as what pretty dimples you've got. So he comes over and I ask in passing if he's going into the hut to say a rosary; and he says no, that it's time to put his cards on the table and make his move. So I tell him maybe the* guaro *has gone to his head, since even though we've known each other a long time, he's*

223

not even my boyfriend. Then he says let's run away together. Would I like him to take me away? I didn't even have to think twice: Let's go. Then for the first time he told me he loved me and I said I loved him, too, because I really did love him as a friend, as a compañero, *and that's the same as loving each other enough to live together, and that's all that's important. Next he says he's been dying for me for a long time now and he didn't have the courage to tell me. I believe him. In a case like this, you have to believe, it's what your feelings tell you to do. So, he's gotten some money together, since he's been thinking about this for a long time; he had his knapsack on him with the money inside ready for us to take off and set up house together. And after that? It was up to God. I say, Let's at least wait until after the rosaries have been said; but he says now's a good time because everyone is distracted with the rosaries. Everyone means my mother, my family, and all the guests. I remember my mother is giving this party so I'll find a boyfriend and then I'm not so nervous anymore; first we needed some help from St. Anthony for the miracle to occur, then we had to get some more help from* Santa Cruz, *the Cross, which I made myself. That was the last time my mother prayed to either St. Anthony or the Cross, because she felt like they didn't do such a good job with the miracle. She would have preferred a formal wedding and not this way we have of running off with our sweethearts to start a family, the way most young people did.*

A half hour earlier you could start to hear bombs explode.

"What are they doing on the other side of the hill?" asks Ticha, who is visiting Jacinto and Juana.

"It sounds like it's coming from the lagoon," Juana says with concern.

"Shit! Grandfather's alone with the boys," says Jacinto.

"Calm down. Emiliano knows how to take care of himself," says Beatriz.

They also heard cannons firing and airplanes flying overhead.

"Things are getting ugly," thinks Jacinto. Every day they get sucked deeper into the war. They get the tail end of the disaster. "Like the tail of a comet," he thinks. "It only brings misfortune."

"You're right," says Jacinto out loud. "We've always lived in the midst of war, but we didn't notice because they didn't used to bomb us or burn our crops."

Beatriz thinks about Emiliano a few miles away. In the direction of the fire. On the other side of the hill. She tries to ease her son's mind.

"As soon as the bombing stops we can go over there. I know if something bad had happened to him my heart would have told me so."

"The sun is about to set and I'm upset that it's too late to go now."

"You know very well our hearts have never lied."

"But sometimes they hide things to prevent us from wallowing in our own misery," says Jacinto.

"I'm worried about the boys, I should have taken them. I hope my papa doesn't run into any problems, he can barely see," Beatriz says.

"And we're responsible for Lucía's children," says Juana about her grandchildren, who had been taken to the lagoon several days before.

They had become used to the awful sound of war and the possibility of falling victim to indiscriminate shelling.

"It's getting dark, I don't know if we'll be able to make it today," says Ticha.

"We'll trust your mother's heart," Juana tells Jacinto.

"If the bombing continues and night falls, we'll leave first thing in the morning."

"All right," agrees Jacinto.

He tries to shrug it off, trust his mother, Beatriz, and his own heart's messages. He didn't want to be removed from what was going on, but he had no idea how he would get involved, or when. The authorities' violence was part of his life. The want. The hunger. The lack of medicine. Always living hand to mouth.

The *guardia* had dominated the country since he became conscious. They were masters of the zone, harsher than the landowners themselves; they maintained order with their rifles poised to shoot, their machetes and the law in their hands—the agrarian law that forced people to work at the haciendas, under the threat of being jailed as vagrants and troublemakers. Each hacienda had its own jails and the means to impose unlimited pain, which would be drawn out until such time as the accused was disposed to work for the *patrón*. Even though they had a small plot on which to plant their own crops, they were obliged to set aside part of the year to produce for the hacienda. In that sense, they had always been at war with the Guardia. Ever since he could remember. But he was also aware that suddenly people were no longer resigned to be submissive to the authorities. And so they had begun to wage another kind of struggle. A type of protest that had never before existed in Cuzcatlán. A war of liberation. Though he didn't fully understand the ramifications.

After that, Jacinto was no longer unsociable. We went to San Vicente, where we had some friends. They had a room where we could hide out and live, in case my mother gave the guardia *cause to come after us. Maybe there would be no problem, but just in case we lay low for a week. During that time Jacinto told me he had to* look for work and he had previously planned a trip to the coast. Meanwhile I would stay there doing housework for our friends, which is how I'd earn my room and board. Jacinto would bring me clothes and whatever else I needed from the coast. I had no reason to complain—like they say, you make your bed, you have to lie in it. We had to live together from now on. He wasn't gone long, he came back to San Vicente every fifteen days, we'd be together for one day, usually Sunday. And we were happy. One day some people I knew told me Jacinto's family and my family had stopped quarreling, because my family claimed Jacinto had betrayed them. His family said my mother had tried to buy me a mate so why was she upset?

I thought the person they ought to be mad at was St. Anthony, since he turned out to be a little too miraculous, as no one had any idea Jacinto would take responsibility for me; they couldn't overlook the fact that Jacinto and I weren't even boyfriend and girlfriend. I'm the one who said so. It wasn't Jacinto's fault.

Soon after, I learned my mama had forgiven him, once she was forced to admit that she was the one who pushed for the miracle.

I had a good time in San Vicente, though sometimes I bit my nails because, you know, the fact that he was gone fifteen days on the coast and we had no chance to get to know each other wasn't exactly what you'd call a treat. I got thinner every day as a result of my first pregnancy. I always felt sick and moody; the only way I got through it was eating hog-plum leaves with salt or green mangoes. That's what being pregnant is about. At that time I got the idea that the mistress of the house was getting tired of me since she complained I wasn't getting things clean enough. And when Jacinto came back from his trips I found out the woman was complaining to him about me, saying I wasn't being nice and she was mad at me. All this came out in jokes and offhand comments.

Jacinto told me to be nice, that he was saving his pennies so we could move back to the village, but he said he didn't want to sponge off his family; instead he was going to try and rent a small parcel, which he already had his eye on, one that had never been tilled before, and maybe we wouldn't need the patrones. All right, I said, let's not go back with our tails between our legs. But one day, during one of his absences, I had had enough. When he came back from the coast, I was gone.

My mother forgave me, but she said I had to get back together with my compañero, I was too young to be a single mother. So I said, all right. I told her Jacinto and I loved each other but lately I was left alone and I decided to come back home; what I really wanted was for Jacinto to come looking for me, so we could be together again; I wanted him to get over his embarrassment in front of my mother and my sisters and come to our hut. Knowing him as I did, I thought it would be hard for him to come to the house, even though I hoped he would, and we could get back together. Well, that's how it happened. One day I got a message from a little girl, who told me Jacinto was at his house and could I come over. I was so happy. Feet don't fail me now, I said, even though the lagoon was an hour's walk from there. My dream was that we would see each other again before the baby was born.

So we talked and I started crying and he told me to stop or I'd have the baby right then and there. Together again at last, I said to myself. Then I told him I'd talked things over with my mother and sisters: if he still loved me he could come and live with me at home, they were expecting us, there was a corner of the hut waiting for us on the other side of the hill.

That afternoon, the girl who gave me the message came and shouted from the street that my mother told us to come back to the hut—the runny-nosed little girl had become the messenger for both sides and she'd already gone and blabbed to my mother that I was with Jacinto. Maybe it was better like that, there wouldn't be any *surprises and everything would work out. All I had to do was convince Jacinto not to be embarrassed, that we should go and put in an appearance at the house, I'd get his things together and we'd go. The blockhead told me that was too much to handle all at once, you go ahead and then we'll see. I spent almost the whole afternoon in his hut trying to convince him. Go on, he said. And so I went. He'll show up, I know he will, I told myself, though I was sad because I really missed him, I had butterflies in my stomach.*

That numbskull. Hardly two hours had passed—it was getting dark—when I heard some pebbles near the cooking fire hitting the post. Shit, the Cipitio, I said to myself. See, the Siguanaba's son always comes throwing rocks near the stove, he loves to stir up the ashes. The Cipitio covers himself with ashes. Well, I got over my fright and went to have a look, and I saw his shadow near the mango tree; or maybe I just sensed it, because I overcame my hesitation and without telling my mother I opened the door to the yard. Hello Jacinto, I said in a low voice. All he replied was, Hi. When are you going to stop being so thickheaded? I asked. Are they asleep yet? he asked back. Well, I said, the men are still out having a good time; it was still early yet. And I heard my mama snoring, I said. Jacinto was glad, you could tell by the way he breathed; in the dark it sounded like a puppy panting excitedly. Or a bellows. We were feeling exactly the same thing. Fat cats. Happy puppies. We almost stopped breathing. He touched my belly to feel the little creature kicking inside. About that time I looked like a garrobo *between two poles, I hardly ate a thing; but my weakness didn't prevent me from hugging him tight, so he couldn't escape; he wouldn't go now that he had dared to come to the house. And he told me he wouldn't ever leave me again, at least not for many months, because he'd saved some money from his job on the coast. Right then I wasn't even thinking about his trips, only that I had him there next to me after not being with him in weeks. He had been*

*on the Balsam Coast, in Sonsonate, that's why he'd taken so long.
I saved money extracting balsam, he says. With that we can build
a hut in a rented field, near my mother.*

*That's where my first son was born, in our own house. We named
him Jacinto, Jacinto Segundo, just so I could hear the name when
his daddy was away; my mama said to give him two names so we
didn't get confused. I named him Jacinto Segundo. My mama
wanted to call him Segundo instead of Jacinto. What difference did
it make, I could call him what I liked.*

*One day we had some bad news; he was only three months old
when he got malignant diarrhea. The minute she saw me the village
medicine woman told me I'd better prepare myself. I asked why she
said that. I have to be honest with you so you're not hurt any more
than you have be, she said. I should expect the worst. I wanted to
cry then and there but the tears wouldn't come, because what she
was saying seemed unbelievable. My God, my God, this must be a
dream, or a nightmare, I thought as I watched the medicine woman
get sad, too. Can't you make him better? I asked. By now the tears
were streaming. I'm doing what I can but I doubt it, she answered,
as she put a wad of chewed leaves on the baby's belly and made
him drink some green herbal water. He's not responding, she said.
How can you tell when they're responding? I asked. When they cry,
she says. While there are tears there is life. I kept waiting for him
to cry. He died that day.*

XIII / MICROBUS TO
SAN SALVADOR

January 9, 1981

AFTER I LEFT HOME, I hardly ever came back; lack of opportunity. Distance. Lack of means. It had nothing to do with forgetting about my parents. Nowadays it's even harder to get to Apastepeque, the best thing is to stay away. The smaller the population the greater the danger for anyone involved in an organization.

After my *compañero*'s death I went to visit the lagoon and Apastepeque, to see my children, my parents, and my grandmother Ticha. I found they had changed. I had never seen them so preoccupied, like they were being harassed by some ill-fated bird of misfortune; so I tried to remain indifferent to my own personal problems. I had actually recovered from my *compañero*'s death. It seems hard to believe you can go back to hoping and dreaming after losing what you most cherish. I think that though our lives have been so battered, though we've endured hunger and all sorts of privation, that is also what has given us such a great advantage as people. No one who has gone through what we've gone through will deny that it is precisely those experiences which have made us strong. Certainly we're not made of stone, but of clay, though sometimes I believe we're harder than the grindstones we made as kids. The harder they hit, the tougher we get. The important thing is to use that strength for

231

everyone's benefit. We don't know what lies ahead, but we have a lot of hope. Moral fortitude is what Great-grandfather Emiliano called our imperviousness to sun and poverty. We need it now more than ever. I believe it's there. I don't know, I'd rather hear other people say it, those who have suffered—it doesn't seem possible to tolerate it anymore, there's nothing else they can do that they haven't already done to us. Emiliano told me it had been going on for more than a hundred years. Since his great-grandfather's time. They hadn't a clue in hell what happiness or joy meant. Others use their material strength to behave like supreme assholes. We use our moral strength to keep from getting worn down, so we can keep on going, so our hopes don't let us down. Someday life will change for all of us. We have to keep telling ourselves that. So we don't forget. That day I stopped by the lagoon to express my sympathies for Great-grandfather Emiliano. "We don't exist anymore," said Beatriz. "Old people are a burden, we get in the way." Don't say that, I protest. Though I know she's thinking about Great-grandfather Emiliano. I don't want her to relive it all again because she gets very sad. However, I can tell she's hiding something from me. Actually it's her eyes that give it away, the way she looks. That's a defect of the poor: we hide our emotions behind our eyes; that's why we don't like to look people in the face when we don't want to be discovered. But I can see it as she defiantly raises her head to the north wind blowing her hair to one side. Then she says that lately her heart hasn't been feeling right. "Touch me, child," she says. I seem to feel palpitations like starfish in her breast. But I don't mention it, because she probably wouldn't understand.

"It's like you're full of caged birds."

"And they want to take off and fly," Grandmother interjects.

I shiver when she says this. A chill runs the length of my

body. I've never had an intimate conversation with my grand-mother. I don't have much chance; when I was little I didn't go to the lagoon very often, particularly after the flood, when they had to cross over to the opposite side. Their house was farther away from us—we had to go all the way around the lagoon to get to where my grandparents lived. And I was all wrapped up in my world and the things I feared: tempests, the *guardias,* drunks, the blazing hot sun. There were other problems, too, like going to bed hungry and waking up without much desire to do anything but earn your daily tortilla.

Each of us guards his privacy like a sacred object. No one talks about what hurts him. Thoughts, ideas—it's best to keep them tucked away in the deep recesses of the hut. Where no one will see them; where not even the sun can penetrate.

"You'll get over it, Grandmother. You just have to get used to it. Great-grandfather would not have been against the war." She said it just to share a crumb of her own optimism with Beatriz. She had plenty to spare, but each person must tap into her own source of hope.

"What I can't get over is why he had to die like this," says Beatriz.

"It was terrible."

"More terrible than you know, my child." And she covers her eyes again to hide her feelings.

I haven't been the same since I left Chalate for San Miguel. I've got my *compañeros,* my work with the peasant federation, my studies—I'm learning the reasons for our poverty and taking courses in nursing so I can be part of the war. She already was. She couldn't tell her grandmother, because she wouldn't under-stand. With my father it's different. I have the feeling he has begun to understand life. She was sure Grandmother would be with the whole family together to the end.

"Do you miss him much?" my grandmother asks.

"Who?" I say, pretending I don't understand.

"Your *compañero.*"

"Yes, I miss him a lot; but what can I do, Grandmother?"

"I'm worried about how you're going to manage alone with two children."

"My parents help a lot, they're taking care of them for me. I think they actually miss having the noise of children in the house."

"We haven't been lucky in the last few years."

"Each person makes her own luck. Maybe we just haven't found ours yet," I say.

"I was referring to your *compañero.*"

"Oh, of course; I also miss his father, I would have liked to have met him and heard what he had to say."

"It's sad," she says, "the things we have to put up with; I wonder if the Lord is testing us to see how far our faith and resignation will go."

"Imagine, at Emiliano's age, what possible threat could he have been to the authorities when they're armed to the teeth like Martians? Sometimes I wonder if they really feel strong or if they're really scared to death."

"Don't let them fool you. As long as they have those weapons they'll never be afraid, they're protected by some force that comes from afar." And I see two tears well up, but her face is impassive. She adds: "Sometimes I think my heart is breaking, child."

"Does it hurt?" I ask.

"It's nothing," she answers.

"It's something," I insist.

"Maybe the Cipitio played with me when I was little," says my grandmother, "and I didn't realize it. Maybe now I'm suffering the consequences."

The Cipitio is the son of the Siguanaba and he falls in love with little girls, coming in the middle of the night to caress them. And once he has won them over with his caresses, he appears before them dressed in coarse white cotton pants and no shirt, wearing a wide-brimmed sombrero. People figure he's not even twelve years old, though he seems younger because he's so short. He is very small and has bulging eyes, big dimples, and a permanent grin. He likes to play with the ashes in the cooking fire. So the first thing you have to do before you go to bed is clean the kitchen. He is a kind of pixie that brings bad luck.

"You never told us about the Cipitio," she says, not believing the story.

"Sometimes you confuse reality and dreams, maybe that's why I never mentioned it."

"You shouldn't believe in things like that," says Lucía.

"Neither believe nor disbelieve," says her grandmother.

Ticha went out into the yard. She said she was going to get water from the well. It was her way of avoiding conversation with her granddaughter. "And give the chickens some millet before they start climbing trees," she tells her.

"Something's going to happen," she says, suddenly filled with a grave premonition. Still she tries to cheer herself up: "Maybe it's just that people can't go on being the same way." Behind the hill, the brightness of the afternoon is like a ball of fire.

Seeing as it was Sunday morning, we decided to go to the lagoon in Apastepeque together to visit Grandmother, Mama, Papa, and the kids. The distance is a little over three miles. That was the day I found her sadder than ever, complaining about the pain in her heart. That was when she spoke of old people getting in the way and of the birds in her breast that wanted to fly. I didn't think anything of it; but at noon, while Papa and I were clearing the far end of the yard and Mama was grinding corn, we heard a shout from in back of the hut. I had a premonition and went flying toward the well, where she had been drawing water. Grandmother was lying on the ground vomiting yellow liquid. I screamed loud enough so Mama and Papa would hear. They came running.

"Go on, Juana," says Papa. "Get some rhubarb so we can make her something to drink. It's bile," I hear him say as he takes my grandmother by the shoulder. "It's her heart," is what I think.

"It's impotence," is what comes out of her toothless mouth. At least that's what I think she says but she's speaking in a whisper. "I'm full of rage." This time she speaks slowly and distinctly as though aware these will be her last words.

"Why rage?" asks Papa. "Just keep calm, it will pass."

After my papa put her on the wooden cot, she answered Papa's question while we waited for Mama to return with the rhubarb. She told us why she was enraged. She finally made us understand that Corporal Martínez was also Pedro Martínez. "Your brother, Jacinto," she told Papa. "Tell Antonia, tell Juana." I don't know if it was because her eyes got full of clouds, like when a big storm is coming, but they stopped reflecting the light filtering through the walls of the hut. I just don't know. All I know is that Papa let her down gently, cradling her head in his arm. "Tell everyone," was the last thing she said.

"It's too late, Juana," says Papa, as she comes in with the rhubarb. My mother dropped the stalks and looked at me, as though searching for an explanation. So I told her, ignoring

Jacinto, who was frozen in place, staring at his mama with great sadness.

"The birds flew," I said, not expecting they would understand.

"What birds?" asks Juana, my mama.

"The ones Grandmother carried in her breast," I answered.

"Is such ingratitude possible?" says Mama, referring to my uncle, Pedro Martínez, for the first time. "Does he really exist?"

"Our misery is to blame for everything, so I don't hold it against my brother. We didn't even know he was alive," says Papa, coming back to himself, as though returning from a long dream.

"It's all so strange, Jacinto," my mother comments. "Suddenly appearing to touch off a tragedy; he's taken both Grandfather Emiliano and Ticha."

"The deaths of the poor, the explanation is always the same," I say to no one in particular, trying to recover from the shock of this unexpected development. I realize we are in great pain and it has numbed our thoughts. An old pain. But we must stay awake.

I never imagined that now, on this trip to San Salvador, I would come face-to-face with Pedro Martínez.

XIV / JACINTO

October 1980

SHE WAS A GOOD woman who might go to heaven. Now that she was about to die he had to think about her the way he'd think about other women like her. Juana running barefoot over the cobblestone streets. Walking under the noonday sun. Jumping over small islands of hay so the plants wouldn't scratch her feet. Running behind Grandfather so she wouldn't be late for the hacienda. Gasping for breath, suffocating. She's been a woman since she was seven. Juana is like her daughter Lucía and her daughter Antonia; she's also like her mother-in-law Ticha. From birth she has been a woman who must live in other women to be transformed.

A calabash filled with water hanging over her shoulder.

From a tender age she's been a complete woman. While other children of the world play, she works, facing hurricanes, thunderstorms, gang bosses, and the authorities.

Tirelessly and without complaint.

Her braids fell over her shoulder when she was little. Then she wore her hair short; after reaching adolescence she kept it shoulder-length. She put *clavelones* in her hair. A red flower that grows by the roadside. Later her daughter Lucía would spruce up her hair with a sprig of myrtle or mignonette. They are the same person. Their stories overlap, their lives overlap. And they have never figured out either the weather's changeability or their own impatience. Living through their own blood. Up and down, like all the poor in Cuzcatlán, where the Southern Sea beats. Where you're always going up or down. Because the roads always go down; or down and then up again. Ascending and descending hills and volcanoes.

Sometimes the roads spill over like rivers. And like volcanic eruptions, spilling over. Always flowing somewhere. Up, down, giving life to the man who has no name.

His heart is the heart of the volcanoes. He feeds the undying land with his blood.

And when he is at the summit of the volcanoes he is a bird and his voice is like the roar of the ocean.

Beatriz has gone off by herself on the paths of God.

Jacinto has been left all alone. Inhabited by strange beings who lift him up in the air so he can touch the face of the sky and the foot of the volcanoes.

Beatriz is also his grandpa Emiliano. Both had the same dreams that never came true. She is also his daughter Antonia and his daughter Lucía. That's why they say the age of man is endless. There is no death, only transformation.

Beatriz has lived the age of a star which might be the age of the red flower she wears in her hair. Like a star. No one can stop her now when she ascends and descends the volcanoes. She can't be held in chains now.

The *zensontle* sings in the tops of the mango trees; it might be the voice of those who never dared sing for fear of breaking in pieces. For fear of shattering the crystalline composition of their feelings.

He feels pain, but not sorrow. Jacinto knows no one can hold back the change in their lives. Neither in his life or in that of Juana or his two daughters.

In league with eternity, the two *compañeros* will not be left alone.

Suddenly he felt sad. Never before in his life had he had this feeling—somewhere between hopeless and impotent, like suddenly getting the feeling that the sun would not come up again. Or like someone had told him it wouldn't rain for a year. He didn't feel like this even when Juana died.

His throat filled with stones. His tortilla refused to go into his mouth. Was it the sorrow which, in spite of disasters and famines, he'd never felt before? Pain yes, when Juana died.

It was when a neighbor came and asked if he knew a certain Corporal or Sergeant Martínez. "No one knows who the hell he is." And Jacinto answered that never in his life had he ever known a person who was a corporal or a sergeant. To him, the *guardias* were like phantoms that passed with death riding their shoulder. They were part of the zone, but he never had any contact with them.

"The name doesn't ring a bell?" the neighbor asks.

"No, it doesn't," replies Jacinto.

"Strange, doesn't tell you anything?" says the neighbor, intrigued. But when he sees Jacinto's eyes fill with shadows he backs off. "Each person has his troubles, though if we can help our fellow man, our help shouldn't be denied," he thinks.

It was the first time Jacinto remembered he had a last name. Never before had either he or his family needed one. It didn't even appear on the hacienda's pay sheet. The gang boss knew them all by heart. "He could recognize us even in bean soup." It was enough for the men running the haciendas to know their first names, and form a mental picture of the way they walked, answered, obeyed, and reacted to shouts and insults. Each of them had his own personality.

"Even horses and oxen don't have last names and nobody

loses them or gets them confused," thinks the gang boss. And that's what he tells the *patrón* when the latter points out that the last names are missing from the payroll. All he sees are Christian names.

There were hundreds of men working on the haciendas. Sometimes there were thousands. Depending on the wealth of the landowner who had appropriated not only the farms but the men to work them. And if you didn't like it, or wanted to escape it, well, that's what the Guardia Nacional was for, they had permission to round people up and return them to their zone of origin, invoking the law against vagrants, thieves, and troublemakers which one of the members of government had had the wisdom to decree.

"That's right," says the hacienda owner, "I never realized dogs don't have last names either." His face was illuminated by this discovery and by the fire of his intelligence. "No problem, then." And with his mind at ease he returns to the city, which he leaves once a year to visit the hacienda. He comes on his Arabian horse, pistol by his side, surrounded by the Guardia Nacional so nothing will happen to him. He's pleased with the protection and zeal afforded by the military government. Perhaps he goes back in his touring sedan, armored against heavy-caliber bullets and flanked with machine guns and hand grenades. He is satisfied with his power, which is based in turn upon the power he himself, with his capital and spirit of free enterprise, bestows upon his rulers.

"You've got to realize, *compa*, I forgot I even had a last name, since I never use it," says Jacinto with an expression somewhere between a shrug and a scowl.

"The same is true for me, but I thought I should ask if you knew Corporal Martínez."

"Listen," Jacinto interrupts, "I've never participated in elections because all the ballots in the zone are filled in by the gang boss himself, he votes for us." His irony suddenly acquires a strain of protest, without abandoning the kind voice and characteristic humility of a farm worker. "The gang boss is the one who elects the representatives and presidents."

"You don't need to tell me," says the neighbor impatiently, wanting to get back to the conversation about Corporal Martínez.

"So what good are last names?" The irony creeps back into his voice as though he's sticking up for himself or trying to take his thoughts back to a former time, when he was young. Remembering his mother Ticha, dead two weeks ago; his grandfather. Deep down he was running away from the remembrance of the past, particularly his beloved dead. His attitude was to see death as another sister; the most natural thing in life is death. Some consider it a gift from God. Jacinto saw death as a final respite from days of rain and sun. Misery, hunger. Disease and injustice. This was his first opening of consciousness as a poor man in Cuzcatlán, where the Southern Sea beats.

For the first time in his life Jacinto felt the need to be dishonest. His heart was telling him something; he knew by the way his chest was pounding. And then he had that feeling which he'd heard strikes men no matter how strong they may be: sorrow. He felt it when a mouthful of tortilla refused to go down his throat. Grandfather Emiliano comes to mind, such an unexpected cause of death during the army's last invasion. Then they come and tell him about the kind of shit Corporal Martínez is up to; however, he chooses to remain ignorant of the corporal's direct participation in the death of his grandfather.

"They say Corporal Martínez clubbed María Pia's *compañero*, Helio. I don't know if you know her, she was working as a tortilla maker at the hacienda."

"Yes, I remember her."

"That's not all. They say the corporal disappeared him, no one has heard from him. And he hit María Pia so hard it broke her arm."

"I'm glad you're telling me this, so we'll be ready for those beasts," says Jacinto, trying to assimilate the message, but without focusing on the fact that it was Corporal Martínez who was committing atrocities in the zone. It couldn't be him, because they never send natives on missions to their place of birth, especially not missions like that—burning huts and disappearing people. The Guardia Nacional was careful not to pit the authorities against their own neighbors and relations.

At that moment Jacinto discovered that his poverty signified a lack of food and material conditions for life. But it didn't signify human misery. The others were the miserable ones. His life had been a struggle to survive, hounded by hunger and the cruelty of the situation in which he lived. That was poverty. He understood the difference between the poor and the miserable. "We're poor, they're miserable," he thought.

The question about his last name, which he had previously ignored, had opened his eyes as well as what some of his neighbors were already calling consciousness. He needed a shove to be able to comprehend it and they had given it to him. He had had to journey across hundreds of years for that little shove, and he carried those years which his fathers and grandfathers had endured with him. Terrible years. Their vitality used up beneath hurricanes, thunderstorms, and the harsh suns of March and April, just for another piece of tortilla and another grain of salt. And who owned those energies? All this they had endured with the patience and reflection of centuries, he and his fathers and grandfathers. But now a new element had been added: now they came to violate his identity, his nature. People removed from the poor, from their way of being; people unfamiliar with their

243

centuries of slave culture, oppressed culture, but culture nonetheless; the physical oppressors came now to rob them of their only wealth: their integrity. Not only did they appropriate their creative and constructive energies, but they wanted to plunder the feelings that emanated from their hearts, which all the centuries of darkness, spoils, cruelty, hunger, and material deprivations hadn't been able to destroy. Feelings which survive time and injustice. In the past they seized their strength for working and dispossessed them of their lands. In the past they had violated their women. They had devoured their children in the haciendas. Now they wanted to turn their feelings into shit. The military instructors of the day, educated in the academies of other worlds, were now experts on souls. That's why they burned huts and disappeared people unnecessarily. They insulted the race, whose own mothers were whores because they had more than ten children; whose sisters were whores because they sought their lifelong *compañeros* at the age of fifteen. The technological culture had come to assault the oppressed culture, which conserved in its roots the traces of an even more ancient culture of poets and warriors.

"Look, that's not all; they already told us what he was doing in Chalate, what he did to José Guardado," a neighbor tells him.

"What did he do?" Jacinto asks.

"They say he tore his eyes out and decapitated him."

"I don't know anything about him. Practically everybody in El Salvador has the last name Martínez."

"I'm only telling you, Jacinto, so you can do something, for the sake of Emiliano, who was an honest man; and for your own sake, because you've never once complained or offended anyone," the neighbor says humbly, aware he could hurt Jacinto; but he also knows Jacinto must wake up and emerge for the benefit of everyone. "You can do something." About Corporal Martínez, known as the Executioner of Chalate, accompanied by William, known as the baby *guardia,* because he was barely twelve years old. It was his job to set the huts on fire and make fun of the victims. He danced to the rhythm of the *guardias'* gunfire, though he himself never touched a weapon.

"But what can I do?" he wonders, wanting to open the window of his heart, look inside, and find the other Jacinto, his true conscience. Not the one hidden beneath the peaceful farm worker. Contemplating his life, quarrying stones, feeding his four remaining pigs because there wasn't enough to feed any more of them, though they got their nourishment from garbage, leftover corn water, and human excrement.

"There's not even enough shit to feed the pigs," he thinks in desperation, still intending to gather his forces to confront the new problem: his brother, Pedro Martínez.

And when he opens the window of his heart, he sees the life of his parents; that of his brothers, whose memory he can hardly summon—if he met them at that moment he wouldn't recognize them; and that of his grandfather Emiliano. And his father Eusebio, whom he didn't know.

Pedro Martínez helped him to look inside, find what his daughter Lucía called consciousness, which no matter how much she explained it he could never quite grasp. "A person discovers consciousness on his own, because it is transparent, it is invisible, it can't be smelled or touched, it can only be sensed, tickling people, tickling poor people like us." That's how his younger daughter explained it, in pretty words. And Jacinto thought that in order for the poor to have consciousness, they had to know who the miserable were. After so many years of oppression they were sending them human wretches who, instead of terrifying them, awakened their need to know life. True life.

XV / MICROBUS TO SAN SALVADOR

January 9, 1981

TODAY IS THE DAY I meet Corporal Martínez. I don't know what will happen when I meet him. Maybe my hands will shake; so what, how can I help it? We're all so sad. I can look out the window at this beautiful landscape, these green mountains and those volcanoes and valleys. The seafoam swirling about the southern coast of Cuzcatlán. But between the landscape and the glass window is my life, which isn't mine alone; it belongs to my entire family, including Corporal Martínez, who could easily have been my father. And Grandfather Eusebio, whom I never knew but whose shadow hovered in my memory. We are sad people. She looks at the sun that dapples the still wet leaves of a cool morning that never wants to end. Those shitty mountains. The way the moisture hangs from their indecisive glance. It doesn't stay in one place, it leaps over cliffs; she looks at the sierras to the north, behind them Chalate and Cabañas, and behind them other celestial cordilleras lost in Honduras. When I feel I'm made of flesh and bone is when I am filled with great hope. It doesn't matter that that very fact makes us shed a tear. We get sad. It doesn't matter. First we were made of wood, but we had no souls, we couldn't speak. Then the gods burned us because we were useless in that form. They also experimented with clay and water, but we dissolved in the rain, we couldn't stand the storms. And our valleys and volcanoes are very rainy. Then they discovered corn in the age called Teosinte. And they made us of corn. They saw then that we could speak, we had souls, which meant we were made to love intensely, we could pass that love on to our children; move our hands, turn our heads, be stirred on dark nights by the moon, the stars, the wind, and the storms. We could be afraid of hurricanes; we were terrified by lightning and torrents of water cascading down from the volcanoes, before, during, and after it rained. As long as there is a soul, there is fear. If there is fear, man exists. We also tremble at the sunset, and at the death of a child we never knew. We have souls. So the gods let us live. It was worthwhile for us to continue in the world, reproducing, growing. But our enemies did not know these things and treated us like shit for centuries and centuries: they beat us, they wounded us and threw salt in our wounds so we would feel unimaginable pain, they decapitated us and nailed our heads to stakes, exhibiting them, to mock those who dare to express human qualities. They hung us from trees in parks. In front of our children and mothers they disemboweled us. They filled us full of holes with their harquebuses and muskets, with their helicopters and planes; they destroyed us with bombs and burned us with white phosphorous. They wanted to extinguish our souls. Precisely that which led the gods to the decision to let us live and continue on earth. They cut off our hands, they poked out our eyes. Our enemies. Do we have enemies? Who are our enemies? How old are our enemies? How long have they torn our fingernails off and ripped out our eyes? Why do they want to exterminate us? Where do they come from? Who the hell invented them? Are the severed heads, charred bodies, and spilled guts real or imaginary? What are they looking for inside our bodies, what do they hope to discover, what frightens them, what worries them? Maybe our hopes are what terrify them. We will survive despite our enemies. We were made of corn. That was the raw material. The rest was a miracle of nature. The enemy will not be done with us until he discovers the secret of our survival. And we will not explain that enigma until he is no longer our enemy. Maybe then we can share the world with the same sensibility. No one knows. They come. We are here. We're not leaving. We live here. It is our land. Our volcanoes, rivers, mountains, lakes, birds of paradise. They will not remove us from here. Over our dead bodies.

"What is your name?"

"Pedro Martínez, at your service."

"The only service you can provide is to tell the truth."

"I already told you everything."

"You've portrayed yourself as an angel."

"I'm a professional soldier."

"A professional killer, you mean."

"I follow orders. . . ."

"And carry them out with your eyes closed."

"That's part of the job. If I don't do what I'm told I'm dead."

"Do you know William?"

"William, the little boy. . . ."

"That's the one."

"Yes, I knew him, but he's dead now. He died in an ambush arranged by you people."

"We're aware of that."

"He was just a boy."

"You people made him a man in the Guardia, you shit all over him, and you yourself are much to blame."

"We gave him food and shelter at the garrison. I can't be held responsible for what he did."

"You trained him yourself and he tagged along with you when

you captured Helio and Emilio in Ilobasco, for example. . . ."

"I don't remember very well. . . ."

"And you beat María Pia and burned Helio's father's hut."

"I don't know because I have carried out a number of operations. I've never been a bastard with humble people, I've always been kind. . . ."

"And you killed José Guardado in Chalatenango."

"Certainly you're aware of the rules of war."

"Murder isn't one of those rules."

"In wartime there are no murders. If we don't kill you, you'll kill us."

"José Guardado wasn't even armed when he went to visit his family."

"He was a leader of the subversives."

"You don't agree that you're committing murder when you cut off his head while his hands are tied behind his back?"

"That wasn't me, it was a private."

"If the private was our prisoner he would say it was you. You're not ashamed, it doesn't affect you, when you treat your own people, people who come from the same place, like that?"

"I'm not one of them."

"They're peasants like yourself. . . ."

"I'm not a peasant, I come from San Salvador."

"So you claim."

"I swear."

"Never mind. I only mention it because I would like you to recall the operation last October in Apastepeque, at which you were present."

"I already told you, I'm a professional soldier, I obey orders, I go where I'm sent."

"Are you aware that a very old man and three others were killed there?"

"The officer in charge is the one who killed the old man."

"And the other three?"

"That was an accident."

"Let's deal with one at a time—you provoked the old man, did you not?"

"We never meant to kill anyone, we were making a search of the hamlet."

"And you ended up burning cornfields and huts."

"Those were our orders, the guerrillas came there to buy corn."

"Did you insult the old man? Don't deny it, because we know what happened."

"I didn't insult him."

"Why, then, did he lunge at you?"

"I don't know, maybe he got nervous."

"Do you know what his name was?"

"No I don't, I never asked."

"You lie."

"With all those names it's easy to get confused."

"I would like you to repent for your crimes, that alone would be sufficient."

"I already told you, *comandante*, there are no crimes."

"Shit, man, a person has to have the patience of Job to deal with you; what about the other three victims? . . ."

"I don't know what came over me."

"You went berserk after the captain shot the old man, so you just got up and started shooting."

"I swear, *comandante*, I wasn't in my right mind, it's just one of those things that war does to you. . . ."

"Do you want me to tell you the old man's name?"

"Go ahead. . . ."

"His name was Emiliano and he wasn't a leader of the subversives, as you call us. With José Guardado it was different. But I guess you don't care whether a person is a leader or not."

"I assure you it wasn't me who killed him."

"He was the grandfather of Jacinto Martínez of Apastepeque."

"I'm at your disposal, my *comandante.*"

"I'm not your *comandante.* And I hope you don't continue
claiming you're from San Salvador."

"You can check my credentials."

"You people make up your credentials."

"Fine. I said I was at your disposal."

"And you don't wish to repent."

"Like I said, I'm a career military man, a professional."

"If you won't say it, I will: Emiliano was the father of Beatriz Martínez. For a long time they lived on the south side of
Apastepeque lagoon, then they moved to the foothills because
the lands were flooded and the landowners decided to grow
rice—"

"I can't shoot, though for the past twenty-five years of my
career—"

"Let me finish—"

"—in order to reach the rank of corporal of the Guardia I
have undergone the worst tests."

"Quit being a martyr and let me finish—"

". . . insults, beatings, humiliations. I'm as poor as you people."

"And you just now figured that out?"

"That very poverty throws so many obstacles in your path. In
order to get to be corporal of the Guardia I had to sweat blood."

"You, too, lived on the south side of the lagoon, you were
born and raised there until the patrols captured you and brought
you to the garrison."

"I tell you, I'm from San Salvador."

"All right, forget it, if that's the way you want to be; all we need to do is clarify some things."

"You want to get truth from lies. I don't know who invented those things."

"If you think I'm lying, it may be time for you to meet someone."

"You give the orders, *comandante*."

"Will you please bring Beatriz in?"

"Listen, *comandante*, you don't need to bring anybody in. That would be a shitty thing to do, real shitty."

"When you killed José Guardado you didn't whine like that. And speaking of shit, you should look in a mirror and see how they've filled your mind with shit, if only you could see inside yourself."

"I never cried a day in my life, *comandante*, until that day in Apastepeque. You've got to understand that we're at war, the same goes for you."

"You're ashamed to meet Beatriz. . . ."

"Look, *comandante*, I don't give a shit whether my family has gone astray. Let them. The gringo advisers have taught us that we should fight our families to bring them out of the darkness in which they live. . . ."

"Bring them out of darkness by killing them?"

"They should listen to reason and there wouldn't be any problems."

"You know something, I don't know whether to take your tears for cowardice or repentance. Anyway, I don't think you deserve to meet a woman as rugged as Beatriz; it would be an offense for you to see her. . . ."

"You do me a favor, *comandante*. . . ."

"Why are you afraid if your conscience is clear?"

"You know best, *comandante*."

"Too bad she is a witness in the trial and therefore must see you."

"Don't do that to me, my *comandante*."

"Let *compa* Beatriz come in."

Corporal Martínez will be surprised. He's not expecting a young woman. However, he will mumble something, a word that sounds like *mama*, stuttering like a child learning to speak. I'll tell him I'm not his mother. Then he will just stare at me, his eyes won't believe what they're seeing. To him, I will be his mother, who left the south side of Apastepeque lagoon. He won't notice that my features merely resemble those of my grand-mother. Corporal Martínez will go back to his childhood, he'll go back in time. Once I see he's recovered, the first question I'll ask will be about his brother Manuel. He will tell me that he died in an ambush near the city of Suchitoto four years ago. He was a *guardia* like me, Mama, he'll say, sobbing. I won't be affected, I won't demonstrate an ounce of compassion. He will keep on talking: Ever since then I swore to take revenge on the subver-sives, because the subversives killed my brother treacherously. I will respond with a question: Who will take revenge on you, on your twenty-five years as a Guardia Nacional, committing atrocities with impunity? He'll answer: Forgive me. How does a man become a beast? I'll wonder. And he'll read my thoughts. He will answer, also to himself: The gringo advisers have made us evil. I will say, out loud this time: No one can make you evil. That is what I will believe then. He will answer: Before the advisers came we had friends and relatives. I can't believe what you're saying, I'll reply, you're just wiping your shit onto your benefactors. Once again he'll say: Forgive me, Mama. He'll keep on crying. I am your niece, the daughter of Jacinto Martínez, I'll

253

reply. But he'll keep on saying forgive me, Mama, forgive me, Mama, as if he were some bizarre creature from the remote past. I'll say: Beatriz is my alias. I use the name in honor of my grandmother, your mother. He'll tell me I'm lying. I'll see him one last time cowering in a corner of the hut, because that is where he has gone to sit while we interrogate him during his trial as a war criminal. Crouching, sitting on his haunches, the way we peasants do, resting buttocks, thighs, and our whole bodies on our legs and the soles of our feet. Because we never had seats to sit on. We invent the means on the basis of our needs. My shadow will fall across him. He will have his hands over his face shading himself from the light, which seconds before I arrive will have been shining brightly. The light will come through the doorway. I will also think he is covering himself because he is ashamed, because of the impotence of being a prisoner. And when he has seen me enter he will withdraw as though physically returning to his childhood. When the *comandante* says my name he won't understand Corporal Martínez's reaction; or he'll understand, but only partially. And when he senses my shadow on the hands covering his eyes, he'll see his mother as she was when he was eight. Afterwards, I'll go back and join the other members of the popular tribunal.

Half an hour later we'll go to the *comandante,* myself and the other *compañeros* of the jury. The *comandante* will ask if we have reached a verdict. We will say we have. He will be surprised when he reads the words *not guilty.* And he'll turn to me, saying he doesn't want to meddle, but he doesn't understand, because Corporal Martínez's crimes have been verified. Then I will ask him what would have happened if we had found him guilty. He'll tell me that he would have been executed, since that is the maximum sentence for a criminal like him, accused of various crimes against civilians. He will say this with emphasis on certain words, as though demanding an explanation. I will explain: By finding him not guilty we have condemned him. The *comandante* will ask why. Because we want him to go on living, I'm going to reply. Then he will insist with his eyes. Up until then I will meet his gaze. We have sentenced him to go on living, I'll explain at his look of surprise. That's no punishment, he'll reply. *Compañero comandante,* all you know is that Corporal Martínez is my father's brother, but you don't know the whole family history, I'll go on. He will ask: What history? I'll answer: It's too long to go into, but someday we'll have enough time and I can tell you then. He'll look at me with his intelligent, profoundly black, and slightly ironic eyes; and a sympathetic smile, as though he wants to use it to give me strength, to lend each other mutual support and hope. He'll understand everything, then; the little story. An understanding that will come once he is aware that from now on we will be bound by eternal friendship.

THE VINTAGE LIBRARY OF
CONTEMPORARY WORLD LITERATURE

"A cornucopia of serious fiction by contemporary writers from all parts of the world...a mix of the *au courant* and authentic art."
—CHRISTIAN SCIENCE MONITOR

"These works appeal intellectually, emotionally, even physically, and transport us out of our own space and time into strange and wonderful other places."
—SAN JOSE MERCURY NEWS

"Most impressive."

—NEWSDAY

"Excellent."

—THE VILLAGE VOICE

"Ambitious...a boon for armchair explorers."

—NEWSWEEK

On sale at bookstores everywhere, but if otherwise unavailable may be ordered from us. You can use this coupon, or phone (800) 638-6460.

Please send me the Aventura books I have checked on the reverse. I am enclosing $_____ (add $1.00 per copy to cover postage and handling). Send check or money order—no cash or COD, please. Prices are subject to change without notice.

NAME _____

ADDRESS _____

CITY _____ STATE _____ ZIP _____

Send coupons to:
RANDOM HOUSE, INC., 400 Hahn Road, Westminster, MD 21157
ATTN: ORDER ENTRY DEPARTMENT
Allow at least 4 weeks for delivery.